THREE BAGS FULL

BLAKE VALENTINE

Published by CRED PRODUCTIONS, 2024.

This is a work of fiction. Similarities to real people, places, or events are entirely coincidental.

THREE BAGS FULL

First edition. March 6, 2024.

Copyright © 2024 BLAKE VALENTINE.

Written by BLAKE VALENTINE.

Chapter 1.

The Boeing 737 banked steeply as the cabin crew dimmed the interior lights. In the darkness, the illuminated seatbelt signs glowed. Below, the gaudy neon spread of clubs, bars and hotels hugging the Mediterranean coast resembled a giant star-spangled blanket. An oasis of promise; a debauched retreat; a refuge. Captain Weir levelled off and listened to the crackle of the radio messages from air traffic control. In ten minutes, the plane would be taxiing across the Malaga tarmac, set to disgorge its passengers into the sultry night air.

It was 2AM Spanish time.

When Weir first started flying the route back in the mid-Eighties, air travel still retained a sense of glamour; Spain was suitably exotic. Back then, the money had rolled in. His comfortable, commuter-belt existence had enabled him to invest in two rental properties on the Costa del Sol. Things, though, had gone steadily downhill ever since; his world of privilege hadn't quite become one of penury, but his existence was no longer one of glittering possibility. It was hard not to feel nostalgic. Now, in the wake of a billion budget air miles, the Costa felt like tarnished silver. Aeroplanes these days, as his colleagues reminded him all too frequently, were just buses with wings. He longed for the days when a pilot's wing badge was an open licence for a leg over; the era when smoking was still permitted everywhere.

Weir engaged the autopilot. If there were no security delays, he realised he might still catch the tail end of a party in the hills. Far-away from prying eyes. A perk of the job. One of the few that remained – he could bury his sorrows in young, willing flesh, all too easily impressed at bagging an actual pilot.

And, failing that, there was always tomorrow night. Or the night after.

The complex in the hills wasn't going anywhere.

Nor were its girls.

* * * * *

Abdellah Rif didn't look up as the plane passed overhead. It was simply a moving mass of lights. A distant rumble of jet engines. An irrelevance.

He levered himself away from the black Bentley he'd been leaning against, dropped his cigarette onto the rough ground, and stamped it out with his heel. The hillside was steep. Barren. Terraces had been carved out and then flattened into patches of ground where new building foundations now sprouted. The surroundings were typical of any construction site – patches of dried grass and weeds had sprouted during delays in the work, and piles of rusting wire lay about.

The land belonged to Rif. But so did most of the land in the area. At least it *had* done. He'd built his first complex thirty years ago. Since then, he'd moved from project to project. Building to building.

Lighting another cigarette, he took out his phone and dialled a number. As the call connected, he looked out towards the shoreline, allowing his mind to wander. There was nothing wrong with the location. There was nothing wrong with any of his locations. But every time he made a purchase, he seemed to move a little further inland. It felt as if a little more of his fortune was being prised away. A step further from the beaches. That – so the high rollers at the Segovia Palace reminded him – was just the price of progress. That was what happened when more and more land was priced at a premium.

But that would soon change, he assured himself.

Rif's new plan would see him right back on the strip. Right back amid the action.

'Well?' he demanded gruffly when the phone was answered.

'It was him,' the voice on the other end of the line announced. The tone was neutral; emotionless.

Rif ended the call.

He was a wealthy man: tailored Armani suit; Rolex watch; Gucci shoes, and cufflinks made by Aspinal of London. He had a stable of women on hand to service his every whim. But he never forgot where he'd come from. Rezza and Hassan were his top choices for a job like this – all brawn and no brains. They'd already softened the traitor up. But it was the boss who'd been wronged. And, at times like this, the boss believed it was up to him to take care of business.

Abdellah Rif remained a man who wasn't scared to get his hands dirty.

* * * * *

Rif crossed the patch of waste ground, approaching the fresh foundations. A bloodied figure was kneeling down. Before them, an open trench was half filled with setting concrete. A row of steel rods protruded, marking a channel in its midst; the dappled surface of the drying mixture glimmered a little in the reflected orange glow of a distant street lamp.

The man didn't move. He tensed a little as the boss' footsteps crunched behind him. Rif drew hard on his cigarette and then flicked the butt into the trench. It landed in a shower of sparks, fizzing a little as it encountered the damp concrete. Sometimes, as Rif knew, people fought back moments before death. Other times, they lay down ready – as if fixing themselves – keen to expedite the process. And, sometimes, they were like the man before him: utterly defeated. Dead already.

'I gave you a job to do.' Rif sighed.

Silence.

He switched to Arabic. 'Want to explain why you failed me?'

Silence.

Rif sighed and withdrew his IMI Desert Eagle. The boss' tone softened, almost imperceptibly. 'Adil… have you said your prayers?'

The kneeling figure nodded, emitting a slight whimper. Had the boss been able to read minds, he'd have seen the man wondering why he ever left his steady job as a chef and decided to chase the riches Rif tempted him with. It was this avarice – he well knew – which had led to his demise. That, and his failure. And the man with the gun didn't tolerate failure.

Rif pulled the trigger.

The Desert Eagle is not a subtle weapon. As the echo of its report rebounded from the breeze-blocked walls of the construction site, Adil's corpse pitched into the trench. Half of his head was now missing.

Before the corpse landed, Rif turned. He walked away from the scene, checking his phone and then replacing it in his pocket. Looking up, he sniffed and nodded. Rezza – now seated in the cab of a cement truck with a pipe protruding from its rear - started the diesel engine. It rumbled into life with a deep roar. The gears crunched. Hassan began directing his colleague as he reversed the vehicle. Once the truck's rear bumper inched level with the edge of the trench, he signalled for him to stop.

Seconds later, concrete began pouring out of the extended chute, spattering the surface on which the dead man lay. The concrete moulded itself to the contours of the cavity; slipping and sliding, it made its way along the trench in a sludgy mass, swallowing everything it came into contact with.

An hour or two after sunrise, it would be set rock hard.

Walking back towards his car, Rif paused. Something caught his eye; a light blinked for an instant and then vanished. He peered into the darkness of the scrub-covered hillside.

Frowning, he shook his head and resumed walking.

As he did, he retrieved the phone from his pocket once more.

Chapter 2.

Trent Rivera was enduring Sunday lunchtime at Jim's Bar. Catering for expats, the English pub was a Costa del Sol institution. Weekdays, it dished up a constant onslaught of omelettes and chips, washed down by cheap booze and accompanied by football. It wasn't Rivera's kind of place – it was too busy; too noisy; too British. But Iris – his 1972 Volkswagen T2 – needed work. He'd been told there was a man that frequented Jim's who could help him in that regard. And so, somewhat reluctantly, he'd dragged himself there.

Rivera was reading a tattered copy of *A Tale of Two Cities*. In the din of the lunch service, though, he was finding it hard to concentrate. Jim's Bar was at the top of a hill. Behind it, the foothills of the Sierra de Mijas rose to become the mountains of the north. Looking down from its sun terrace, drinkers had a clear view all the way to the twinkling Mediterranean. But the entire establishment looked washed up and burnt out. Plastic parasols still bore sun-faded emblems of tobacco companies from yesteryear, and the tacky street sign advertising the establishment resembled a relic from when the Vauxhall Viva reigned supreme.

Shirtless children with buzz-cuts careered around, feral from sugary drinks, and covered in transfer tattoos. Meanwhile, rotund diners compared the relative merits of their Sunday roasts while sinking pints of imported British ale. Rivera, nursing a blackcurrant and soda water, began to feel jittery. The only saving grace was that – when he'd arrived – the Fulham game was being broadcast. The screen was hung on the wall, surrounded by dozens of decorative Union Jack flags, and set next to a portrait of the Queen. That he, a lifelong fan, would be able to watch his team, made the prospect of his stay a little more bearable. But then, the barman had bowed to the pressure of the punters and the channel had been switched.

United were playing at home.

*****

When Rivera left the Army, he'd been offered a stark choice: walk or be pushed. He'd chosen the former. After his last tour of duty in Afghanistan, he'd come to the realisation that he was brilliant at killing people; decent at languages; reasonably competent at cooking; good at finding things out, but not much use at anything else. He'd come home haunted by some of the things he'd been involved with while in uniform. They plagued him, torturing him until their whispers became a never-ending roar.

He never thought he was the type of person who'd crack, but – eventually - he'd broken down entirely. Before, he'd thought such things only happened to other people. He was used to stress; used to threats; accepting of the hands of fate. On his first night in Basra, his Commanding Officer had made him and a fellow soldier draw lots. Rivera had been given the less desirable assignment. But he'd lived. The other man hadn't. After that, his job in the city had been relatively simple: he was more-or-less a chauffeur for high-ranking officials, and an improvised mechanic whenever he was required to be. His time as taxi driver coincided with the worst days of the IED campaign. It was a life without logic: some of his friends made it. Others didn't. It was simply the luck of the draw.

Rivera had never fired his weapon in Iraq. He reasoned you could get used to anything – it simply became your life. So, the continual beeping of the infrared radio transmitter signal used to trigger roadside ordnance became his soundtrack. He still slept at night.

Afghanistan, though, had been a different story. Hence the hollowed out husk of a man who came back to Hammersmith, and flipped.

His then girlfriend called him a loser; a drunk; a junkie. The representatives from the army who'd come to serve him his marching orders were more diplomatic: they termed it PTSD. But they weren't any more sympathetic about what he'd done. He was given a discharge on medical grounds.

And that was that.

Shortly afterwards, Rivera had spent most of his money on Iris. He'd stumbled upon the campervan when she was sitting on the forecourt of a backstreet garage in Hammersmith. It was love at first sight. The name came from the sprig of purple and yellow flowers painted on the driver's side door. Unbeknownst to Rivera, the Silverfish also came with an additional passenger: Rosie. The tabby cat – of indeterminate age – had appeared in the ex-soldier's rear-view mirror a short time after he'd driven the vehicle away.

She'd been there ever since.

The Army clerks recommended he should draw early on his military pension. He'd followed their advice. It didn't make him a rich man. But it kept him in food and clothing. And, when the money ran out, he took whatever work came his way. He'd dug ditches; poured concrete; carried hods and worked as a doorman. He'd even picked up a few shifts working as a short-order cook. But, beyond that, he also had a range of more specialist investigative skills he'd picked up in the services.

Sometimes, circumstances called on him to put them to use. He didn't go looking for trouble, but he found it hard to walk away when he saw injustice being done.

Most of the time, though, he was content to ramble from campsite to campsite, taking things at a slow pace. Reading books, looking after Rosie, and wrestling demons from his past.

Spain, though, was different.

Spain was a holiday.

Spain had been Betsy's idea.

But now Betsy had gone home.

* * * * *

The couple had met in the north of England; they'd both been working in the same place. Rivera was still running away from his breakdown while Betsy was escaping a break up. The couple uncovered a vast web of deception and helped the police shut it down. Afterwards, Rivera was left with what had been termed a discretionary payment. And Betsy – having no other plans – had tagged along.

Driving Iris through France, they'd soaked up culture, and generally taken life easy. Their loose plan had been to keep travelling until the money ran out. Naturally, things happened. Before long, the couple were more than just travelling companions. And, romantically entangled, they spent most of the late winter in a small commune close to Biarritz. Once spring announced itself, they crossed the Pyrenees and then headed south until they ran out of land. Unlike any of his previous women, Betsy cast a spell on Rivera. He was so besotted he'd even considered proposing.

It had been a blissful existence; they'd moved into an apartment at the start of summer. Iris was a faithful servant, but the Spanish heat turned her interior into a sauna. Rivera argued they could tough it out, but Betsy had insisted. Besides, she'd claimed it wasn't fair on Rosie - the cat had accompanied them throughout their travels.

Then Betsy's father had been taken ill.

She'd headed home to look after him. Rivera had offered to accompany her, but it had all been very sudden. One morning, she'd received a phone call, and that same evening, she was on a flight out of Malaga. They'd spoken vaguely about dates, and she'd made noises about wanting to come back and join him in the sun. But she'd remained in Britain.

He'd stayed in Spain, finding labouring work on a nearby construction site and spending lonely nights thinking of her. Now, though, sitting in Jim's Bar, he was consumed by guilt. Rivera was no stranger to such a sensation. With Betsy, he'd quelled his tom cat-like behaviour, but – of late – he was once again being driven by his below-the-belt psyche. Last night had been typical. For him, casual sex was what a hit of heroin is like to a recovering junkie: a momentary fix before the onset of self-loathing.

He couldn't remember where Sharon had said she was from. Blackpool? Blackburn? Burnley maybe? He grinned ruefully as he recalled his late mother's assertion that anywhere north of Watford may as well be covered in permafrost. The youngish lady from the north was well-oiled by the time she lurched over to Rivera in Lineker's Bar. She'd asked him four questions. Are you married? Do you have any kids? Have you got a big cock? What's your name? The realisation that he could have done literally anything carnal to the woman in question had spurred his animal brain. But now it was the memory of those actions which filled him with disgust. In Sharon's hotel room, the two friends she was on holiday with had watched the couple gyrating from their adjacent beds. When he was finished with her, they'd asked him to stick around. He'd wanted to retreat, but had been drawn back to the fray.

His remorse was made worse by the incessant piss-taking he suffered the next day on the construction site. When he'd removed his shirt during a cigarette break, his co-workers had seen the giant, talon-like claw marks rent across his back. He looked like he'd been savaged by harpies.

Chapter 3.

Saïd mopped at his brow. It had been punishingly hot outside at dawn. It was already the kind of heat that feels like a physical adversary. Now, though, beneath the sheeted dome of the polytunnel, the midday sun was beating down, and the temperature was almost unbearable. He removed his gloves and wiped at his weeping eyes with the back of his hand. Then, he took off his baseball hat for a moment, adjusting the rough stitching at the rear where the rag-like strip of material was attached to protect his neck. He straightened his back and winced. Most of the guys who'd been working there for five years or more had already developed permanent stoops. Many of those who'd been working any longer were well on the way to early graves. He didn't want to be one of them.

He feared he wouldn't have a choice.

Saïd looked out into the distance over Pontiente Almeriense and then shielded his eyes. This was the heart of Almería's Plastic Sea. Wave after wave of greenhouses stretched; they were a continuous mass, hugging the undulating foothills and shimmering in the sunlight. Here, in the oven-like warmth, the bosses grew cucumbers; watermelons; peaches; peppers, and tomatoes. Each day, innumerable box loads were loaded onto trucks that arrived to make collections. From depots, the produce made its way into the peaceful, sanitised, air-conditioned aisles of supermarkets all across the continent.

The owners' companies turned over millions of euros every month. They lived in lavish, pharaoh-like luxury, frequently holidaying in luxurious climes, and sending their offspring to private schools and colleges. While their bank balances grew, they remained blissfully unaware of the misery and suffering their profits were built on. People like Saïd were at the foot of their pyramids. Other than a handful of overseers, Almería's Plastic Sea featured very few Spaniards. Mainly, the greenhouses ran on immigrant labour.

Some of it legal.
Most of it not.

Chapter 4.

'Alright, mate?'

The ex-soldier frowned, squinting slightly as he looked up at the man standing before him.

'Rivera, right?'

Nodding, the seated man slowly shook the proffered hand. The newcomer's palms were soft – Rivera assumed it was from tanning oil. He looked slathered in it.

'Name's Les Fletcher.' The new arrival's south London accent had a rasping timbre. He lowered himself into a chair, belched, and immediately lit a cigarette.

Rivera chewed his lip. Fletcher had dark hair flecked with grey that looked like it had been permed. He sported a Magnum PI-style moustache, and a gaudy Hawaiian shirt unbuttoned down to the middle of a protruding paunch. A thick gold chain was hanging from his neck; the medallion slung on the end of it resembled an Olympic medal. He wore salmon-pink chinos and a pair of deck shoes, and was bronzed to such an extent his skin almost looked like leather.

'I hear you've been asking after me?'

Rivera nodded. 'I need some garage space. My T2 needs some TLC.'

'Roger that. Well, you've got the right bloke,' the other man grinned. He reached into his pocket and deposited a business card on the table. 'Carvajal Rental Cars. That's me,' he announced proudly, pointing to the embossed logo. 'I've got a workshop out back. We can talk terms.' He stood up suddenly. 'Here,' he pointed at Rivera's half-empty glass. 'Let me get you a proper drink.' He grinned. 'That looks like the kind of watered-down sherry my gran would've drunk.'

Before Rivera was able to protest, Fletcher had stood up and was moving away towards the bar. He turned. 'You're eating, aren't you?' The ex-soldier opened his mouth to reply no, but the other man spoke first. 'Course you fucking are!' he grinned. Though there were families with young children present, he didn't check his use of expletives. For a moment, the ex-soldier wondered if he should say something to caution him about it. But then a man who was surrounded by his offspring at a nearby table, spoke up.

'Their Sunday roast is fucking fantastic!' he bellowed. 'More like Bradford than bloody Benelmádena!'

Fletcher nodded enthusiastically. 'Don't worry – I'll order for both of us...'

Chapter 5.

Saïd – like most of Pontiente Almeriense's immigrant workforce – had come from Morocco. Illegally. So, when the bosses told him to work from dawn until dusk, he did. Anyone complaining would simply be told to leave the site within the hour and not return. There was always the threat of the Guardia Civil if a worker became really uppity, too. And, if the bosses wanted to call in the big guns, they would mention the Kbir. Recently, the Moroccan mafia had done battle with eastern European gangsters who'd wanted to take over their turf. They'd more than held their own. When it came to agriculture, the Kbir skimmed off profits from the Plastic Sea; disrupted production wasn't in their interests – they were more than happy to violently make examples of disobedient workers.

So Saïd worked.

All day.

Every day.

He was a dinghy cast adrift, and at the mercy of the Plastic Sea. There was no such thing as a day of rest in Pontiente Almeriense. A day when you didn't show up was a day you didn't get paid. And, if you missed two days in a row, the chances of a job being there on the third were minute. There were no contracts, and an almost unlimited pool of replacements stood ready to take your place if you faltered.

No official terms or conditions.

You worked, or you didn't work.

You got paid, or you starved.

Every day was the same. At night, in the hovel he'd constructed, Saïd dreamed visions of ripe watermelons; succulent peaches, and emerald cucumbers. When he'd arrived in the country, he'd envisaged opening a restaurant. Now, he simply hoped to stay healthy long enough to work a way out of the fields for his sister and himself.

But the chances were slim. Saïd was an educated man – at least he was once. But that meant nothing here. He knew that much. Brains came a very distant second to brawn. And anyone asking questions was seen as a danger.

There were no shops on site. And so the bosses set up a company store. It was here where the workers purchased food and drink. The prices – of course – were massively inflated. But the workers had no choice – they were like miners of old; steelworkers from the days of unregulated industry. Shackled to the store. Indentured servants. Slaves.

That was why so many of his friends changed profession once the Kbir came calling. His cousin, Ishaq, was one of the few who'd resisted – but he was so naïve that not even the gangsters wanted him shuffling around as part of their crew. Then, there was Arraf – but he'd arrived in Spain nearly five years before. He wasn't quite Kbir, but he was certainly heading in that direction.

Saïd knew what the Kbir was. But he wanted no part; he knew what they'd do to Nour.

* * * * *

Years before, he'd made a promise to his mother. Propped up on pillows, she'd looked hard at him with her dying eyes, giving him strict instructions to look after his sister. The family home had been a breeze-blocked hut with an earthen floor and a corrugated iron roof. It had electricity but no running water. Compared to the Plastic Sea, it felt like paradise.

The next morning, Saïd's mother had died. He and Nour had left Drâa-Tafilalet a week later. But he'd remembered her words.

So he went on working. Picking. Sorting. Carrying. Loading. He scratched at his arm. It was welted from the pesticides that were continually sprayed. Most days, the crops were misted while the pickers were working. It was a perk of undocumented labour: the bosses could do what they liked. There were no masks. No protective clothing. They calculated there was more money to be lost from pausing picking than from losing a worker. After all, pickers were easy to replace.

And this was business.

The scabs covering his arms were forever being knocked off and then reforming; they wept pus and attracted flies. They became infected and Nour had to dress them as best she could. Then there was the cough; breathing in fumes all day long had given Saïd a constant wracking wheeze that woke him up in the night and made him constantly short of breath. His eyes were always swollen red, and he'd developed the stumbling gait of an old man. Sometimes, he felt twice his age. Other days, he felt nothing at all.

He wore gloves, at least. After one shift working without them, he'd purchased a pair. It was a lesson he'd learned quickly. His hands had swelled up to almost twice their normal size and had kept him in burning agony for days.

Saïd's constant fug of chronic exhaustion sometimes made it difficult to distinguish whether he was asleep or awake – he saw crops before his eyes in either state. And his worries weren't dispelled by dreams any more – they were invariably variations on the same theme: him lying dead, and Nour being forcibly removed by the men in the pickup trucks.

He squinted towards the mountains, dreaming one day he might simply walk over them and never return. The idea there was a free world so tantalisingly close beyond made his heart hurt. But he knew he'd never get there – he owed the bosses more than he could ever repay.

A barking voice brought him back to the present. 'Break time's over buddy boy!' The shout came from the end of a row of tomatoes. 'Get back to it ...or I'll dock you an hour.'

Saïd sighed. Bent back down to the base of the vines.

And started picking.

Chapter 6.

From the balcony outside his office in the Segovia Palace, Abdellah Rif surveyed a corner of his kingdom. His exclusive members' club with its spa hotel and its conference facilities was the finest place on the Costa.

For now.

With his next venture, he planned to outdo even himself. But for today, he was happy. At least reasonably happy. Or as happy as an endlessly ambitious workaholic could ever be.

It was his birthday. His *actual* birthday. Not that anyone else would have known. His mother, father, and brother were all long dead.

There would be no celebration today.

He looked out, watching as a dark coupé wound its way along the approach; lush gardens bordered an eighteen-hole golf course. *His* golf course. The establishment's three luxurious restaurants catered to the region's glitterati. Rif employed three Michelin-starred chefs to work on his premises – he was determined that no finer food would be served on the Costa. He pressed flesh with celebrities on the up and those on downward spirals who still crossed the threshold.

His threshold.

But it wasn't enough. It would never be enough for him.

He stared out. From his vantage point, he could see all the way down the mountain. As his eyes roved over the arroyos and ravines that cut through deep rocky reds and dark barren browns, they passed over sleeping whitewashed villages nestled in nooks and crannies. Endless olive groves stretched coastward, hugging the slopes. He placed a hand upon the balcony. The Segovia Palace was a replica of a Moorish building – its white stuccoed walls were inlaid with delicate terracotta designs and rounded windows. The east and west wings each had an angular tower that rose above them, while the central section – where Rif had his quarters – was dominated by a glittering domed roof.

*****

In the distance, pressed up close to the coastline, the landscape changed; the high-rise towers of coastal hotels rose against the shimmering blue of the Mediterranean where his next project lay. It was – he promised himself - the one that would change everything. The one that would make mere mortals look upon his works and despair. He'd spent three decades manoeuvring himself into a position where he felt ready to strike.

Rif looked out further into the hazy distance. He stared out across the sea and saw, looming on the distant horizon, the murky, shadowy outline of the African coast.

Morocco.

Home.

Once.

Chapter 7.

Rivera's rule was simple: he limited himself to a pint of beer at any one sitting. The only time he gave himself a pass was at Christmas. Or to celebrate a birthday. Or when Betsy encouraged him. But at all other times, his sobriety was strictly observed. His breakdown had been prompted by a bender of booze and drugs that had made him lose all control. He didn't scare easily, but that had made him afraid.

With Fletcher treating him to lunch, it had been all he could do to prevent beer being forced upon him. In between raising toasts to Arsenal, the other man talked endlessly. The bronzed, moustachioed figure looked halfway between a darts player and a night club crooner. It felt as if the only time he wasn't speaking was when he was inhaling on a cigarette. He was a force of nature – albeit one now rather ragged around the edges.

'What did you think?' Fletcher asked, belching contentedly. 'The food?'

'Oh – er – very nice,' Rivera nodded, smiling weakly.

'Yeah? I thought the beef was a little overdone myself. But it's cheap as fucking chips.' He eyed Rivera's empty glass. 'Another?'

'No thanks.' The ex-soldier shook his head. 'I'm going to fetch my motor.'

* * * * *

'Right!' Fletcher announced enthusiastically as he opened the large corrugated iron doors with a screeching sound. He stood back as an oven-like cloud of heat was released. 'Why don't you bring her in?'

Rivera did as requested, backing the Silverfish slowly into a corner and then cutting the engine. The workshop felt like a cave compared with the glare of the forecourt outside. Fletcher mopped at his brow with a handkerchief he'd removed from his pocket. The smells of oil and petrol were acrid.

'Catch,' Fletcher called out, throwing a set of keys to the ex-soldier.

'What are these?'

'Well, I figured you'll need some wheels for a little while, no?'

Rivera shrugged.

'Mates' rates.'

Silence.

'What kind of car is it?'

'Oh, don't worry – it's a crap one,' Fletcher smiled. 'That's why it's so cheap. Fifty a week - euros. Renault 19. Electric blue.' He paused. 'Once upon a time, it was blue anyway. Now it's pretty much held together by rust... Anyway, it's parked fifty yards down the street. Alpha 0849 Charlie Sierra.'

Rivera eyed the other man and then nodded slowly. For a moment, he was transported back in his mind to another inhospitably hot location. 'Thanks. I appreciate it.'

'No worries. Now – let's take a look at the old girl, shall we?' Fletcher cleared his throat.

'You sure? Don't you want to wait until it's cooled down a little? It's hotter than a firecracker in here!'

'No, let's get going. There's no time like the present. But I might be a bit slow today. You know, on account of the beer.'

Rivera nodded.

Chapter 8.

Rif left Morocco in the early 1980s. It had been easy then. His countrymen were allowed to pass freely – there were no visas required for the many, many men who worked in the fields, or the catering industry, or on construction sites. It was only later that attitudes hardened. Before that, people could come and go almost as they pleased. Communities sprung up, and there was plenty of work as the country – shorn of Franco's iron grip – began to fondly embrace capitalism. Rif's brother had preceded him by three years. His boastful correspondence had included money. He'd claimed he was setting up a business. Building a house. On another occasion, he'd said a new job had become available. The letters were regular.

And then, one day, they'd stopped.

Rif's mother swore it was because he was too busy. His father suspected the elder sibling had met a girl. Rif knew he was dead. The younger sibling had never believed what the letters claimed. He knew what his parents didn't – or *wouldn't* say: that a Moroccan man was a non-person in Europe.

But he'd agreed to go looking. He was ready to leave, anyway. The small world of his family was tedious to him; he was surrounded by a lack of ambition that didn't fit with his view of the world. When they put him on the bus, he made all the right noises: he'd write; he'd send money; he'd find his brother; he'd be home soon. But Rif was never going back. He'd had enough of hanging around at the bus station with all the other street kids, clamouring for the opportunity to shine the shoes of new arrivals. He'd tired of going door-to-door collecting payments for the men who ran numbers from cafés in town. And he was sick of scraping by; of picking pockets and mugging people for small change.

Once he was gone; he was gone.

* * * * *

His first job had been in the north. He wasn't called Rif back then. Khalil was his name. Abdellah Rif was another picker who worked beside him in the orchards – a man besotted with the new arrival. So, when Khalil killed a fellow picker late one night after an argument, it was Rif who helped him dispose of the body. It was an accident. A disagreement over a game of cards. The pair of them knew the dead man – a migrant – would have no paper trail. They all knew how men drifted in and out of the ranches and fruit farms as they followed the harvest. So someone being there one day and not the next raised few eyebrows.

After that, the pair became inseparable. Rif doted on Khalil. And Khalil made promises – he asked questions to which the good-natured Rif proffered honest answers.

By the end of the summer, Rif had a plan – he was intending to return home. To study. But that didn't tally with the other man's ambitions.

So, late one autumn evening, Khalil strangled him.

Chapter 9.

Rivera worked steadily. Methodically. Sweat poured from his face. He'd picked up some automotive skills in the Army, but it had really been Iris, a Haynes' manual and a great deal of trial and error that had been his teachers.

Throughout the ex-soldier's huffing and puffing, Fletcher stood by like a well-meaning nuisance, dabbing at his glistening brow.

First, Rivera backed the T2 onto a pair of blocks, raising it about five inches off the ground. 'I'm going to drain the engine oil,' he announced. 'Can you disconnect the ancillaries, please?'

'Er, yeah – remind me, can you?' Fletcher sniffed. 'It's been a while. I mean, since I've worked on a camper and all.' He scratched at the back of his neck. 'My fleet these days – the cars are all brand new, you know?'

Rivera grunted and did the task himself, frowning. Next, he removed the carburettor air cleaner, undoing the hose that secured the end of the intake pipe, and releasing the clips holding it to the support bracket.

'Nice!' Fletcher belched as he observed the ex-soldier from behind.

Rivera straightened himself and looked hard at the other man. 'Do you think you could check out the drive shaft connector for the fuel injection, please?'

'On it.' Fletcher nodded confidently. He stepped around the other side of the van and then reappeared. 'Yep,' he nodded. 'All good.'

Silence.

Rivera frowned.

'What? You don't trust me?' The other man tilted his head slightly. 'I've been in this game nearly all my life. Man and boy.' He blustered and hitched up his belt.

Rivera sighed, setting down the spanner he'd been holding. 'Except you haven't, have you?' he began.

'How do you mean?'

The ex-soldier raised his eyebrows. 'Number one: your hands are too soft. There's no way you've worked on cars with skin like that. Number two: the T2 doesn't have fuel injection. When you went around the back, you just counted to five and walked back... Anyone with any kind of awareness about cars would know that.'

'What?' Fletcher laughed uncomfortably. 'You're a fucking chancer!'

'Number three: you used the Nato phonetic alphabet when you gave me the car registration.'

'Loads of people do that!' the other man protested. 'You'll find fucking dog walkers round here that use it... probably.'

'Maybe. But very few say *Roger that* in conversation.' Rivera paused. 'Not unless they've been in the military. Or the police. But definitely not if they're a car salesman.' He gritted his teeth. 'That's what I think, anyway.'

Silence.

'So what? You don't think I'm on the level?' Fletcher laughed uncomfortably.

'No – not as a car man, at any rate.' The ex-soldier shook his head. 'So... what are you? Police?'

'You know,' Fletcher sighed. 'I reckon it takes one to know one. Your cover story's not so fucking good either. You don't spot things like you've spotted unless you've been in the game.'

Rivera shrugged. 'What you see is what you get. I never claimed to be a car salesman, did I?'

'No. But all that hippie bead bullshit doesn't fool anybody, either.' He paused. 'Copper?'

'Negative.'

'Military?'

Rivera shrugged. 'Some. I've done a bit of investigating too, but it was a while back.'

Fletcher nodded. 'Thought so. Anyone who would vouch for you? I mean – officially. Back in Blighty?'

'Yeah. Why?'

The other man sighed and looked hard at Rivera, weighing his words carefully. 'I've had my eye on you,' he announced. 'Nothing fancy. Don't worry – I've not been queering you up or anything. But I'm running a thing here. An investigation. Nasty business, but I've got an in.'

'Good for you,' Rivera shrugged.

'Yeah,' Fletcher nodded. 'But the police here. Some of them are good guys – at least I *think* they are. But...'

'...you can't be sure?'

'No, and some of them are fucking useless. So I might need some boots on the ground I can call on.'

Rivera chewed his lip and stared back, pensive. 'What's it got to do with me?'

Fletcher shrugged. 'Well, you look like a guy who can handle himself. I can put you on the payroll if you like?'

'Yeah?'

'Yeah. I'll even chuck in the Renault for free if we can drop this ridiculous me-pretending-to-be-a-mechanic lark.'

Rivera laughed, drily. 'This was never about the garage space, was it? You were just looking for a chance to talk to me, weren't you?'

Fletcher said nothing.

'How long have you been watching me?' the ex-soldier pressed.

'Couple of weeks. On and off.'

'Why?'

'Let's just say I had a hunch. And once you started asking around for a workshop, I figured I'd make an approach.'

The ex-soldier's expression clouded. 'You had me checked out already, didn't you?'

Fletcher nodded. 'A little.' He dabbed at his forehead; he was sweating even more profusely now.

Rivera began walking towards the doorway.

'There are people who speak very highly of you, you know?' Fletcher called after him.

The ex-soldier shrugged and carried on walking, squinting against the vicious onslaught of the sunlight. Shimmering heat danced above cars parked on the road outside. Beyond them, a truck's transmission protested as its driver ground the gears; the vehicle climbed wearily up the steep incline outside the garage.

'So, what do you reckon?' Fletcher enquired once the engine noise had subsided.

Rivera paused in the middle of the forecourt; a silhouette. He turned. 'I'll think about it.'

Chapter 10.

Rif's murder had been a spur-of-the-moment decision.

Afterwards, Khalil took the dead man's bag before casting his body into the swollen water of a nearby river. He'd dragged the corpse to a high bridge and dropped it where the current was strongest. With a sharpened blade, he'd removed the last digit of each of the man's fingers and done the same with his toes. Afterwards, he'd used a pair of pliers to tear the teeth out of the corpse's mouth. He scattered the digits as he walked away: food for the wildlife. The teeth, he'd buried.

* * * * *

Three years later, Abdellah Rif had moved south, switching to the construction industry where he muscled his way into a number of lucrative contracts. He learned the trade and painstakingly assembled a team good enough to undercut many of his Spanish competitors. Moroccans would work harder for longer than their European counterparts. And Rif's boys would work harder and longer than anyone else.

Ever since, Rif had been on an upward trajectory; he'd grown wealthy beyond his wildest dreams and possessed the kind of power he'd never imagined possible. But now, there were those who were throwing obstacles in his path. He didn't approve. His business strategy had always been simple: if someone got in his way, he crushed them. Every time. It was an approach that had never failed. Its continued success made his latest challengers all the more surprising.

Then there was the camera flash he'd seen. The idea of an errant print emerging was not something he'd countenance. As a result, his heavies were running names; leaning on people. Abdellah Rif believed the world should work on his terms – anything else was an irritation.

He rose from his chair and returned to the office.

There was – as he liked to remind himself – no rest for the wicked.

Chapter 11.

Rivera sat on the balcony of his rented apartment. The temperature was already climbing. He'd been there for an hour - watching the sun rise over the swimming pool was a morning ritual. As dawn changed the tableau to the brilliant hues of *A Bigger Splash* by David Hockney – an enormous Western Montpelier Snake habitually slithered across the rough grass and swam a width. The ex-soldier was yet to capture it on film in a way that made it look as impressive as it truly was, but he'd vowed to keep trying.

Fletcher's offer dominated his thoughts. But the lack of clarity about what he wanted set alarm bells ringing. Rivera reasoned it either meant Fletcher didn't have much information, or that he was worried the details might put him off. Neither possibility filled the ex-solider with confidence.

As he pondered, he smoked his second cigarette of the day. Later, it was simply too hot to light up, so his tobacco was restricted to the shade of his apartment. Renting the place had been Betsy's idea – Rivera had been in the market for something a little more rustic. But, after they'd vacated the T2, she'd wanted a pool and a sea view.

So that's what they ended up with.

Latinaja was a complex nearing the half-century mark. Roofed with terracotta tiles, its grounds featured flower beds and lawns of buffalo grass. Over the years, it had gone through various phases: rich retreat; package holiday destination; drug den, and now, a mid-market resort. Betsy had loved it. Most of the inhabitants were permanent residents, and there was a strong sense of community. The view from the balcony took in the brilliant turquoise of the shared pool below. And, at a distance of around two miles down the hill, was the glittering sheen of the Mediterranean.

It was a view Rivera never tired of.

But now Betsy was gone. Although it wasn't technically a break-up, it *felt* like a break-up. Not having her with him made him realise how much he wanted her to be with him. So he did what he always did in times of anguish: he stubbornly refused to think about whatever it was that was bothering him.

Betsy had been the breadwinner, taking on freelance work as a copy editor. He'd protested at first, but she'd insisted - the cash he'd left Britain with hadn't lasted beyond France. And the arrangement worked; she set up a little office in the apartment, and he spent his days heading out into the hills. Rivera's great passion – other than working his way through paperback versions of literary classics – was bird watching. It stilled his mind. Unlike most of his fellow ornithologists, though, he didn't use binoculars. Instead, he peered at kestrels, kites and Spanish eagles through a military-grade sniper scope liberated from his previous employer.

* * * * *

It was up in the hills he'd run into Pancho, a dreadlocked PhD student conducting funded research. Since Betsy's departure, the wildlife photographer had become a sometime flatmate. His latest project was sponsored by the University of Madrid. Nights saw him tramping the hills and setting up camera traps in search of Iberian Lynx. The project would, he'd explained to Rivera, form the foundation of his doctoral thesis.

Pancho paid a little money whenever he stayed over, but it wasn't enough to keep Rivera from the daily grind. So, the ex-soldier had taken a job working construction. He simply turned up as part of a crew each morning and followed instructions, working on the building of a new complex. It was brutal, boiling labour, but he could feel himself growing fitter each day. After half a year of idle living, he was back in shape.

Rivera rose, stretching. He picked up his Dickens paperback and tucked it inside his rucksack. The contents of his bag were simple: a book; his sniper scope, and six litres of water. As he stood, he tied two bandanas over his head so they trailed down, covering his neck.

* * * * *

The apartment was medium-sized. It had a living room, two bedrooms, and a galley kitchen with a breakfast bar. When Betsy and Rivera moved in, it had still been cold. The tiles on the ground had been freezing. Walking across the floor on a chilly morning had felt like traversing a frozen lake. Now, though, their coolness was welcome. Each evening, when he returned from work, Rivera removed his shirt and lay down for ten minutes, letting the tiles drag the heat out of his back.

As he opened the door, he unlocked the barred grille covering it, and stepped onto the footbridge linking the apartment to the road. Rivera was about to lock up when he spotted the tall, skinny frame of the photographer approaching. He wore a gilet and khaki shorts. Pancho's dreadlocks were tied loosely back, and he sported a pair of mirrored sunglasses. Unlike most of his peers, he still used film. Rivera had questioned him about digital photography once, but the other man had looked at him through sad, dark eyes, and accused him of heresy.

'Any luck?' Rivera enquired.

'Maybe,' the photographer yawned. 'The traps were sprung, anyway. But we won't know until the film's developed.' He paused. 'Right now I'm dead beat - I'm going to hit the hay. It's too hot for me.'

'But you're Spanish!'

'Exactly, hombre. We steer clear of the midday sun – we're not mad dogs or Englishmen...'

Rivera nodded, grinning. It always amazed him how well Pancho spoke English – the photographer's fluency was the legacy of a couple of years spent in London. He peppered his speech with slang and idioms; the ex-soldier swore the photographer's English was better than that of most of the men and women he'd served with in the military. Rivera clapped his friend on the back and then walked over the rough parking area hewn out of the hillside. Before, he'd parked Iris there, but now Fletcher's formerly electric blue Renault 19 had pride of place. The ex-soldier climbed in and started the engine. It coughed a couple of times and then roared into life. Rivera engaged the clutch and edged down the road in the direction of the coastline, towards Torremuelle. Here, he would collect Miguel and Gonzalo – they were on the same construction crew.

The price of their lift: lunch.

It was an arrangement that suited Rivera perfectly. He dined well on their dime each day in a hole-in-the-wall café they knew: bocaillos; patatas bravas; paella; pinchitos; tortilla espanola, and empanadas. Today, in response to their merciless ribbing about the scratches on his back, he'd decided he would request even *more* of a banquet.

Chapter 12.

Saïd was already awake as the sun rose on the El Barranquete shantytown. Once the fingers of dawn light found their way through the flimsy walls of his abode, there was no escape. No chance of sleep.

The home he shared with Nour was constructed from off-cuts and salvaged timber. All the homes the workers lived in were. They were simple dwellings that had to be rebuilt half a dozen times each year – whenever there was heavy rain or high wind. He'd left Morocco seeking wealth and luxury; his mother's house would have mocked his current abode.

Saïd pulled aside a blue tarpaulin sheet that was stretched between crates and a sheet of corrugated iron. He believed it was better than sleeping under the stars. But only just.

In winter, they froze. In summer, they baked.

There was no sanitation. Nor was there much in the way of hope. The only thing driving the pair onwards each day was the fragile dream of escape.

* * * * *

When Saïd first arrived, he thought El Barranquete would be a short-term measure. At least that's what he'd told himself. But now, it was a way of life. He only wished he could accept it as his lot. His curse was an active brain which constantly reminded him of a world beyond where he was. He loathed the books he'd read. Despised the lectures he'd sat through – they'd made him unable to simply switch off in the way his fellow workers seemed able to do. The fruit picker donned his gloves and picked up the crumbs of his breakfast. On his way to the greenhouses, he would throw it in the quarried out space that served as a refuse tip.

But dumping it there didn't stop the rats.

They were everywhere; at sundown, they'd swarm through the bivouacs, returning to their burrows in a seething mass of blackness. In the morning, they'd emerge again, searching for sustenance. During the day, they were left to roam free. People had little money for poison in El Barranquete. Food was more important.

Of course, the greenhouses were surrounded with traps and bait stations – the crops they protected were valuable. But the workers weren't; the shantytown was like a third world corner of the first world.

Sometimes Saïd wondered if he and Nour were the only ones who still felt anything. Those surrounding them walked around glassy-eyed. Comatose. It wasn't just that they'd given up on life; they shut out the world with whichever chemicals they could procure.

From the company store, the workers purchased food. For everything else, they used the Narcotraficantes. The Narcos dealing drugs for the Kbir rolled through each night in giant Ford Rangers. Unopposed, they set up stall at the edge of El Barranquete. There were drugs to stay awake. Drugs to keep you going. Drugs to numb you to the monotony of your life. Drugs to kill the pain. And drugs to prompt sleep deep enough to shut out the cockroaches the workers shared their hovels with.

All of them were expensive – more than the sailors of the Plastic Sea could afford. And so, the workers were all in debt to the Narcos. If they weren't already in thrall to the company store, the Kbir made sure they were all but owned by them instead. Their daily pay went to the men in the pickup trucks, and it turned into a vicious cycle from which they would never escape. Unless, like Arraf, they changed sides.

Everyone obeyed the Kbir. There was no arguing with them. And if anybody was foolhardy enough to try, the punishments they meted out were more than sufficient to dissuade anyone else from following suit. They were the law. The Kbir *always* got what they wanted.

And they wanted Nour.

* * * * *

Saïd yawned. Moving away from his hovel, he joined the exhausted army of emaciated fruit pickers trudging towards the greenhouses. It was a scene played out innumerable times in history; the dispossessed making their helpless way towards another shift where they would be exploited by those in power. Reaching the perimeter fence, they were held in place until their names were written down by the overseer.

For the first time that day, a familiar thought crossed Saïd's mind. It was a thought he'd think a hundred times before sundown. A thought that plagued him. Torturing him constantly.

He could work for the Kbir.

The offer was there. As time wore on, his moral stance felt more and more ridiculous. Arraf had spoken to him about it the last time they'd met up. 'I promise you, cousin,' he'd explained. 'It's easy money. You load the truck. You drive the truck. And then you unload the truck. That's it. Simple. You do what you're told and don't fuck up, and you get out of this shit hole.'

But Saïd knew it would make him a powerless man. He was already a powerless man. But if he went to drive trucks for the Kbir, he would just be switching one form of powerlessness for another.

Living in El Barranquete, he wasn't confident he could protect Nour. But, if he went to work for the Kbir, he *knew* he wouldn't be able to.

He'd heard about what they did with girls like her.

Chapter 13.

'They filled this one in quickly, didn't they?' Miguel frowned as he turned to Rivera and swigged from an oversize can of carbonated energy drink. It sometimes seemed like he lived on the stuff.

Although he couldn't always respond, the ex-soldier's Spanish was now good enough to understand most of what his colleagues said. In the military, he'd done intensive courses in Pashto and Dari and had also received instruction in basic Arabic. The language of the construction site, though, was not something he'd been tutored in – it was simply something he'd picked up.

'Who was working here over the weekend?' Gonzalo asked as he surveyed the scene. The concrete that had been poured into the foundation trench was now set hard. It wore a light coating of dust. The worker frowned. 'They must've had the truck here to finish up this lot.' He prodded at the solid grey foundations.

'Maybe Cesar drafted in some extras?' Ishaq shrugged.

'I guess...' Rivera said, unconvinced. He cast an eye across the site. 'They don't seem too fussed about making us work hard this morning, though?'

He nodded over towards the Portakabin where the bosses and architects usually hung out. Cesar was sitting on a folding chair, smoking a cigarette and scrolling through his phone. The architects hadn't yet arrived. Nor had the surveyors. It was a typical Monday morning – everyone knew how hot it would get, and nobody was in a rush to leave the shade.

'What are you saying, senõr?' Miguel asked.

'Probably nothing,' the ex-soldier sighed. 'But if they're paying people overtime to pour concrete on the weekend, they must *really* want the job finished.'

'So?' Miguel shrugged.

'So, I'd have thought they'd want to *tener a raya* on Monday morning too. Surely?' Rivera replied.

Gonzalo chuckled. '*Tener a raya*! You're picking up the lingo!'

'Yeah, crack the whip – I like it. Not bad for a *guiri*!' Miguel laughed.

Guiri was a term the workers banded around any time they passed Bar Lineker down on the seafront. Miguel and Gonzalo would shake their heads and mutter under their breaths at the scene they saw: lobster-hued tourists sitting in the direct sun consuming all-day English breakfasts and watching re-runs of Premier League football matches; bunting strung up overhead, and chalked up blackboards advertising special deals on jugs of sangria. It was here that Rivera – an occasional visitor - had encountered Sharon and her harpies.

From the Portakabin, Cesar whistled.

'Time to get working, ladies!' he bellowed as a collective groan sounded. 'Scaffolding's going up today. The truck will be here in fifteen minutes.'

Chapter 14.

On the other side of town, the day began in a very different fashion. Camilla Pérez was going places. She was a million miles away from the squalor of El Barranquete, and the heat and drudgery of Rivera's construction site. That she was on an upward trajectory was evident to anyone who crossed her path: the car; the clothes; the manner. She revelled in the fact that some of those under her command referred to her as a force of nature. With her husband Sergio, she'd built a real estate business from the ground up. They'd started with nothing, and it was due to her dynamism they'd smashed through barriers placed in their path.

A decade ago, they'd had a small flat close to the port. They'd made good on the scraps thrown to them by larger agents. Now, they owned three large houses. Their children went to fee-paying schools. They skied. They had country club memberships. And they rubbed shoulders with the best and brightest in Costa del Sol society. Pérez was being talked about by the kingmakers who facilitated paths into politics, and her husband was doing more and more investing overseas.

Three months ago, Sergio had inked their largest contract yet. They'd diversified – from simply selling properties, they'd moved into renovation and remodelling. Their next project was to be their most significant. One of the smaller shoreline hotels - a 1970s block - was a shadow of its former self. The Pérez family planned to return it to its former glory. Not only would it make their name, but it would make them a fortune. Ten years before, making a million had seemed insurmountable. Now, though, making a dozen times that suddenly seemed realistic.

This morning's meeting was in a private member's club with a German company called Rhineland Kapital. Her Mercedes had been valet parked. The location wasn't a surprise to her – the bigger the money on offer, the more exclusive the surroundings had become. As the Pérez family had moved into higher stakes, so they'd begun to deal with foreign investors with deeper and deeper pockets. Their organisation had a success rate of around seventy percent in such meetings – she knew this was, in no small part, due to how she presented herself. She aimed for elegant but unapproachable, attractive but unavailable.

As she swept into the boardroom carrying a leather laptop case, she was greeted with a familiar sight: a polished table; embossed document folders in each place; crystal decanters filled with water, and a duo of money men wearing identical suits who sported humourless expressions. The only surprise: the absence of her husband. He was due to be there alongside her.

The men at the other side of the table shook her hand. She apologised for her husband's tardiness and suggested they make a start. At this, each of them opened their folders.

Reading silently, Pérez looked up, surprised at a sudden interruption. The door opened, and an uninvited guest arrived.

'This is a private meeting...' she began.

'I know,' the man walking across the room nodded. He was dressed in an expensive suit. Beneath his smile was an air of menace. He looked at the two Germans. 'Gentlemen,' he announced. 'If you please...'

The two men stood casually and swiftly made their way to the door. As they did, another man entered the room. He was darker than the first; younger; more muscular. Despite his immaculate suit and impeccable manners, he carried an undeniable sense of threat.

'What's going on?' Pérez frowned. Her voice was confident, unwavering. Her heart, though, was suddenly beating faster at the intrusion.

'Just someone who wants to talk to you... Miss Pérez,' the new arrival smiled.

*****

Abdellah Rif didn't believe in small talk; he'd trained his enforcers to avoid it too. Didi had learned well. Of course, the woman would never know of the connection to Rif. Nor would she ever learn Didi's name. When she called the police, as she doubtless would, she'd simply report him as a Moroccan – the trail would then go cold. But, just to be sure, Rif was playing the back nine of the Segovia Palace's premium course in the company of the mayor and several of his advisors at that very moment. Plausible deniability never hurt anyone.

The visitor ran his eyes over the woman, smiling thinly, saying nothing. As he approached her, his associate set up a portable projector and connected it to a laptop.

'Listen to me...' Pérez began.

'No,' Didi sighed, as if in bored irritation. 'You listen to me. I'm not here to fuck about, and I'm certainly not here to be dictated to by a woman.' The venom of his statement hung in the air; the implied threat was like a barb to the woman's heart. Instantly, the visitor recovered his poise of politeness. 'We are in the same business, after all, madam.'

'We are?'

'Yes,' the man nodded. 'The hotel you recently purchased. My boss is buying it from you.'

Pérez frowned. 'No,' she insisted. 'We've signed the contract it's...'

'...just a piece of paper,' Didi interrupted. He chuckled. 'My associate has a new contract here for you to sign.' He nodded. 'That way, the ownership can transfer to the rightful party.'

Pérez's eyes widened as he slid a piece of paper across the table to her. The woman couldn't quite compute the other man's certainty, or the way he'd quashed her expectations of the meeting so entirely. She gasped as she scanned the contract. 'But this is a fraction of the value!' she exclaimed. 'It's...'

'...a fair offer,' Didi interrupted. 'There's subsidence – you might have been unaware...'

'Absolutely not!' Pérez's expression hardened. She banged her palm against the surface of the conference table.

Didi sighed. 'This is business.' He smiled. 'I understand – I make an offer. You reject that offer. So I'll make another offer. Yes?' He paused. 'You know where El Caminito is?' he asked.

The woman frowned and then nodded slowly. 'But...'

At this, the man's associate pressed a key on the computer. The generic hotel screen saver switched to the live feed of a terrified man.

Her husband.

Pérez gasped. 'Sergio!'

* * * * *

Sergio Pérez was sat in the family car next to the precipitous El Caminito bend. His wrists had been lashed to the steering wheel. There was no audio, but as her husband's sweat-drenched face stared at the camera, Pérez cried out imploringly, her mouth shaping utterances of pure desperation.

'It's a terrible shame,' Didi sighed. 'People drive too fast around that bend all the time.' His tone hardened. 'You've got two minutes to make a fucking decision. Either you sign this and he lives, or his brakes fail.'

Silence.

'You can't fucking do this!' she spluttered, eventually.

'On the contrary, Ms Pérez,' he shrugged. 'I *am* doing this.' The visitor paused. 'I'm just doing my job...'

'But you'll ruin us!' She stifled a sob.

The man nodded at his associate. Suddenly, the picture changed. Involuntarily, Pérez raised her hand to her mouth and stifled a cry. 'You have beautiful children, Ms Pérez,' Didi continued. The screen displayed still photographs of Lucía and Lucas – her daughter and son. 'It would be a terrible shame if something untoward were to...' He gestured vaguely in the air, all the while regarding Pérez with cold intensity.

'I'll sign,' she announced, grabbing the paper and scrawling her signature on it.

The visitor nodded, satisfied. His associate swiftly packed away the laptop and projector. 'It – er – goes without saying this meeting never happened,' the man smiled. 'Otherwise...' He paused, allowing the unspoken threat to sink in. 'How many phones do you have?'

'Two,' she stammered.

Didi narrowed his eyes. 'You're sure that's the truth?'

Pérez nodded.

'Place them in your bag,' Didi instructed. 'Your belongings will be left with the valet. You will be able to collect them when you leave. A hotel employee will be stationed outside the boardroom door for the next ten minutes.' He narrowed his eyes. 'They may be wearing a hotel uniform, but they work for us.' He paused. 'Do not try to leave during that time. Understand?'

The woman nodded, tears streaming down her face.

'After that, you're free to leave as you wish. You might even be tempted to call the police.' His countenance darkened. 'But if you do, then maybe you won't recall too many details of what happened here.' He paused, letting his words linger. 'We have many friends on the force.' His expression brightened once more. 'It's a pleasure doing business with you, Ms Pérez,' the visitor smiled.

Chapter 15.

'Can I stay then?' Ishaq repeated.

'Yes.' Rivera sighed in frustration.

'Nice one!' Ishaq punched the air in celebration. The young, skinny construction worker poured the remnants of a bottle of water over his dreadlocked hair and held up a hand for Rivera to high five. The ex-soldier, unenthusiastically, acceded. Ishaq was one of the few people that made Rivera feel old; his boundless energy was such that, even now, at the end of a working day – when the rest of the crew were dead on their feet – he brimmed with enthusiasm.

For the last week, he'd been pestering Rivera to permit him to sleep on his sofa for a night. The youngster had barraged him in Spanish. When he'd claimed lack of comprehension, he'd switched to English. And then, when the older man took to ignoring him, he'd changed to Arabic.

Rivera couldn't win.

Ever since Ishaq had seen the giant advertisement on the seafront that boasted of a big-wheeled extravaganza in the fenced off parking lot of a closed-down supermarket, it had been all he talked about. But Ishaq's family lived miles away. He didn't drive, and each morning he arrived at the construction site at the end of a series of bus transfers.

So Ishaq had sought out Rivera as a soft touch. His methods of persuasion were far from sophisticated. He was like a four-year-old in the way he simply barracked his listener, grinding him down in a war of verbal attrition. He'd begged and cajoled until his fellow construction worker had relented.

Rivera sighed, placing his hands firmly on the youngster's shoulders. 'If you say one more word. And I mean only one more word, then the deal's off. Understand?'

Miguel and Gonzalo laughed. They'd both delighted in the youngster's antics. The two construction workers had a bet riding on how long it would take the ex-soldier to cave in.

Ishaq opened his mouth to speak and then closed it again, nodding instead. He had the bright-eyed look of an innocent puppy that had been promised a walk.

* * * * *

Later that evening, Pancho and Rivera stood in the kitchen looking across the breakfast bar at Ishaq. The young construction worker hopped excitedly from foot to foot. He'd upped the pace of his excited patter as he described everything he knew – and much that he didn't – about the monster trucks event.

'You're stealing my look!' Pancho grinned. As he stood opposite the dreadlocked Ishaq, it was difficult not to note the resemblance between the two men. Both were tall. Both were rail thin. And each of them wore their hair in an identical fashion.

Rivera smiled. He stroked Rosie as she ate a sachet of food. Ever since being in the apartment, she'd become an indoor cat. But being confined hadn't seemed to bother her. She'd simply compensated by spending almost all her time asleep. The ex-soldier hadn't missed having to clear her daily offerings of mice and rats.

'Right then, you,' the ex-soldier turned to Ishaq. 'I'll drive you down to the seafront if you like?'

'What – you want to come to the show?' Ishaq blurted out before covering his mouth.

'No...' Rivera laughed. 'But you dancing around and talking all the time is driving me insane.' He shrugged and shook his head. 'I'll be glad to get you out of the apartment! I don't think I can take any more talk about big-wheeled trucks!'

Ishaq grinned a little sheepishly.

'Can I ride along, senõr?' Pancho enquired. 'I'm catching a bus to Malaga. I've got a load of films that need developing in my buddy's dark room.'

'Dark room?' Rivera shook his head. 'Dark ages more like! You do know that digital photography's all the rage these days?'

Pancho shrugged. 'Sometimes, the old ways are the best.' He paused. 'Anyway, this is coming from a guy who drives a 1972 T2. And, yesterday, I saw you reading a book... that was made from paper!'

'Touché!' the ex-soldier laughed.

Pancho grinned. 'I should be back at the weekend. That OK? We might even have a hunter who'll help us out for a couple of nights with tracking. We know where the Lynx go at night, and we've mapped some of their trails. What we haven't yet worked out exactly is where they go in the daytime.'

'The Iberian Lynx,' Rivera explained, addressing the frowning figure of Ishaq. 'He photographs them.'

'Cool,' nodded Ishaq before returning his gaze to the lurid colours of the monster trucks leaflet.

Chapter 16.

'You think?' Saïd frowned.

'I know,' Nour insisted, annoyed at her sibling's disbelief. Her dark brown eyes opened wide in an earnest expression. 'I wouldn't say so if I didn't!'

It was just after sundown. The pickup trucks of the Kbir had recently departed. The dust from their wheels still hung in the air. Some of the residents of El Barranquete had lit fires to cook food. Most, though, were simply lying on the ground in exhaustion. Nour and Saïd had eaten well for a change. Today, she'd been moved into a different section for the first time. There'd been an extra twenty euros in her pay at the end of the shift.

'I know what I saw,' she insisted. 'Hashish.'

'What do you know about hashish?' her older brother frowned. His tone was dismissive.

She sighed. 'I don't walk around with my fucking eyes closed all the time. We live in El Barranquete. Remember?' She sighed. 'Things happen here.' Nour's eyes narrowed at her brother's reaction. 'What? You think I don't know what the guys in the pickup trucks do?'

Silence.

Saïd tutted. 'So talk me through it then, if you know so much.'

Nour smiled. 'I knew you'd be curious!'

'What?' he protested, a little defeated. 'I just want to know what Arraf does. I mean, *really* does.' He paused. 'Enlighten me.'

Chapter 17.

The sun deck outside Jim's Bar in the early evening was quiet. Rivera sat with Fletcher in the bat-heavy twilight. Far out to sea, the dying light was a bruised thumbnail of dark purple on the horizon. The pair of them looked down at the twinkling lamps sparkling across the hillside. Only three of the other tables in the place were occupied. Inside, some of the more long-serving customers had a bridge club. It had been running for so long that the management gave it prominence – regular card-playing customers meant regular income and no trouble. Other regular boozers gave it a wide berth.

Fletcher's eye was drawn to an aged female bridge player who'd just lit a menthol cigarette. 'Jesus, look at the state of that!' he grinned. 'If I was twenty years older...'

Rivera said nothing.

'Her skin's like an old fucking handbag.'

'Pot, kettle,' the ex-soldier shrugged.

'Maybe it's Babs Windsor?' Fletcher joked.

'The rental car company is legitimate, right?' Rivera pressed, keen to get back onto the topic in hand.

'Yeah,' Fletcher nodded. 'I check the cars out and check them back in. The bloke that used to run it is a fellow called Keith Michaels. He's gone on sabbatical – he's still taking the money. I mean – he kind of oversees it. But the Met's moved him elsewhere for a while. The usual stuff. He doesn't mind, though. He's been here forever – he started out with a fleet of Fiat Pandas. Imagine!'

Rivera smiled. 'So, why are you here?'

'Well,' wheezed the other man, leaning in conspiratorially. 'That's a long fucking story.'

Chapter 18.

Nour shrugged. 'A truck came along. Everyone knew it wasn't a normal truck, even though it looked the same. Same markings. Same everything...'

'...but?' he interrupted.

'In the back of it, the boxes were only half full.'

'Of what?'

'You don't catch on very quickly, do you, brother?' She paused and shook her head as if in disappointment. 'What do you think they were half full of?'

'But they can't transport drugs like that,' Saïd frowned. 'Surely?'

'No.' She shook her head. 'They don't. I was sent in with another girl. They had raw garlic on the top half of each crate. To mask the smell, you see? So, first of all, we removed it.'

'Yeah?' Saïd frowned.

'And then we shifted all the boxes. They were numbered, and the hash was wrapped in plastic. Throughout the day, I put numbered crates onto each of the trucks that came along to take vegetables. Sometimes it was three or four. Sometimes only one. They even gave me a clipboard!' She paused. 'It's quite the system they've got going on – I reckon there were over two hundred crates in total.'

Saïd nodded. 'Why you?'

She shrugged. 'Because I can read.'

'And you agreed to it, though?' Her brother frowned. 'Why? You know what we said...'

She shrugged. 'What? Twenty euros no use to you?' Nour sighed. 'Did the food we ate tonight not fill your stomach?'

'Of course,' he protested. 'But that's not what we do – you and me. We get by the rest of the time, don't we?' His expression was pained.

She shrugged.

'What?' he pressed, his tone growing irritated. 'We've never gone hungry before. Have we?' He shrugged. 'I mean – we haven't always eaten like we ate tonight. But... you know what I mean, right?'

'Yes brother, it's a life of luxury.' She cast her arm around. '*Really* it is.'

Silence.

Nour turned back, facing him. Angry. 'What else was I going to do? If I didn't do it, they'd have fired me. You know that. And they'd have fired you too.' She sighed. 'Because that's how they work.'

'But Nour...' Saïd's tone grew heavy. 'The moment you have anything to do with the drugs, you're working for the Kbir.'

She laughed. 'And you think they can't reach us if not?'

He shrugged. 'At least our way we don't... you don't...'

'What?' Nour spoke with irritation.

'You know what I mean,' Saïd insisted. 'They want you. You're young. They want you for...'

'Go on. Say it,' she spat.

He sighed. 'You know what happens to girls who go to work for the Kbir? They're whores. They take them up in the hills and...'

'...sell them.' She sighed. 'I know.'

He turned, glaring at her. Indignant. 'You know?'

Nour shrugged. 'What is it with you and this whole babe-in-the-woods bullshit?'

Silence.

'I promised mama. Remember?' Saïd hissed eventually. He spat on the ground and turned, ready to speak. Then he changed his mind. 'I'm going to sleep,' he sniffed. He pulled the blue tarpaulin aside and crawled into the hovel.

Nour remained sitting, staring out across the surface of the Plastic Sea as it shimmered in the moonlight.

Chapter 19.

'Chas Edwards,' Fletcher announced. 'He's the reason all of us Old Bill came out here in the first place.' He looked at Rivera. 'Name mean nothing to you?'

The ex-soldier shook his head.

'That's why I was first posted to this area.' Fletcher took a long drag on his cigarette. 'It was the Costa del Crime back then, my son. You ever hear of the Great Train Robbery?'

'Of course. What was it – 1960s?'

'Sixty-three.' Fletcher nodded. 'Edwards was one of them. They plastered their mugs all over the press. I reckon they were as well-known as YouTubers are now – for a while, anyway.'

'So, how come he ended up here?' Rivera frowned.

The policeman shrugged. 'It was all to do with the law. Or lack of it.' He paused. 'You see, in the late seventies, a loophole opened up. There was an extradition treaty – it had lasted for a century or more.' He sipped at his beer. 'Then it expired. And it meant that if you were a British criminal here, you couldn't be shipped home. It was insane. You could have been tried by a jury, found guilty back in Blighty, and banged up. But if you escaped and made it over here, then you were all good.'

'And that's why you were here?'

'That's right,' Fletcher nodded. 'We were monitoring Edwards. He'd been in South America for a while in the early seventies. They reckon he flew over on a false passport and then got back on a fishing boat. And then he'd nearly been caught back in the East End living under a new name. A leopard like him didn't change its spots, you see. He was wanted for a jewellery heist and he'd been implicated in a gangland hit too. The idea was to try to tempt him out into the open – get him to Gibraltar. So, I was tasked with getting more dirt on the bastard.'

'And did you?'

'Oh yes,' he nodded. 'But someone else got there first. They never solved it, but I think his past caught up with him. One day he was living the high life, and the next he wasn't.'

'Dead?'

'Yeah,' Fletcher replied. 'Hit man. In the garden of his villa. Only about three miles from here, as the crow flies. Someone showed up on a moped.' He shook his head. 'Ironic really – the place was like a fucking fortress. But, anyway, out he stepped, and whoever was visiting – they capped him. And that was that. Dead as a fucking dodo.'

'They never found them, then – the killer?'

'Negative. Then it all became about the *omerta* – nobody wanted to name names. There were no grasses. No snitches. So the whole thing is still open and on the books. It'll never be solved now, though.' He shrugged. 'After that, the force couldn't justify keeping my squad out here, so they shipped us home. Back to the Smoke. Rotherhithe.'

'You've not suddenly started chasing the killer again?'

'No, no.' Fletcher shook his head.

'So what's the deal, then?' Rivera enquired.

Fletcher cast his eyes around furtively and then leaned in. 'Does the name Abdellah Rif mean anything to you?'

The ex-soldier shook his head, frowning.

Fletcher lowered his voice further. 'Moroccan. Everyone knows about him. Well, everyone who's been here a while. You can't swing a cat round here without hitting something he owns. But he's an enigma - he just kind of appeared one day. Emerged like Stalin out of the fucking Politburo and then started bumping off any would-be Trotskys. And he's been growing ever since. Construction. Hotels. Restaurants. Drugs. Racketeering. Prostitution. You name it.'

'And where do you fit in?'

The policeman sighed. 'Well, his organisation is pretty shady, obviously. It's called the Kbir.' He paused. 'You should google some of this shit, you know?'

'Yeah – I'm trying to do one of those digital detoxes,' the ex-soldier shrugged.

Fletcher frowned. 'I know a bloke who did the same thing once – he'd got addicted to online porn.'

'No comment.'

Silence.

'Anyway,' Fletcher went on. 'We haven't been able to infiltrate it in the usual ways. We're not Moroccan for starters.'

'No kidding.'

'But I've got an in. Something that'll work. *Might* work.'

Rivera nodded.

Fletcher drew on his cigarette. 'Back in the day, all the East End gangsters used to move out to Essex. Then, in the eighties, they all came here. And if you ever wanted to find them, you'd go to the Segovia Palace. You know it?'

'That big place up in the hills?'

'Yeah.'

'But you said those days are gone, right?'

'That's right,' Fletcher nodded. 'The gatekeepers have changed. But the location remains. It's still all about the Palace. Only these days it's Rif's place.' He paused. 'He's tarted it up too, in fairness – it looks like quite a classy joint these days.'

'And it's legitimate?'

Fletcher laughed. 'Well, it's legitimately his. But the money he used to buy it... well.'

'So what are you going to do?' the ex-soldier frowned. 'Get him on tax evasion?'

'He's not Al fucking Capone!' Fletcher paused, incredulous. 'I mean – he's *like* him, but they don't make mistakes like that any more. Not guys like him. They have people to hide things now. The money gets washed clean. *Really* clean.'

Rivera nodded. 'And I fit into this how exactly?'

'I'll let you know. Plans evolve.'

The ex-soldier sighed. 'You're going to have to give me more than that if I'm going to put my neck on the line.'

'Just bide your time, mate,' the policeman grinned.

Chapter 20.

Tatiana took a long drag on her cigarette. She sucked it right down to the filter and then ground it out against the uneven brickwork of the wall. Moss and creepers clung to the stonework. A leaking gutter had cast a long, dark stain down the faded whitewash. In the early evening it looked almost like a Gothic castle fallen on hard times.

Torre de los Boliches was quiet.

But it was quiet for much of the time. It was only after midnight that things changed; that was when the cars began to arrive.

Tatiana cast a glance along the deserted quadrangle. It was spookily lit by the pale glow of the moon. Down the middle of the shale path, grasses and weeds had sprouted – there was little need to remove them.

A guard stood – a dark silhouette in the distance. Occasionally, the tip of his cigarette flared like a firefly.

A warm wind whipped up, blown over the water from Africa. A wind whispering of the Sahara. Tatiana scratched at the track marks on her forearm, wondering once again how she'd ended up where she had.

She knew, of course. But it felt like another lifetime.

*****

Once upon a time, Torre de los Boliches was destined to be the biggest resort on the Costa del Sol. Positioned up in the hills, it was private; secluded even. As a gated community, it was designed to cater to the higher end of the tourist purse. It was a potential gold-mine. Not bad for an overlooked patch of scrubland.

But then the credit crunch happened.

When production of the complex was completed in 2007, the first half dozen of its 200 apartments had already been sold. By late

2008, though, there were still 180 remaining on the market. With the global economy tanking on the back of defaulted sub prime mortgages, the value of the apartments plummeted. Promised riches suddenly seemed to glitter only with the empty reflection of rhinestones.

And the prices kept falling.

The gates had been closed for good in 2009 - at least to the public. Only two residents had still been in situ. They were closeted away in penthouses that had consumed almost all of their savings. Their plan had been to wait out the recession until the euro picked up again. They consoled themselves with the idea the markets would inevitably rise again at some point.

But then the Kbir moved in.

And when they did, they made the residents an offer they couldn't refuse.

Leave.

Live.

* * * * *

Torre de los Boliches was still exclusive; it catered only to a certain kind of clientele: people with significant disposable wealth. But its target audience had changed. Before, glossy brochures had been emblazoned with aquamarine swimming pools. Genteel retirees were depicted strolling carefree through its shaded walkways arm-in-arm. Rainbow-like floral arrangements lined the paths.

There were no brochures now.

No couples.

Just young women and rich old men who visited them in the night.

When he'd taken the place over, Rif had picked it up for a song. He'd seen its potential immediately: a high-class clip joint attracting moneyed punters from all over the Costa. The Russians had largely controlled vice up to that point. They'd tried to muscle in on some of the building trade, so Rif saw a counter-punch into their territory as simply being tit-for-tat. Just desserts. He knew once the first few customers left satisfied, word would spread. Discretion was guaranteed; security assured. And the prices charged reflected its exclusivity.

It became such a source of revenue that Rif had taken to running a nightly coach service from the Segovia Palace right to its doors.

* * * * *

Tatiana absent-mindedly rattled her balcony, frightening away a pair of pigeons. She scratched again at her forearm, cursing. Her skin was white; pasty. She was trapped in an endless groundhog day, devoid of charm. She very rarely saw the sun.

Few of the nightingales who serviced the guests did.

The old sensations sprang upon her suddenly. An ache; a pain; the onset of the shakes. Tatiana sensed the first pinprick droplets of perspiration beginning to break out on her forehead; the feeling of listlessness. It would soon be time for her hit. Her daily dose. That's how they ruled her, keeping her in thrall to the needle. They'd done the same thing ever since she'd arrived.

It was the same for all the girls.

They had no choice. Emil - the so-called doctor who dispensed the shots - was accompanied by an armed guard each time. No arguments. No fuss.

Tatiana lit another cigarette, exhaled deeply, and leaned her head against the cool of the wall, trying to still her mind.

Memories of Russia flooded back.

But that had been long ago. A lifetime. She'd been young then, and strikingly beautiful. Dmitri – her handsome, strong husband - had insisted they leave. She didn't blame him. It was a stark decision: he could run away or go and fight in Chechnya.

So they'd left. Of course, it wasn't a move that was officially sanctioned. He'd confided in her and no one else; certainly not his patriot parents. One night, they'd simply slipped away.

They'd promised Igor – a smuggler – they'd pay back the enormous amount of money they owed. They'd met him in the back room of a bar, along with a crowd of his prison cronies. Fixing them in his cold, expressionless stare, he'd outlined the terms; he'd made them aware of the dire consequences they would suffer if they tried to cross him. They'd both made promises, swearing their loyalty. But once they were over the border, they'd given his people the slip.

They'd opted, instead, to disappear.

It worked. They got clear. Over thousands of miles of late-night bus journeys, they'd covered their tracks. They were satisfied they'd dropped from the grid. Then, under false names, they'd worked their way around the Baltic until they reached Italy.

And then Dmitri died.

Chapter 21.

Fletcher returned with two drinks. Beer for him, and soda water for Rivera. He set them down on the table next to an ashtray.

'Makes me depressed sometimes,' the policeman sighed as he sat down.

'Are you having a crisis of confidence about your shirt?'

'My shirt?'

'Yeah – I'd be depressed if I was dressed like that. What do you call that shade – Technicolour yawn?'

'Cheeky sod!' Fletcher shook his head. 'No. It's this Rif bloke that makes me depressed. The new breed. These Moroccan gangsters...' He shook his head. 'They've got no chivalry.'

'What, and the Brits were better?'

Fletcher sniffed, looking pensive. 'They had a certain... quality. A kind of classiness about them.'

'You're joking, right?' Rivera raised his eyebrows. 'What's classy about paying a river man to ditch bodies in the Thames? They coshed the driver in the train robbery, remember? He was just a normal bloke – a family man. And what about Brinks-Mat – those fucking security blokes were covered in petrol, weren't they?'

Fletcher shrugged, defiant. 'I don't know – there was still something charming about things back in the day.' His eyes twinkled. 'You'd go up to the Segovia Palace, and they'd all be there. Sharp suits. Molls on their arms. Dunhill cigarettes. Dry Martinis. Tips flying around the place. Hatton Garden jewellery. They looked good – I'm telling you.'

Rivera frowned. 'I do worry that all the sunshine must've addled your fucking brain.' He sipped at his beverage. 'Just because they had nice threads didn't make them good! Even if they weren't all killers, they all *knew* killers. They robbed people. Beat people. Busted heads. Mistreated women. Ruined lives...'

Silence.

'What? Too philosophical for you?'

'They had a code!' Fletcher insisted, a little hopefully.

'Bollocks!' growled Rivera. 'What made them any better than the new breed?'

'Well... I could understand what they were saying, for starters.'

'That's just racist!' the ex-soldier protested, shaking his head. 'Being a bastard isn't to do with borders or languages – you know that. There are twats and good people everywhere. A criminal's a criminal, right?'

Fletcher grinned. 'When it comes to banging up criminals, I'm colour blind. But – you see this lot hanging around on street corners in tracksuits. Gold chains. Football shirts. Baseball caps. It's uncouth. They'd slit your throat as soon as they'd look at you.'

'Oh what? And the Krays wouldn't have?'

He shrugged. 'At least they were always good to their dear old mum.'

'Yeah, because she was fucking terrified of them!' Rivera scoffed.

The policeman looked across the table and shook his head, taking a deep gulp of his drink. 'You're an obstinate bastard, Rivera. You know that?'

The ex-soldier laughed. 'You've only known me five minutes. You don't know the half of it.' He put his drink down. 'Anyway, tell me what I'm needed for, then I'll decide if you can put me on the payroll. So far you've been nothing but nostalgic.'

Fletcher grinned.

Chapter 22.

Tatiana and Dmitri had both dabbled in heroin before reaching Bari. But it had been there, on the shore of the Adriatic, that they'd both developed a real taste. At first, it had merely been an experiment; a leisurely pursuit. But where they'd started out partaking after work, they soon found themselves working so they could partake.

One afternoon, she'd returned from a café and found him lying still. His skin was pasty, and his eyes were lifeless. The syringe was still hanging from his arm.

Minutes after was the moment she truly realised she was hooked. She found herself shooting up the remains of his supply, combing his pockets for cash, and making herself scarce before summoning an ambulance.

After that, it had been a downward spiral. Her looks had already started to suffer under the onslaught of the needle. She was still attractive, but where looking good had been effortless, now there was an edge of desperation to her appearance - a hunger glimmering just below the surface.

A year later, she'd become one of dozens of eastern Europeans plying their trade on roundabouts along the beach road of the Costa del Sol. They shared rooms in cheap apartment blocks. Shared clients. Shared needles. Occasionally, the Nacional de Policía would cart them off to the cells for soliciting. But most of the time, they let them well alone.

They knew what went on.

Everyone did. And rounding up a load of street walkers made for giant piles of paperwork. So long as they kept themselves reasonably scarce, they were allowed to carry on.

* * * * *

Then, one night, she was ushered into the back of a big black Bentley with tinted windows and driven up to the hills. There was going to be a party – that's what the driver had told her. The exchange of words had been short – she realised she was being given no choice.

She'd been in the hills ever since. These days she had some privileges – it was her job to keep an eye on what the Kbir called their new acquisitions. She'd protested. But she had no choice. Without the work, there were no drugs. And without the drugs…

So she did what she was told.

And somehow, she'd become one of Rif's favourites. He'd drag her out on his arm to soirees and then make her suffer whichever indignities his most esteemed guests dreamed up. Sometimes he'd watch. Other times, he'd send her off with an associate while he talked business.

It was at one such evening that she saw him.

Igor.

And her past came tumbling back. It was unmistakeably him. Older now. But then, so was she. He hadn't seen her – she was certain of that. Miletski didn't look massively different to how he had in the back room of the bar years before. He'd simply scrubbed up a little and put on an expensive suit, but he was still the same man. She'd tried to tell herself it was a one-off – an isolated incident. But if he was consorting with Rif, he'd be at the Segovia Palace again. And men like Igor didn't forget debts.

Chapter 23.

Fletcher leaned in close to Rivera. 'I want Rif,' he hissed.

The ex-soldier frowned. 'You said he's untouchable?'

'*Was* untouchable. I think the wheels are coming off a little, though. The fucker's taken his eyes off the prize – he's got complacent.'

'Really?' Rivera chewed his lip.

'Yeah, he's got some competition, so they say. There are people muscling in. He's got the Russians on one side, and the Albanians have been giving him gyp too. For decades he's had things his own way – but now the eastern Europeans are circling like vultures. Word is that he's going soft.'

'I've heard that before.' Rivera pursed his lips, unconvinced.

'But I think we can set him up,' Fletcher insisted. 'Frame him. Honestly!'

Rivera narrowed his eyes. 'Honestly? That doesn't sound very honest, Fletcher.'

The policeman shrugged.

'But the courts will chuck it out, won't they?' the ex-soldier went on. 'They'll say it's inadmissible. You know how this kind of thing works. Evidence obtained under duress. Unauthorised wire taps – I've heard it loads of times.'

'So, we have to do our best to expose the whole thing. I mean *all* of his operation.' Fletcher sighed. 'We've got a chance here – an in. We need to take advantage.'

The ex-soldier scratched at his head. 'Let me get this straight. You're going to infiltrate a foreign organisation. You don't speak the language. You're not trusted by them. And then, you're going to do a fix-up job.' He paused. 'I think you're insane. To be honest, I think you're just playing out some little Flying Squad fantasy. Only trouble is... it won't fly.'

Fletcher laughed. Then his voice hardened. 'I've been after this bastard for three years, Rivera. I nearly had him, and then he slipped away. He's a fucking monster – he thinks he's Teflon-coated. But I'm going to get him this time. I promise you.'

The ex-soldier frowned. 'With who? Who's the in?'

Fletcher dropped his voice a little lower. Rivera could only just hear it above the warm wind tugging gently at the canvas of the lowered parasol. 'I've got a girl.'

'Lucky you.'

'Not like that,' Fletcher protested, rolling his eyes. 'She's one of them. A hooker. She's shit scared. I've cut her a deal.' He paused. 'Immunity. Witness Protection. That kind of thing.'

'Do you have that kind of power?' the ex-soldier frowned. 'What are you – in bed with the commissioner or something?'

'No.' He shook his head. 'But there's a guy I know here who can grease the wheels. Interpol.'

'Really?'

'Yeah – he can pull all sorts of strings.'

Rivera narrowed his eyes. 'So why's he not going after Rif himself? I mean – he'll have sufficient resources, right?'

Fletcher sighed. 'He is. But it's my informant we're using, so it's my gig.' He paused. 'He's Dutch – he reckons the Kbir are responsible for most of the drug trade that ends up going through Rotterdam. So... we get Rif and we close down that leg of their operation. It's like a mutual appreciation society.'

'So, they can put deals on the table?'

'Yeah.' Fletcher leaned back. 'They can indeed.'

* * * * *

'Have you seen this?' Fletcher enquired, unrolling a newspaper and flattening it out on the table.

Rivera scanned the headline:

ALONSO FERRERA STILL MISSING.

He nodded. 'Yeah – sad.' He paused. 'Why?'

Fletcher sighed. 'We think it's a kidnapping. And we think it's got Rif's fucking paw prints all over it. He's worried about something – at least that's what I reckon. That's why he's lashing out. Usually his targets are rivals, so we can't work out the link. But we've picked up a little chatter – seems like he's spooked. This guy's a doctor. Spanish.'

'Can you prove it's him?'

'Negative.' The wind whipped up again. Fletcher looked off towards the coast before turning back to face the other man. 'There's worse...' he said quietly. 'Much worse.'

Silence.

'You going to tell me?' Rivera pressed. 'I mean – you keep dangling these nuggets of information and all...'

Fletcher sighed. 'You know about the dark web?'

'A little,' the ex-soldier nodded.

'Well... we can't link him to it, but his associates have got things on there. At least that's what our experts reckon. They think he's using it to monetise things – it's some grisly shit, too. Only lately, they've been stepped up.'

'Why use the web?'

Fletcher shrugged. 'It's easy. To scare people. Remind them who's in charge.'

Rivera nodded. 'How bad are we talking?'

'*Really* fucking bad.'

Rivera frowned. 'Do I want to see?'

Fletcher shrugged. 'If you're going to come on board, I think it's only fair you know the kind of person we're dealing with. He's an arsehole. Ruthless. Mean. Cruel.' He paused. 'All of the above.'

The ex-soldier puffed out his cheeks. 'Is this about Ferrera? This – whatever it is, I mean?'

'No,' Fletcher replied. 'We think this is something else.'

Rivera sighed. 'Go on.'

'We can't trace it,' the policeman began. 'We've had all sorts of IT experts involved, but the place it's routed from just keeps bouncing around too fast. The moment they think they've got a fix, the signal pops up somewhere else. It's a kind of encryption our guys haven't been able to get their heads around.'

'So what's it got to do with you?'

The policeman sighed. 'The poor fucker involved has a placard hung around his neck. It looks like a scene from a summary execution or something.'

'Yeah? What's it say?' Rivera pressed, intrigued.

'I'm a snitch from the Costa del Sol.'

'Well, it's hardly sophisticated, is it?'

'It doesn't need to be.' Fletcher shook his head. 'He has a noose around his neck. And he's positioned outside. It's in real time, so sunset and sunrise correspond with here.' Fletcher paused. 'We know there's a pool, but if you send a drone up to look, you can't move for pools around here, can you?' He paused. 'Anyway, he's gagged and his hands are tied behind his back. But even that's not the biggest problem.'

'Then what is?'

'His feet are resting on a giant block of sugar.' The policeman paused. 'It's covered in ants. I mean – millions of them now. More and more all the time. So many it doesn't even look like sugar any more. It's just a seething, wriggling mass of hungry insects and...'

'...when they've eaten their way through the sugar, the man dies,' the ex-soldier interrupted.

'Exactly. And what's worse is that it's become like a dark web pay-per-view snuff movie – they're calling him *Sugarman*. You've got psychos all over the globe glued to their screens, cheering the ants on. Our computer people have told us there are even people running books on how long he's going to last. They think it's Rif's people doing that too.' He paused. 'Sick bastards.'

Silence.

'Anyway,' Fletcher continued. 'That's Rif for you. If you come on board, you're not going on stakeout... you're going to war.'

Rivera nodded. 'I appreciate the warning.'

Chapter 24.

Rif ended the call. He leaned back in his luxurious leather chair, looked across the mahogany sheen of his desk, and stared through the windows. Idly, he played with the crystal paperweight on the desk before him. It was solid. Heavy. He'd once used it to smash the skull of a subordinate. His other ornament was a scorpion sealed in amber. The creature was forever set in a pose, suggesting it was ready to strike. Rif called the artwork *Don't-fuck-with-me*.

Replacing the paperweight, he frowned.

Alonso Ferrera had been a good man. At least Rif *thought* he'd been a good man.

Once upon a time.

But the doctor he'd trusted had failed him. So, he had to die.

It was the same with Adil.

* * * * *

For years, everything Rif touched turned to gold. His construction firm had gone from strength to strength; his workforce increased year on year, and the number of buildings bearing the name of his organisation grew on an annual basis. In truth, Abdellah Rif didn't believe in charity – not unless it was an act of charity that benefitted him and him alone. But he'd realised it bought him favours. He'd realised he could use donations to leverage influence. So he did what he needed to do to secure future contracts.

With each property acquisition, his influence grew even further.

But then, one day, he ran out of luck.

* * * * *

The plan had been simple.

Rif wanted to buy Castillo Football Club. He had no great interest in sport, but he saw the potential benefits being an owner would bring. FC Castillo was a reasonably big club. But Rif believed it could be huge. It was in a prime spot next to the Mediterranean. And with investment, he believed he could make it into something enormous. The team's shirts would bear the name of his construction company and he – Abdellah Rif – would bask in the glory they would go on to achieve. Not only that, but he'd heard of sports washing – he knew the more money he ploughed in, the cleaner it would become.

And when it came time came to sell, he would simply flog his purchase to the highest bidder.

He'd bought most of the board. That was easy. And the club was nicely positioned for promotion to La Liga. Once that happened, he knew its value would soar. It was then the work would really begin. Rif's plan was to gamble big; he'd sink everything he had into the club in pursuit of European qualification.

Rif had little doubt that, if they secured a Champions' League place, a rich sheikh would come calling. And once that happened, he'd sell up and disappear into the sunset with all the profits. It would, he was convinced, fast-track him towards being part of the establishment. With a seat at the high table, his image would look as fresh as the emerald surface of the stadium's hybrid turf.

The deal was on the table. The money was ready.

But then came a problem Rif had not foreseen.

Chapter 25.

Miguel and Gonzalo climbed out of Rivera's car a short way down the street from Bar Lineker. A large banner advertising a karaoke night had been hung across the deck.

The two Spaniards looked from Rivera to the bar, and then back again. They smiled meekly.

'What?' he shrugged. 'Just because we're from the same country doesn't mean we're all the same.'

'Mierda!' laughed Miguel. 'But you still go there!'

'Only occasionally!' Rivera protested. 'It's not my fault – there's a certain type of lady I have need of every once in a while.'

'See you tomorrow senōr,' Gonzalo grinned, slapping the roof of the car.

Pensively, Rivera watched the two men walk away. Away from the beach, the building fronts grew older; more faded. And the shops suddenly began catering for locals rather than the tourists. The gaudy neon emporiums of the coast road became grocery stores and hole-in-the-wall taverns. The ex-soldier looked on as the two workers turned beneath a fire escape and disappeared into an alley.

Rivera pulled away. Then he stalled. Fletcher's Renault 19 hadn't failed him yet, but it was an obstinate drive, nevertheless. Iris had her quirks and frequently complained when being driven. But Rivera always felt it was worth it. She was a character, after all. The Renault, though, had no such charms. It stalled, on average, three times a day. Miguel and Gonzalo had taken to cheering each occurrence – they'd even offered to light a candle for the car the next time they went to confession.

It was time – the ex-soldier reflected – for him to make a concerted effort to fix Iris. He knew he'd have to brave the oven-like interior of Fletcher's lock-up once again, but her engine was currently in pieces, strewn across the garage floor.

Rivera's Haynes manual had been bedtime reading for the best part of a year. Some sections were almost imprinted upon his brain from him scouring them so many times. He'd been leafing through it the previous evening before falling asleep, and needed to collect it before heading up the hill to Carvajal Rental Cars.

He only hoped Ishaq wouldn't still be there. The youngster had been asleep on the sofa in the morning when Rivera had shaken him awake, dreaming of monster trucks and reeking of alcohol.

'What time did you get back?' the ex-soldier had enquired.

Ishaq had held up four fingers, groaning.

'So... work today?'

The youngster had flipped him the bird and then turned over to continue sleeping.

'OK,' Rivera shrugged. 'I'll tell them you're sick.'

Chapter 26.

Rif's nemesis was Ignacio Ibanez. Throughout his lifetime, he'd taken umbrage with plenty of people. Some had become clear enemies, while others simply faded into the shadows. Few, though, had ever crossed him as spectacularly as Ibanez.

The nightclub crooner turned hotelier had made a last-minute bid for FC Castillo. And it had been accepted. Rif had beaten him to the ownership of Torre de los Boliches years before, and had publicly gloated afterwards. It was a detail the Moroccan had conveniently forgotten. When the deal for the football club was agreed, the crooner had only had slightly more capital to plough in than his rival. But he was Spanish. Even at the lofty heights he'd reached, Rif knew that in some people's eyes he'd always be an immigrant.

And that's why the board changed its mind.

As soon as he heard of the Ibanez coup d'état, Rif began plotting the other man's downfall. Consumed by hatred, a red mist had descended. Revenge had become his raison d'être – everything else had gone by the wayside.

* * * * *

The club's most valuable asset was Nazir Rabbat. The Moroccan international was a superstar in the making. Born and raised in the foothills of the Atlas Mountains, he'd been signed by Casablanca as a youngster. He'd then moved to Auxerre and now, at a mere nineteen years of age, the outgoing owners – for their final act - had signed him. Though he had little interest in the day-to-day running of the club, Rif had developed a fondness for the youngster – he saw his rags-to-riches story as a reflection of his own.

But now the club was the property of Ibanez.

Rif, hell-bent on vengeance, knew that with Rabbat plus an injection of fresh cash, prospects for promotion were good. It would – he feared – see Ibanez taking all the glory for the foundations he'd laid. So, he paid the young player a visit, and made him an offer he couldn't refuse.

But he refused.

* * * * *

The demand was simple. To secure pole position in the segunda division, Castillo needed to defeat bottom-of-the-league Cartagena. So Rif decided Rabbat and his teammates should throw the game. He'd place a series of massive bets on the outcome he desired. That way, he'd get rich and could begin to instigate Castillo's demise. Without promotion, the investment Ibanez had made would plummet in value. It would – Rif assured himself – serve as sweet revenge until he could organise something even better. More than anything, Ibanez would lose face.

But Rabbat hadn't complied.

Not only that, but in a show of defiance, he'd scored a hat-trick as his new club put Cartagena to the sword, and secured the league's top spot. Watching on the giant screen in his office, Rif saw the striker rush to the corner and blow a kiss to the camera after scoring his final goal.

He knew it was a gesture meant for him. The boss' second-in-command was a man named Amrabat. When he'd entered the office to ask a question soon after the goal had been scored, Rif had been so enraged that he'd flung his crystal paperweight at the other man.

For almost the first time since he'd left Drâa-Tafilalet, he felt like he'd lost hold of the reins. Someone else was pulling the strings. Rif was a control-freak – he couldn't bear the idea another person's agenda was being enacted.

Someone wasn't following orders.

Rabbat had wronged him. So he sent Adil to kill him.

* * * * *

It was to be a straightforward hit. Adil would enter the complex where Rabbat lived; he would be disguised as a gardener. The young footballer lived in an exclusive location inhabited almost exclusively by Spaniards and Caucasian foreigners. The chefs; the gardeners; the litter pickers and all other maintenance staff were North African. It gave Adil an aura of invisibility. After all, what was one more Moroccan to the men on the gate? His orders were to enter the footballer's apartment, disable the alarm system, lie in wait, and make the kill.

Simple.

But it had gone wrong.

The first Adil knew of his failing was when Rabbat shook him awake. The hit man had secreted himself between the bed and the wardrobe and waited. He'd known the footballer would be out at training for most of the day, and he'd been right. He'd spent the morning idly flicking through the channels on the enormous flatscreen. What he hadn't planned on doing was falling asleep.

When Rif looked back, he realised he'd made the wrong choice: Adil was a football fan. Rather than shoot his quarry, Adil stared at him; wide-eyed; star-struck.

Nazir Rabbat wasn't just a pampered footballer who'd been wrapped in cotton wool on his journey through a series of sporting academies. He'd grown up in Beni Mellal.

The Smith & Wesson 1006 had been cast aside as Adil had lain snoring. When it was aimed back at him, the hit man saw how the hand of his opposite number didn't shake. His finger simply whitened on the trigger. Seeing Rabbat levelling the firearm, it was clear the footballer had handled a gun before.

And, at that point, Adil told him everything.

Before the police removed him, the two men solemnly shook hands. Adil might have been spared. But Rabbat's hat trick had propelled him onto the radar of several huge clubs. Three days later, news broke that he was moving to England. The bid triggered a massive buyout clause, which meant that – all of a sudden – Ibanez was in line for a huge pay-out.

Adil ran.

That Rif risked looking like a fool was unacceptable. That the police were now sniffing around for details of the botched hit, only made things worse.

So Adil had to die.

That – Rif reasoned - should have been that. The gangster had a lifetime's worth of making problems disappear with quicklime and cement. But he'd caught sight of a camera flash in his peripheral vision. It was distant, but the prospect of the execution having been caught on film remained a loose end.

And Abdellah Rif didn't care for loose ends.

Chapter 27.

Crossing the road outside Latinaja, Rivera nodded at Pablo. The gardener seemed ageless. People said he'd been there tending the grounds ever since the place had opened. There were even rumours he'd farmed there before that. All Rivera knew was that the gardener had been a perpetual presence since he'd arrived, and that he was the cheeriest man he'd ever encountered. Seeing the ex-soldier, Pablo looked up from beneath his broad-brimmed hat and beamed.

'How goes, senõr?'

The ex-soldier shrugged. 'You?'

'I'm an old man. If I get to work with the sun on my back and eat a meal in the evening, then I'm happy.' When he wasn't discussing football, Pablo had a habit of talking in profound, philosophical utterances.

'San Miguel on Friday?'

'Of course!'

Rivera smiled. Since Betsy had left, he'd taken to drinking a beer with the gardener at the end of each week. They didn't talk much – they simply sat outside his tool shed and looked towards the coast as the shadows lengthened.

'Your guests? How are they?'

'I don't know what you're talking about!' Rivera grinned. He was pretty sure nobody ever followed the rules about sub-letting or reporting guests to the office. And he was certain Pablo would never say anything. He'd never mentioned Pancho, and he certainly hadn't talked about Ishaq.

'*Lots* of guests, senõr...'

Rivera grinned and then held a finger to his lips. He realised Ishaq had clearly not been an incognito lodger. He frowned, wondering what kind of domestic squalor would greet him in the apartment. 'I'll see you Friday.'

'You will,' the gardener grinned.

Rivera waved and crossed the footbridge.

Entering, his eyes took a moment to adjust to the darkness. Inside, the shutters were still closed. Rivera picked his way carefully across the lounge. As he did, Rosie rubbed herself against his legs, mewing.

Navigating the gloom, Rivera reached the French doors. He turned the handles and flung them wide, then he reached for the cord to open the blinds. The light of the late afternoon flooded in. Rivera glanced around.

Ishaq was still stretched out on the couch.

Rivera stared at him for a long moment.

The youngster was dead.

The ex-soldier dialled 112.

Chapter 28.

'No.' Saïd shook his head. His expression was taut; adamant.

'Why not, cousin?' Arraf frowned in disappointment. It was dusk in El Barranquete. The last slivers of sunlight were disappearing over the horizon far out to sea. Crows were cawing above the refuse tip at the edge of the settlement. The two men smoked Arraf's cigarettes and stood facing each other. The visitor was wearing a Barcelona shirt and a New York Yankees baseball cap. His designer tracksuit bottoms overhung expensive white trainers, and he wore a thick gold chain around his neck. The men who worked for the Kbir knew their wealth might not last forever. They tended to flaunt it in ways that made their attire look almost uniform. Saïd, in contrast, was clad entirely in washed-out denim and wouldn't have looked out of place in a Dorothea Lange photograph.

'It's not my kind of thing. I've told you before.' Saïd repeated his oft-proffered argument. By now, it was more like a thin-worn mantra.

Arraf shrugged, watching the dark figure of Nour walking towards the refuse tip. An enormous rat made its unhurried, fat-bellied way across the path behind her. She bore a bag of refuse slung from one arm. In her other hand, she carried a large, empty plastic container. El Barranquete was like a desert. But to grow crops, the farmers had to irrigate them. Even unscrupulous overlords couldn't deny their workers water. So a pipe had been diverted to the shantytown. It was here, each evening, Saïd's sister made her pilgrimage, filling up the containers they'd use for drinking and washing. On good days, the residents purchased bottled water from the company store – if not, they had to drink the brackish, metallic-tasting liquid from the hose.

Arraf nodded towards Nour. 'Well, it may not be your kind of thing. But do you really think that living here is *her* kind of thing? You think that's what your mother would've wanted?'

Saïd narrowed his eyes.

Chapter 29.

Tatiana drew heavily on her cigarette. She'd already worked her way through half a pack and she'd only been awake an hour. It was no matter; the Kbir controlled the pirate tobacco trade - her Marlboros came from Al Hoceima. The supply was all but unlimited. She yawned - the dope had made her sluggish.

Another dreadful night lay ahead. But all the nights were dreadful. Here, they were simply hamsters on a wheel, going endlessly round until they fell off.

She and her fellow employees would drink and smoke until midnight. Many of them would punctuate their evenings with bumps of cocaine in an effort to numb themselves. And then the cars would come. In ones and twos at first. After that, the coach would arrive, filled with punters. Rich men. Wealthy enough to afford Rif's prices, at least. Men with catalogues of depravities. It was a cattle market. The girls were meat, and the Kbir sold by the pound.

Many of the visitors, when outside of the complex, were well-respected lawyers; bankers; politicians; high-ranking businessmen. But here, they dehumanised their prey; divorced themselves from any kind of wrongdoing. The girls – they assured themselves – were escorts. They were keen to earn money for themselves before returning to their home countries. It was an easy lie for them to swallow. Handing over stacks of euros, the men somehow convinced themselves the girls operated willingly. They conveniently overlooked the armed guards and the nightingales' skeletal frames; their haunted eyes. They saw what they wanted to see.

The girls' reward? A dawn-light shot in the arm. Then sleep.

Tatiana knew it couldn't go on.

But, until she had another option, she had to carry on as if nothing had changed; arousing any kind of suspicion might be fatal.

She wouldn't be the first victim of not following orders. Torre de los Boliches was a place where humans were chewed up and spat out – wrung out until they weren't even really human any more. Tatiana knew she was close to that state. But somewhere deep inside, she kept a tiny glow worm of light burning.

Hope.

Chapter 30.

Arraf sprinkled snippets of information into his conversations with Saïd. Over time, the latter had pieced together a picture of the Kbir's operations. The headlines he'd known about already: drugs; intimidation; control. But, scraping beneath the surface, he was reluctantly impressed at the complex nature of their set-up.

The organisation was careful with their trucks. Their fleet bore the logos of a wide range of different companies. All of them were genuine, and all drivers had dockets and documents to prove it. None of them exceeded the number of hours they were allowed to drive. None of them drank alcohol or got high when they were on the road. None of them broke speed limits. None of them presented as being anything other than regular, honest employees. They were well paid but powerless.

Once you drove for the Kbir, you drove until they told you they didn't want you to drive any more.

Or they promoted you.

Or you died.

* * * * *

Arraf had driven trucks all over Europe, never asking questions. He simply loaded where he was told to load and unloaded where he was ordered to unload. He'd made money along the way, and dragged himself out of the life he'd loathed before. But he remained concerned for his cousins. And annoyed at the pride that prevented them from accepting his offers.

Each time Arraf saw him, Saïd seemed to have grown more withered; more haggard. He knew what working on the Plastic Sea did to people. He knew that sleeping in a bivouac would kill him. Even before the pesticides did. Saïd wore his age like a death mask. Living

– at least living in El Barranquete – was a young man's game. If he wasn't careful, Arraf knew his cousin would soon be too old for it.

And then there was Nour.

The Plastic Sea was no place for her.

It was no place for anyone.

So he persisted, encouraging his cousin to accept. Saïd said no. He didn't care for himself; he never had. But, this time, when Arraf had mentioned Nour again, he'd hesitated.

'You don't meet any old men in El Barranquete, cousin. This place fucking eats people.'

Saïd had shrugged.

'And you sure as hell don't meet any old women,' Arraf had continued.

Silence.

'I hear you're moving up in the world.' Saïd changed the subject.

Arraf nodded. 'Yeah – and there's space for you because of it.' He looked hard at his cousin. 'So, promise me you'll think about it. OK?'

Saïd dropped his cigarette butt onto the rough ground and stamped it out. 'I'll think about it,' he muttered, keeping his eyes averted from Arraf's searching gaze. 'But not a word to Nour.'

Chapter 31.

At eleven o'clock in the evening, Tatiana gathered the girls together in a room with soft lighting and sofas. In the corner, a bar was built into the wall. It was her job to serve drinks. To make merry. To exchange pleasantries with the customers. And, if they wanted to pay a premium, it was her job to accommodate their wishes.

The room served as a waiting area. It was here the girls gathered in between servicing customers. Rif insisted they had raffle ticket numbers tacked to their tops.

No names.

Every night, the numbers were changed. He didn't like the idea of favourites; he didn't want customers being fussy. Unless they wanted to pay extra – then they could do what they liked. They were welcome to enjoy the services he offered. But they were still *his* services. *His* rules.

Many years before, in a cold land where winter's dark was perpetual, Tatiana had been a promising student. An ice dancer – she'd skated on the frozen lakes around her hometown. Occasionally, she tried to remember what the cold felt like. The *real* cold. The cold that seeped into bones. The cold that left people dead if they stayed out in it too long. The kind of cold where if you were to spit, it would freeze solid by the time it hit the ground, scudding across the snow and ice. It was the memory of such cold that she retreated to from time to time – far away from the barren, dusty, scorched hillside where she was situated now.

The promising student who spent much of the year trussed up in furs was a million miles away from today's scantily clad madam. The taut curves of her body that men still found attractive remained remnants of her previous athletic prowess. But the room she was now in resembled a trading floor. Tatiana explained the day's pricing structure. Rif kept his ears and eyes open, and he made adjustments to undercut his competitors; to lure in potential high rollers. Prices fluctuated; it was a stock market of vice.

She laid out the night's plan: how many euros particular activities cost. How much money additional indulgences were worth. How much to charge for extra participants. How much of a premium was owed if the punters didn't want to use protection. Inadvertently, she'd become the go-between; a Sonderkommando. Years before, she'd read books about those Jewish prisoners forced to aid the murder machine of the Shoah, while knowing all the while that, soon enough, they would suffer the same fate as their victims. She wondered how they'd managed to close their minds to the horrors before them.

The heavily made-up faces around the room nodded in bored irritation. They'd heard it all before.

Finally, Tatiana explained when they were permitted to press the panic button that would summon the security guards. They would remove the punter and, if necessary, physically educate them about the error of their ways. It was a vanishingly rare occurrence, though. The rule was that the button could only be pressed if an employee was being throttled so viciously they were on the verge of blacking out.

It had happened three times before.

Twice, it had been too late.

But getting rid of bodies was not something that worried the Kbir. They were steeped in such practices. It was a numbers game; easy come – easy go. There were always new girls who could be brought in.

Rif didn't care – the fine he charged for death by misadventure suited everyone: Rif got richer; the punter got to feel like they'd dodged a bullet, and the stable of nightingales was refreshed with new personnel. When he'd taken over Torre de los Boliches, Rif's people had installed hidden cameras in each of the rooms. It was –

he'd informed his inner circle – an insurance policy. Discretion was the word he used most when talking up the after hours entertainment on offer. No names. No CCTV. Nothing that could place any of the punters there.

Unless he needed to.

The death of a nightingale was when the hidden cameras came into their own. It was a simple case of leverage. Rif rarely cared about the loss of life. But there was no harm in squeezing money when opportunity presented itself. In such an event, the security guards conveyed the punter into a waiting room, where they were served with drinks. Then, when Rif entered, he played both good and bad cop. He began as their friend. Patted them on the shoulder. Gave them a cigar. Served them another stiff drink. Assured them the authorities would never be told. Then, he'd bring in the worst of his mercenaries; the scar faces; the ones whose very expressions spoke of a bloodlust that could never be sated.

'It's like this...' he'd explain, heavily; regretfully almost. And then, using a remote control, he'd switch on the enormous flat screen on the wall of the room.

As the guest viewed the footage of their earlier actions, Rif continued his explanation. 'Like I said, the authorities won't be informed. But it's a complicated thing - making footage disappear. There are always difficulties. And unless we take care of them quickly, footage can find its way onto the internet. We can never be too careful. We have to double-check that everything's been destroyed – you know... to avoid anything unwanted coming to light.'

After the threat was made clear, it was simply a matter of horse-trading. Once a figure had been agreed upon, Rif proffered a handshake and that was the end of it. It wasn't as if he dished out receipts; he simply walked out, leaving the traumatised punter breathing what they believed were sighs of relief.

Nobody would ever discover the whereabouts of whichever girl had perished. Rif's construction company was forever erecting buildings. Many of their reinforced concrete foundations were bolstered by bodies in need of disposal. And, if they weren't cemented into the hillsides, there were myriad other ways of making them disappear, anyway.

Death, as Rif was fond of reminding people. Was just a part of life.

And anyway, the deaths he was obscuring weren't the kind that would trigger police searches. They were nightingales: runaway girls; junkies; under-the-radar workers; criminals. The girls usually went by other names – they certainly weren't officially documented. And there was nobody to report their absences, anyway. In short, they were the kind of people who could simply shuffle off their mortal coil without leaving so much as a footprint.

Tatiana cast her eyes around the room once more.

'Any questions?'

Silence.

Chapter 32.

Rivera had been officially incarcerated twice before. The first time was in the Army – he'd had an altercation with a fellow recruit during basic training. The argument had seemed innocuous enough, but in the charged, macho atmosphere of the intense 14-week period, fights were de rigueur. Men were being turned into killing machines; they took on the attributes of blunt weapons. The result was a swift descent into violence. His commanding officer put him in solitary confinement for 24 hours in an attempt to teach him a lesson. The second time had been in Hammersmith during his breakdown; his girlfriend had called the police, demanding they took him away. He couldn't remember much of the event – he suspected his narcotised state was a factor, but also that his amnesia was borne of shame.

The charges hadn't stuck – the arresting officers had realised he was in the grip of PTSD. Rivera had been self-medicating the traumas he'd developed since shipping home from Afghanistan. The cocktail of booze and drugs left him bloated and increasingly volatile. When he looked back, he couldn't remember exactly what had triggered the incident, only that he'd lost control completely. Rivera had never threatened the girl – it had been the furniture in their rented flat which had borne the brunt of his rage. But he was led away in handcuffs and slapped in the cells, nonetheless.

Being in a cell once again brought it all back. A prison is a prison. If a person's liberty is stripped away, the location makes little difference: the experience is universal.

Chapter 33.

Sunrise. Tatiana exhaled and settled back onto one of the leather sofas as the last punter departed - the man staggered drunkenly and grinned, leering. The air was thick with cigarette smoke. She turned out the lamps one by one as the other nightingales were ushered out and back to their rooms. The cleaning staff would come on shift in mid-morning.

The gates were guarded, but the sentries were lazy. She knew that much. On occasion, she'd slipped past them. But they all did from time to time. The place ran on favours – it was easy to find amenable guards. The type of favours they required were entirely predictable. And in exchange, getting out – if only for a few hours – was always a possibility. They couldn't go far, but sometimes not far was far enough – anywhere outside the grounds felt like respite.

Further down the corridor, Tatiana saw Emil making his rounds. The guards called Emil the doctor. He wasn't – he was just the man with the needles. Each morning, the girls were given a shot. The guards knew it would knock them out and that most of them wouldn't surface until sundown. Unlike the guards, Emil didn't seem to avail himself of the girls. But that somehow made him more sinister. His approach was methodical; mathematical.

That's how Rif wanted it.

When the nightingales surfaced again, the whole process started over. And Emil was on hand to top up their doses.

The guards only had to keep half an eye on the nightingales. They knew they were bound by the invisible bonds of addiction – even if they ran, sooner or later they'd have to return for their medicine. It was an inevitability.

Their passports had been confiscated long ago. And none of them had phones.

There was no escape.

Tatiana knew that.
But she had a plan.

Chapter 34.

When Rivera was processed at the National Police Torremolinos Benelmádena, the desk sergeant had – at first – assumed he was just another drunken *guiri*. He'd been brought through the rear entrance, straight from the yard, and made to remove his jewellery. On average, a dozen or so British troublemakers were processed each night. Cheap booze and plenty of holiday cash made for a potent combination. The reverse sweet-spot, where revellers seemed to combust, was usually at the finely balanced point between being paralytic and also feeling jilted.

Rivera had been compliant. He'd made a thorough examination of the crime scene after calling the police. The ex-soldier hadn't resisted arrest. Hadn't protested. He was aware of how things looked: a young man who he'd worked with was lying dead in the apartment he rented. As it stood, he was the guilty party.

'Anything to say?' the arresting officer demanded once Rivera had filled in and signed a series of papers. He spoke in English – the language in which most of his business was conducted.

The ex-soldier spoke bluntly. 'Phone call.'

'Excuse me?'

'Can I have my phone call, please?'

The desk sergeant, hearing what had been said, simply held a receiver aloft.

Rivera called the number for Carvajal Rental Cars. Fletcher wasn't there, so he left a message.

And then, knowing nothing would happen until various wheels began spinning, Rivera simply walked to his cell, accompanied by two Spanish officers. He fixed his expression to one that was both hard and hateful. He knew prison politics were much the same as those in the military - people manoeuvred for dominance. No weakness could be shown.

* * * * *

It was the smell that hit him at first. The box-like room stank of urine, fear, and hopelessness. From above the bunk, the ceiling dripped. Constantly. Rivera lay on his back, sweating, watching as a drop of condensation crawled slowly across the grouting above him. It reached an intersection where it pooled with other droplets. Then, after the bubble swelled with remnants of dust and dirt, it wobbled, and fell all the way down through the foetid, humid air of the cell until it landed on the thin, bare mattress.

He drifted off, sleeping intermittently. There was nothing else to do. At first, Betsy drifted into his thoughts. He lamented how far the dream he'd had with her had soured. Then, he banished her memory – the place he was in was not befitting of such sentimentality.

Later, as evening turned into the early hours of morning, his rest was broken by the sounds of people being dragged down the corridor outside. Some swore at their captors in Spanish. Others in Arabic. And some of the snarled streams of vitriol were spat out in bitter Anglo-Saxon.

Then the door of his cell swung open.

Chapter 35.

Fletcher's single visit to Torre de los Boliches had been approved by both his commanding officer and a representative from Interpol. It being rubber-stamped had been delayed – the ethics of funding a serving officer visiting a brothel remained a grey area. But it was a rare opportunity, and he looked like any other punter. He was fat and bronzed, and had the same arrogant, jowly visage as the rest of the visitors. The other punters picked raffle numbers from the nightingales who were draped around the room like terracotta china dolls. They'd popped Viagras en route and had spent the latter part of the journey boasting about their prowess. On arrival, they'd swiftly made their way to private rooms. Fletcher, though, headed for the bar.

'This one,' he'd announced loudly, pointing at Tatiana. 'I want this one.'

'She'll cost you extra, senõr,' a guard explained as he wandered over.

'Name your price,' Fletcher smiled, laying a wad of banknotes onto the bar. He presented as a man clearly used to getting his own way. The guard nodded, grinning.

As Tatiana had led him out of the bar and down the corridor towards a private room, he slipped a fifty euro note into the breast pocket of the guard who was now manning the door. 'This should keep you out of trouble, eh?' he'd laughed, patting him on the shoulder.

Once they entered the room, he sat on the bed. 'Do they have cameras in here?' he asked.

The nightingale had turned away from him; she was removing her clothes, draping them over a chair. She turned and narrowed her eyes. 'Why?'

'Tatiana, right?' he'd whispered.

'Yes,' she'd nodded, her eyes widening.

'I got your message.'

Chapter 36.

The man stood at the entrance to Rivera's cell was huge; his neck was thick, and his tattooed arms bulged with muscle. He wore a black wife-beater vest, over which a chain thick enough to anchor a yacht lay. He was unshaven and had gapped teeth twisted into a grotesque smile. The man's throat was inked with a series of swirls, and his head was shaven. The scalp of Rivera's new cellmate glistened in the dim, anaemic light. Curling his lip, he sneered in cold command.

'I'm Antonio,' he announced in Spanish. Behind him, the door swung closed.

Rivera didn't move. He lay back on the mattress, his hands placed behind his head, and simply watched. At the same time, his mind was awhirl with a million calculations. More than anything, he was wondering why he – a man supposedly accused of murder – should suddenly have a cellmate.

Looking at the other man, he was certain it was no accident. That he'd been allowed in without removing his jewellery was enough of a sign, but the fact he was regarding the ex-soldier with such hatred only confirmed his suspicion. There is a certain type of prisoner: a thug; a killer; the kind of man who would think nothing of murdering someone if it might buy him a favour or two. Antonio looked like that kind of man.

Rivera knew there was no way the charge on him would stick. Fletcher would see to that even before the police examined the scene properly. But it clearly suited someone to have a *guiri* in the frame. The ex-soldier pondered: the whole thing stank of a set-up; what was unclear was who stood to benefit.

If the ex-soldier was dead – he reasoned - he wouldn't be able to protest his innocence. The force would simply fudge the paperwork; claim an administrative error – an unfortunate mistake due to overcrowding. Ishaq's death would then be attributed to him, and any investigation would be swept under the carpet. Rivera was no stranger to such approaches; he'd seen enough of them in the Army. He'd had to unpick and unravel them in myriad investigations. Looking at the man entering the cell, he believed he was almost certainly part of such a plot.

By the time the door clanged shut, Rivera's mind was made up.

There was a moment of silence as the echoes of the sliding bolts died.

Antonio looked at the man on the bunk. 'That's my fucking bed,' he announced. The Spanish spoken on the construction site was – for the most part – rough and ready. But Miguel and Gonzalo sometimes conversed more lyrically; poetically almost. Antonio's utterances had no such charm.

'Terribly sorry old chap!' the ex-soldier announced in English, springing himself upright and onto the floor in a fluid motion. As he did, he kept talking, affecting the accent of an effeminate aristocrat. 'You know how this lot are, don't you just? I mean, I asked them for a copy of *The Times* and they gave me *The Telegraph*.' He looked at the other man, affecting an expression of horror. '*The Telegraph*! I mean, really… what is the world coming to?'

Antonio frowned, mystified by the other man's actions. The camp English utterances were incomprehensible to him. But he was also having to recalibrate his plan. He'd been wrong-footed – he'd been told the other man was smaller than him. He was. But he was also used to the effect his intimidating presence had on people - he'd expected his cellmate would be cowering in the corner. But that wasn't the case.

Rivera knew that by placing himself on the floor, he'd surrendered his advantage of higher ground. But he also knew Antonio's initial intention would probably have been to dump him on his head. It would – the ex-soldier reflected – be exactly what he'd have done had the tables been turned. Then, the authorities would simply be able to claim the deceased had fallen out of bed.

Antonio frowned. As he did, Rivera moved towards him, talking constantly. He was trying to narrow the angle between him and the other man. The cell was small; most of the floor space was sandwiched between the bunk and the wall. Rivera reasoned Antonio was the type of fighter who would favour a run-up; the kind of man who would need room to swing. He knew the closer he could get, the better.

In a boxing ring, there would have been no contest. Rivera knew that only too well. But he was a street fighter. Antonio was so big, he'd probably never lost a fight. He'd have been used to having the upper hand; he wouldn't be the type who'd be familiar with thinking on his feet. And, as the ex-soldier well knew, that could make someone complacent.

Complacency could make a person hesitate.

And, sometimes, a split-second of hesitation was all the time required.

* * * * *

Rivera saw Antonio's shoulders tense as he moved towards him. He stared at his adversary's wall of muscle. The other man began to raise his arms, suspecting that – were his target to have the audacity to attack him – he would go for his head. It was that thought the ex-soldier was banking on.

He was also grateful the officer who'd admitted him hadn't bothered to remove the laces from his boots. So what if one more idiotic Englishman had hanged himself rather than facing up to his crimes? The ex-soldier had kept his boots on while lying on the bunk. It was a lesson learned in the Army.

You never knew when you might have to move.

Rivera dodged and crouched down. He wedged his left sole between the foot of the wall and the concrete floor, and used it to launch himself forward. As he did, he let himself fall, sliding low like a footballer making a challenge.

Antonio, confused, grabbed at the empty air where Rivera had been a second before. Then he stepped forward. Meaning all his weight was on his rear leg when the ex-soldier hit. It was one of Rivera's favourite moves. His boot made contact; almost all of his body weight impacted just beneath his cellmate's kneecap.

There was a crunching noise, accompanied by the popping of tendons and ligaments. As the other man's knee bent the wrong way, it sounded like the felling of a tree. For a moment, he remained standing, his weight suspended in the air. Then he crumpled.

Antonio roared. Shocked. He hadn't imagined he'd have any trouble pulverising the other man. But, for all his strength and frightening demeanour, he was a stage fighter – he was intimidating enough to win fights without having to fight them. He certainly wasn't used to being attacked. And he was a poseur – he was used to strutting and preening himself like a steroid-pumped prima-donna; his gym-built body wasn't designed for combat. He'd certainly never experienced pain like the agonising sensations now coursing through his body. He clutched at his wound. For a moment, a flicker of fight surfaced; a part of him forlornly considered mounting a rear-guard action, but then he rolled over.

*****

Unlike his opponent, Rivera had never lost his animal instincts. The Army hadn't taught him anything he didn't already know – it simply made him more dangerous. Once the other man was on the floor, the ex-soldier knew the contest was all but over. It became a simple case of mathematics.

As Antonio rolled, he clutched involuntarily at his ruined knee, leaving his head unguarded. Rivera took the opportunity to thrust his thumb deep into the other man's eye socket. Wrenching at it, he used it as a pivot. He then pushed the other man's bulk away, and smashed the heel of his boot down across the bridge of Antonio's nose, putting all his weight behind it.

The other man groaned, gushing blood.

Rivera, hyper-aware, heard the viewing panel in the steel door slide back. He smashed his left fist into the already ruptured nose of the other man. There were - he reasoned - two possible outcomes: he would kill Antonio, or the staff would restrain him. Either way, it would result in him being alone once more. Which improved the chances of Fletcher being able to free him. The authorities wouldn't be able to rustle up someone more dangerous than Antonio at short notice – he was confident of that.

A key hurriedly scraped in the lock, accompanied by urgent shouts and hurried footsteps. As officers streamed into the cell, he punched the fallen man on the side of the head with his right fist. The outside light from the corridor spilled into the room.

He raised his left fist once more, but before he could deliver a killer blow, Rivera was grabbed roughly by multiple pairs of hands. Officers bundled him into a corner, away from his unconscious cell-mate.

He didn't resist.

Chapter 37.

Rif's rule about phones was absolute. He wanted the nightingales captive. Caged birds.

That was why the men entering Torre de los Boliches had their phones confiscated. It was done with good manners and a friendly tone. But those were the rules. Rif believed his girls to be manipulative hustlers. Without phones, though, he reasoned, there was little chance of them securing escape routes. He wanted them hermetically sealed; utterly cut off from the outside world. For the most part, that's what he got. But just because the boss made demands, it didn't always mean they were implemented to the letter.

Tatiana had believed that the only way out of Rif's clutches was through death.

Until one night, an opportunity presented itself.

* * * * *

The customer was called Terry. At least that was the name he'd given. He'd demanded a private audience with Tatiana. Usually when visitors were blind drunk, they were denied access to the top nightingales. But it was a quiet night.

And Terry had deep pockets.

Carlos checked his phone at the door, giving the man a numbered ticket by way of receipt. Then Terry staggered down the corridor with his chosen woman.

Once inside the room, he passed out on the bed immediately. The protocol in such circumstances was for the nightingale to go through the punter's pockets; to liberate as much cash as possible. Tatiana had gone about this business. But then she realised the man had a second phone.

She knew there were hidden cameras in the rooms. All the girls did. But she also suspected the film was only reviewed if something bad had happened. Something *really* bad. A drunken man with a picked pocket wouldn't be likely to trigger any such action.

So, Tatiana dropped the man's wallet beneath the bed. As she bent down, acting like she was trying to retrieve it, she grabbed his trailing hand and held his thumb to the screen of the phone.

It unlocked.

It was a moment she'd planned for – she just never thought she'd have the opportunity. The number she searched was for an international agency focused on victims of trafficking. It was the top item listed on the search. Keeping the bed and the sleeping man between herself and the camera, she clicked a phone icon that placed a direct call. Her message was short.

Concise.

She gave the details she needed to, and then hung up, erasing the number from the phone's call records.

Three weeks later, Fletcher arrived.

Chapter 38.

'Interview, senõr,' the arresting officer announced to Rivera, taking in the scene before him. Two officers were still guarding Rivera while medics attended to the writhing, gurgling, semi-conscious Antonio. One of them held a truncheon against his throat, while the other kept a hand on the butt of his holstered handgun. The officer shook his head, frowning. 'The Comisario wants to speak to you.'

Rivera stood motionless as a set of handcuffs was locked onto his wrists. 'You've charged me with murder, right?' he began. His tone was calm; impassive.

'Yes,' the arresting officer replied.

'Then why the hell was *he* put in with me?' He nodded towards the man on the floor.

The officer eyed him coldly for a moment and then shrugged. 'Administrative error. It happens all the time...'

* * * * *

Comisario Ramos looked irritable. Doubtless – Rivera mused - he'd expected to be dealing with the unfortunate slaying of a foreign prisoner rather than having that same prisoner sat, looking daggers at him. It was shortly after 4AM – the Stasi's favourite time for interrogation; the time when people were at their lowest ebb; the time when prisoners' defences were down. But, it seemed, the tables had turned. The official regarded Rivera contemptuously. He had deep lines on his forehead and bags beneath his eyes. The man opposite, in contrast, looked wide awake.

'So, Senõr... Rivera,' he began. His accent was strong. 'Did you kill Ishaq En-Nesyri?'

Silence.

'I'd advise you to answer if...'

'I did not.' The ex-soldier's reply was blunt.

Ramos sighed. 'You can save us both a great deal of time by admitting this, senõr.' He paused. 'He was in your apartment. There are no witnesses.' The Comisario pushed his glasses back up to the bridge of his nose.

'But I didn't do it,' Rivera repeated, coldly. 'I arrived home and found him. That's it.' He paused. 'And I'd like an answer as to why a gang member was permitted to enter my cell with the express intention of killing me.'

The Comisario waved his hand dismissively. 'We'll get to that,' he explained. 'Accidents happen. It was just an unfortunate mistake. Do you have an alibi?'

'I do. I was at work until four o'clock.'

'Can anyone verify that?' he enquired.

'Absolutely,' Rivera replied. 'But before I give you names, I want assurances – I want my own cell; I want a lawyer, and I demand that a representative from the British Consulate is present.'

Ramos nodded, disinterested. 'We'll be talking to your co-workers in due course. What about the apartment? Could anyone have been spotted going in or coming out?'

The ex-soldier shrugged. 'Maybe. I just found the body – it's up to you lot to work out what the hell happened... I have no idea.'

The Comisario tutted and then sighed. His eyes narrowed. 'It doesn't look good for you. You realise this?'

Silence.

'Nor does the fact you gave me that outraged gorilla as a cellmate,' Rivera answered eventually. 'Anyway, when you establish the time of death, you'll know I wasn't anywhere near. What possible motive could I have had?' the ex-soldier protested. 'Of course, you'll find my fingerprints all around the apartment. But it's *my* apartment, isn't it?' He paused. 'How did he die? I couldn't see any obvious wounds; no abrasions...'

Ramos narrowed his eyes. 'We've been doing a little digging into your past, senōr. You've done some investigating yourself. And...'

There was a commotion in the corridor outside. An angry voice was raised. Despite protestations, the door was opened forcefully.

'Comisario, I'm sorry. I...' the arresting officer apologised as he followed the newcomer into the room.

The entrant waved him away in irritation, holding his credentials out to Ramos.

'Interpol?' The Comisario shook his head, frowning. He opened his mouth to speak again, but was shut down instantly. Ramos' expression was one of bewilderment; he couldn't understand how the situation was seemingly spiralling out of his control. The new man vastly exceeded him in rank. His paymasters hadn't briefed him on the possibility of such an occurrence.

'I'll take it from here, thank you,' the newcomer said brusquely. He was a man with red hair and very pale skin. The gritted teeth underpinning his expression were a clear indicator of his impatience.

'But...'

'I'll speak to you outside Comisario,' the man announced. 'When I'm finished here.'

'How long will that be – er – sir?'

The new man turned, annoyed. 'It'll take as long as it takes. You, Comisario, will wait outside in the meantime. No interruptions. Do I make myself clear? And I want all audio-visual monitoring equipment turned off.'

'But...' Ramos interrupted.

'Do I make myself clear?' the newcomer's tone was icy.

The Comisario nodded and meekly exited the room.

Chapter 39.

'The cameras are behind the mirror,' Tatiana explained to Fletcher. 'Right in the centre.' She spoke in a low voice; hurried.

The policeman nodded. 'So, if I stand with my back to the wall, I'll shield you, right?'

'Yes,' she replied, frowning.

'Right.' He cleared his throat nervously. 'I'm going to stand here facing the bed. If you get on your knees and – er – act, then anyone watching will believe that's what you're doing. Right?' Fletcher felt his blushing cheeks burning.

Tatiana nodded. 'Correct.'

The policeman took a deep breath. 'And while you're acting... you can explain things to me.'

'Don't look at me,' Tatiana hissed.

'What?' Fletcher frowned.

'Tilt your head back. Look at the ceiling, not just at me. Otherwise, they won't believe you. That's what the other customers do – at least most of the time. Just don't move too much – if they only see your back, they won't think anything's wrong.'

'Oh – er - very well,' Fletcher shrugged.

* * * * *

Fletcher left the room knowing Tatiana was willing to go on record as an informant. He also knew he'd have to source methadone for when he managed to extract her. She explained what went on at Rif's place in the hills, and how it worked. He didn't know everything by the end of their conversation – but he knew he had enough to build a case.

In response, he told her it would take two weeks. He'd given a time, a date, and a place. The policeman knew he wouldn't be able to get another message to her, so he'd just have to hope she'd make the planned rendezvous. There was no way of confirming; if he tried, he risked blowing her cover.

Until then, she had to hold her nerve. There wasn't a moment when she didn't worry about discovery; the only nightingale who'd come close to escaping before was Svetlana.

That had been two years ago.

The discovery of her betrayal had taken place on the water. Rif had taken a group of nightingales on board a chartered yacht to service a collection of wealthy businessmen. It was the usual set-up: champagne; cocaine, and luxurious surroundings. He'd ordered the girls to dress as French maids. From time-to-time, one of Rif's associates would peel away and drag one of the girls into a private room. Then, after a few hours, Svetlana had been spotted using a discarded phone. The guards had pursued her to the prow of the boat.

And then she'd thrown herself overboard.

Svetlana's body had never been found. But Tatiana clearly remembered the mix of horror and utter resignation on the girl's face as she teetered on the brink. She still remembered the involuntary scream she'd unleashed as her friend had tumbled. But, even as she held her hand to her mouth, a lecherous businessman began pawing at her from behind. The nightingale still recalled the way the anchor was dropped. A dinghy was lowered over the side to circle the area lest the body should surface. It wasn't for rescue – it was to recover any evidence. None of the men would mourn Svetlana, but they didn't want a barnacle-encrusted corpse coming back to haunt them, either.

Five minutes later, the party on-board was back in full swing.

Chapter 40.

'I'm sorry about the delay,' the newly arrived Interpol agent announced to Rivera. 'These bloody cowboys are clueless.' He sighed heavily. 'Anyway...'

'German?' the ex-soldier enquired.

'Dutch.' He held out a hand for Rivera to shake. 'Frans Mühren.' The man on the other side of the table paused. 'Fletcher contacted me. I understand he's spoken to you about a few things.' The agent paused. 'Anyway, more of that later – let's sort out our current problem.'

Rivera nodded.

'Tell me. What's your version of events?'

'You've read the notes, right?'

'I have, but I want to hear things from you.' Mühren frowned. 'I know you've been an investigator, so you've probably got a decent idea.'

Rivera nodded. 'Ishaq was at some monster trucks event – I'm not sure what it was called, but it was in the parking lot of a supermarket.'

'Can anyone confirm that?'

The ex-soldier frowned.

'Procedure,' Mühren shrugged. 'I've got to give Ramos something, otherwise he'll start complaining he's been frozen out.'

'Well,' Rivera sighed. 'I gave him a lift down to the seafront. My buddy Pancho was in the car too – he's a photographer. He's in Malaga at the moment, but he'll be back here at the weekend.'

'Good,' the agent nodded. 'We'll talk to him. And then?'

'He'd been drinking - Ishaq. He wasn't devout. Clearly.' Rivera slapped absent-mindedly at a mosquito that was in the process of biting his arm. 'He arrived back around four in the morning. Clattering. Tripping over stuff. When I left for work, he looked dreadful -

so I left him there, on the sofa. And when I arrived back, he was still there. But he was dead.'

Mühren nodded, echoing the Comisario's words. 'It doesn't look good, you know?'

'I realise that,' the ex-soldier nodded. 'I was in the apartment with him and there are no other witnesses. But if you establish the time of death, it should place me at work.'

'I believe you. Don't worry about that. We'll prove it and get the charges dropped soon enough. The Spanish authorities will be a headache, but they'll do what they're told. My real problem is why the hell anyone would want to kill this kid?'

Rivera shrugged. 'I know. And after examination of the crime scene, I see no motive either.' He paused. 'You might turn up something more with DNA analysis, but this, to me, looks like a professional hit.'

Mühren frowned. 'How?'

'Too clean. No bruising. No signs of struggle. I couldn't even work out how he died. No wounds. You wouldn't get that if it was a robbery. There was no sign of forced entry, either.'

'So what's your gut feeling?'

The ex-soldier looked hard at the other man, chewing his lip. 'Chloroform.'

'Really?' Mühren raised his eyebrows. 'Bit old-fashioned, no?'

'Maybe,' Rivera shrugged. 'My hunch is that a person knocked on the door, and Ishaq – thinking it was the postman – answered it. There would probably have been a few of them – whoever they were.' He paused. 'You should probably talk to the gardener at Latinaja – he mentioned seeing a few people.'

The Interpol agent nodded. 'Why chloroform?'

'Well, no struggle. And no sign of how he died. They could've held a rag over his mouth - just kept it there until he stopped breathing. You'll have to check when you get the blood work back from the morgue.'

'I will,' Mühren nodded. 'And...'

'...and then there was the slightly boozy smell,' Rivera interrupted. 'It fits with the theory – chloroform, I mean. I thought it was the scent of the alcohol toxins at first, but now I'm not so sure.'

'We'll check it out,' Mühren said.

Silence.

'So... Interpol?'

Mühren nodded. 'Fletcher told me you were sitting on the fence about whether to get involved with us. Is that still the case?'

The ex-soldier narrowed his eyes. 'Do I get to look into who killed the kid if I say yes?'

'You do.'

'Then I'm in.'

'Good.' Mühren produced a couple of forms. 'I'll need you to sign here. This is a police one stating that – as a person of interest in the case – you won't leave Almería.' He held up another one. 'This is an official secrets document.' He glanced down at it. 'It's the usual stuff – keep your mouth shut. And if you don't, you're toast.'

The ex-soldier took the pen that was proffered.

The Interpol agent sighed. 'If our friends were involved in this, I shouldn't think we'll find much. And if it *was* a hit, they'll have used professionals. False plates. No prints... they're good.'

'But why Ishaq?'

'My question exactly,' Mühren replied. He sipped at a bottle of water and replaced the lid. 'I see no reason for killing the kid. And I can't see how he was a threat to anyone. So we're missing something. Our friends operate with impunity, but even they don't go round killing people for no reason.'

'Drugs?'

'Drugs. Vice. Construction. Hits. You name it. It's proving any of it that's the problem.'

Rivera frowned. 'Ishaq was just a big kid. He liked monster trucks, for fuck's sake. There's no way he was some great criminal mastermind.'

Mühren nodded. 'I agree – at least that's how it looks. But he was Moroccan. Family ties and tribal things go pretty deep with that lot.'

'Yeah, but he'd have mentioned something. The kid never stopped bloody talking. We had to ban him from telling us about his dog having a litter of puppies. If he was involved in something, there's no way he'd have been able to keep quiet about it.'

The Interpol agent nodded slowly. 'But killings like this don't just happen. You know this already, though - Fletcher's made me well aware of your record. So you know how the world works.' He paused. 'You think Ishaq was just collateral damage?'

'Maybe,' Rivera shrugged. 'But for what? Even if he was just caught in the crossfire, why were they in my apartment in the first place? It makes no sense. It's not like I have anything to steal.'

Silence.

Mühren slid a card over the table. 'You think of anything, call me. Cut that guy Ramos out of the equation, though. He's off the table now.' He paused, letting the statement hang in the air. 'And talk to your friend – this guy Pancho. Can you call him?'

Rivera rubbed the tip of his finger across his eyebrow, itching a bite. 'Negative. He's a bit of a hippie. He kind of pops up and then disappears.'

The Interpol agent sighed. 'Well, the minute he pops up again, talk to him. He'll need to be questioned, anyway.'

'Really?'

'Not in a bad way. He'll just need to be eliminated from the inquiry.'

As the pair stood up, Mühren shook Rivera's hand. 'I know Fletcher flies a little close to the wind, but he's our best chance with this.' He looked hard at the ex-soldier. 'He trusts you – so you must be the right kind of guy to help out. Do what you can. But try to keep your head down – things like these are bad for investigations.'

Chapter 41.

Rif seethed. But he spent plenty of his time seething. Lately, it had simply become his natural state. It was as if a boiling mass of anger perpetually percolated within him.

He wasn't winning.

To lose was unacceptable.

Second place – to his mind - was always first loser.

But nothing was ever enough for him. He was a man who thrived on action. A man of boundless energy. Anyone that got in his way, he disposed of. It had always been like that; ever since he'd become Abdellah Rif. He was – he repeatedly reminded himself – one of life's winners. Winning had become a habit. It was simply the way he conducted business.

That's why the Ignacio Ibanez affair had hit him so hard. No matter how he tried to convince himself otherwise, he couldn't help feeling he was the loser. He could dress it up as boardroom bullshit – he could even claim it had been racially motivated. But the bitter truth of the matter was that he'd failed to win.

Of course, Rif had lost before. But he'd always seen it coming. He'd done whatever was necessary to limit losses; to turn defeat into victory. He'd redrafted boundaries; altered parameters; reframed things, so he remained number one.

This time, though, he'd been completely taken by surprise. He'd shaken hands. He'd signed cheques. He'd slid envelopes brimming with cash across desks. But it hadn't worked; it felt like the rug had been ripped from beneath him.

Rif wanted revenge. Ibanez was the target, but, in the meantime, anyone he could strike out at would do as a temporary measure. He'd even sanctioned Amrabat's online snuff movie. The victim – one of Doctor Ferrera's assistants – was a nobody. His death would be long and drawn out. But it was doing little to sate the boss' bloodlust.

* * * * *

Access to Ibanez was not easy to come by. But Rif could be patient when he needed to be. Everyone had an Achilles' heel – the boss had learned that long ago.

For Ibanez, it was vanity. The tabloid press gleefully reported his many plastic surgeries. His ageless face looked like it had been ironed into a static, featureless, two-dimensional mask. It was ridiculous, Rif reasoned – utterly undignified for a man of his age. His liposuctioned stomach was ripped. It couldn't, however, obscure the sagging leather hide of his antiquated skin. But it clearly worked for him, massaging his Viagra-fuelled libido. The paparazzi regularly photographed him with young women on his arm.

So Rif had hatched a plan.

Doctor Alonso Ferrera was Ibanez's personal physician. For an exorbitant fee, he'd promised to do Rif's bidding the next time the former nightclub crooner went under the knife. Instead of a facelift or a chin tuck, though, Rif wanted the surgeon to focus on the patient's nether regions. The cosmetic enhancements Ibanez was being admitted for would turn into something very different. Something nightmarish.

Rather than take the life of his nemesis, Rif wanted to ruin his lifestyle. He wanted the fallen lothario to suffer. And he wanted Ibanez to know exactly who was responsible.

But the doctor had double-crossed him. He'd taken Rif's money, and then, having alerted his regular employer to the threat posed, accepted a huge reward from Ibanez too.

So Alonso Ferrera had to die.

Chapter 42.

'I still can't believe it!' Pancho shook his head at Ishaq's death once more. He'd spiralled swiftly through the five stages of acceptance once Rivera had delivered the news.

The photographer rarely smoked, but he now sat on Rivera's balcony, drawing hard on the hand-rolled cigarette he passed back and forth with the other man. There was little to say. Both of them understood *what* had happened; they were both struggling with *why*.

'You're not just a builder, right?' Pancho asked abruptly, after a long silence.

'What makes you say that?' The ex-soldier narrowed his eyes.

Pancho frowned. 'I can't see how they'd let you out of jail so quickly otherwise. As far as anyone else knows, you're a murderer. And they haven't got another suspect yet, have they?'

'Not that I know of.' Rivera shook his head.

'Right – so you've got connections,' Pancho nodded. 'You must have. So... are you some kind of lawman or something?'

'Was,' Rivera replied. 'But that was a while back.'

Pancho nodded and stubbed the cigarette out. 'Why Ishaq then?'

The ex-soldier shrugged. 'That's the bit I don't understand. I've done investigation work before, but it's not helping. I see no answer here.' He paused. 'The only thing I know is that it looks like a professional hit.' He looked at Pancho and then back over the pool towards the distant Mediterranean. 'But why they chose Ishaq is anyone's guess.'

'You think it was a Moroccan thing?' Pancho asked.

'Maybe. But if he'd been in trouble, I think he'd have said.' Rivera smiled wryly. 'The kid could never keep his fucking mouth shut about anything.' He grinned a little. 'We'd have never heard the bloody end of it!' He shook his head. 'He was a good kid, you know? An idiot, but an idiot with a heart of gold.'

Pancho nodded. 'It must have been a shock though – you finding him, I mean?'

'Yeah.' He turned and looked at the photographer. 'For a minute, I thought he was you – with the dreadlocks and all...'

'Fuck!' Pancho's eyes widened, and he sprang suddenly to his feet. 'Wait here!' he muttered.

'What?' Rivera demanded. But Pancho had already headed inside.

Chapter 43.

Rif was a man with more money than he could spend in many lifetimes.

But it wasn't enough.

It never would be. The Moroccan was too narcissistic to realise he was a narcissist. The longer he lived, the fewer people challenged him. Being feared meant people simply became yes-men in his presence. After years of such treatment, his brain had rewired itself to believe it was simply the natural order of things. Being untouchable meant he acted with impunity. He was convinced he was a genius; a higher order of human. But the slightest of slights would send him into a tailspin. His few close confidants never questioned his tantrums. To have done so would have involved ascribing an element of logic to an entirely illogical being. When it came to their boss, they understood the *what* and the *how*; there was no *why*, though. No explanation.

His ego was eggshell thin. And suddenly that shell had been shattered; Rif felt vulnerable. It wasn't a sensation he cared for in the slightest. Since Ibanez's action, he'd veered between combatively seeking revenge, and a defeatist streak of self-destruction. Failure wasn't something he'd learned to deal with before.

Nazir Rabbat was gone. He was untouchable now. Rif seeking revenge there would simply trigger a holy war – even in his state of embittered hatred, he wasn't willing to risk that.

He'd learned that Ignacio Ibanez wasn't the kind of man his people could simply despatch, either. That had been a bitter disappointment. Rif would happily have ordered the hit, but there were only so many bribes that could be placed before someone would ask the wrong kind of questions. Only so long inquiries could be misdirected before his motive became clear.

So, Rif made a new vow: if Ibanez went big, he would go bigger.

Plan B.

Chapter 44.

'What the fuck that was about?' Rivera frowned. He eyed Pancho with incredulity as he returned to the balcony and sat down heavily, a cold beer in each hand. He handed one to the ex-soldier.

'Are we celebrating or something?' Rivera began, uncertain.

'No,' Pancho replied. 'We are most definitely *not* fucking celebrating.' He sighed. 'I just needed something to take the edge off.'

Silence.

'They took my camera,' Pancho announced. His tone was blunt. The ex-soldier narrowed his eyes, unsure as to whether it was the violation of the sacred bond Pancho believed existed between man and camera that was the issue.

'Who?' Rivera pressed.

'Whoever killed Ishaq.' The photographer replied.

'Really?'

'Yes.'

'You're sure?' Rivera frowned.

'Definitely,' Pancho nodded. 'It was here when I left. I only took the films with me. And Ishaq wouldn't have taken it.' He paused. 'Would he?'

'No.' Rivera shook his head. 'That kid was a lot of things. But he definitely wasn't a thief.' Rivera sighed and shook his head. 'I did an inventory of everything after I found him. Guess I'm losing my touch – I thought you'd taken your camera with you.' He looked over at the photographer and then narrowed his eyes. 'You jumped up pretty quickly back there. I mean, I know you love your camera and all, but... something you want to tell me?'

Pancho pursed his lips and exhaled slowly. 'Yeah. I think so.'

* * * * *

'It was when you said he looked like me when he was lying on your couch,' Pancho explained. 'That's when I started joining up the dots. That's what I think might have caused this whole thing.'

'Go on,' Rivera pressed, frowning.

'One night last week I was out in the hills on the trail of a lynx.'

'OK...'

'Some of my camera traps are near your construction site. I put them there because I reckon the lynx must have to pass close by to get to some of the other places they've been spotted. It's quite a good location really – I mean, there's nobody around at night, so there's always a chance of some decent pictures.'

'You're not making much sense, Pancho,' Rivera frowned. 'Get to the point, *amigo*.'

The photographer sighed. 'Well, last week, those traps were all sprung. All the ones by the site – that is.'

'So?'

'So, it's never happened before.'

Rivera shrugged. 'Foxes? Wolves? Cats? Dogs? There must be plenty of them around, right?'

'Maybe, but they're set up so they can only be triggered by larger animals.'

The ex-soldier frowned. 'So, what are you saying?'

Silence.

'Who owns all the property around here?' Pancho asked, eventually.

'Well, I work for Cesar. Why?'

'No – he's just the overseer.' Pancho shook his head, irritated. 'Construction around here is all run by gangsters, isn't it? The Moroccans. What do they call them – the K'Thraa?'

Rivera nodded. 'You mean the Kbir, right?'

'Exactly!'

The ex-soldier narrowed his eyes. 'Look – I'm an investigator – *was*. You were right about that; I've heard some pretty roundabout explanations before, but you've got me stumped. I know I'm not the sharpest tool in the shed, but you're going to have to paint a picture for me. Please!'

Silence.

Pancho sighed. 'When I was growing up, people used to tell stories about Cucuy.'

Rivera's brow furrowed. 'Who?'

'Cucuy – I think this is his doing.'

The ex-soldier shook his head. 'Mate, I don't have a clue what you're on about.'

Chapter 45.

Over the years, Rif had purchased packages of land and properties all along the coast. He'd continually shuffled them; shifting and manoeuvring. Where he usually blitzkrieged his way through life in bulldozer-fashion, here he'd exercised patience. Here, he was playing the long game. And here he was, nearly ready to bring Plan B to life. If he couldn't emasculate the former crooner, he vowed to eviscerate him economically.

To raise capital for the FC Castillo purchase, Ibanez had sold the Hotel ¡*Arriba España*! It was a sale completed only weeks after he'd made his final bid for the club. By then, Rif already had his sights set on various paths of retribution. He'd ducked, weaved, and pivoted, bouncing off the ropes of the ring until he was ready to spring back. He took no chances; the deception was perfect.

The company Ibanez sold to looked entirely legitimate: a consortium of German and Russian businessmen.

It wasn't anything of the sort.

* * * * *

The lawyers and bankers who oversaw the sale were well-paid and respectable. They wore fine suits and spoke with immaculate elocution. There was nothing about them which would have raised eyebrows in any boardroom. They propelled the purchase with a quiet air of professionalism. They were teetotal- treadmill-running-vegan-dieting-jet-setting examples of clean-cut sophistication.

The deal was swiftly done.

Unbeknownst to Ibanez, though, the ¡*Arriba España*! now belonged to Rif. Once the deeds were signed, it became the final piece of his puzzle. He'd engineered myriad boardroom coups over the years, but he'd never had one where he'd paid so much money for a one-off operation. The lawyers and bankers were all kept on enormous retainers. Now they'd kick-started Plan B, he'd tasked them with seeing it through.

The new owner of Spain's most exciting up-and-coming football team was extremely wealthy. But he wasn't so wealthy that he hadn't overstretched himself. He was all in for Champions' League glory, just like Rif had once intended to be. But that left him vulnerable.

Meanwhile, Rif owned the hotel. And with it, the Moroccan owned five of the largest beachfront hotels on the Paseo Marítimo; they were all positioned next to one other. Nobody knew the truth – they were owned by shady organisations that were fronts for other, even shadier organisations.

Plan B was the building of a super casino. Rif would knock down each of his hotels and build an enormous new one that would dominate the front. It would be on a scale not seen outside Las Vegas or Dubai. He knew he could do it; officials would be bribed; a new Fuengirola marina would be constructed; a Disneyland for deep-pocketed gamblers would be established. A new destination for the super-rich would spring up, and he'd be king.

Ibanez would be history.

Chapter 46.

'Cucuy...' Pancho sighed. 'He was like a – how you say? – bogeyman.'

The ex-soldier narrowed his eyes.

'He was the night prowler. People used to say to keep your nose clean, or Cucuy would get you.'

'So we're talking about a fairy tale?' Rivera enquired. 'This is fiction, right?'

'Not so,' Pancho insisted. 'Cucuy was real. Cucuy was the Kbir. Cucuy was the person who buried people beneath swimming pools, or in the concrete uprights of freeway bridges.'

Rivera frowned.

'You said Ishaq looked like me,' Pancho said heavily. 'So what if they thought we were the same person? What if they'd been looking for the guy who was known for wandering around the hills at night and taking photographs?'

'Why?'

'Well, what if one of those cameras wasn't triggered by an animal? What if it was triggered by a person? And what if it saw something it shouldn't have?'

The photographer's words hung in the air for a moment.

'Like what?' the ex-soldier asked, eventually.

Pancho rolled his eyes. 'Use your imagination.'

Rivera nodded slowly. 'Go on...'

'Well, the cameras are pretty well hidden, but they'll flash sometimes.' Pancho spoke earnestly. 'What if someone saw a flash but couldn't find the camera? What would they do then?' He paused. 'If it was Cucuy, he'd want to silence people. So maybe it's the same with these guys? Surely they'd decide to look for the photographer? After asking around, they'd have been looking for a skinny guy with dreadlocks. And that would have led to your place eventually, right?'

Rivera nodded grimly. 'So that's why they took the camera. To destroy it.' He sighed. 'So now we've got nothing.'

'Unless there's something on the film,' Pancho replied.

'What?'

'I use film, remember? And the film's in Malaga.'

'How long until you find out what's on it?' Rivera enquired.

'A few days, I guess – my friend will let me know if there's anything interesting.' Pancho paused. 'You think this might be the reason?'

Rivera shrugged. 'Well, if there's something incriminating on the film, it would be a motive, wouldn't it?'

Pancho nodded. 'What now? Police?'

'Not yet. I think you should stay indoors – keep out of sight.' He paused. 'I'll need the address of your friend. I'm going to collect that film – so you'll need to let him know I'm coming.' The ex-soldier paused. 'Cucuy, right?'

'Yeah, Cucuy,' Pancho nodded. 'This feels like his kind of thing.'

Chapter 47.

Fletcher wasn't happy. The half hour he spent in his local café each morning for coffee and cigarettes was usually his favourite part of the day; a chance to watch the world waking up, backlit in glorious, razor-sharp resolution by the rising sun. It was a moment of mindfulness - a chance to read the local paper.

There was, though, nothing about the day's headline which made him feel relaxed. Thanks to quick talking and promises of future favours, he'd managed to make the journalists leave Rivera's name out of their reports. But the rest of the details were there. And that was only the English-language papers. The officer's conversational Spanish was passable, but his vocabulary didn't stretch to deciphering broadsheets.

If the story stuck around, he worried it would risk blowing the cover of his undercover recruit.

* * * * *

Fletcher knew Tatiana would be unreliable. Picking a prostitute as a key witness was an enormous risk. He'd encountered junkies before too – they were always in thrall to their next fix. But he also knew the nightingale was scared. It wasn't just the dope; she was a prisoner too - they had her under guard. And even if she *did* escape, she had no money; no passport. It wouldn't be long until she felt the creeping onset of withdrawal. Her captors knew that much; it was like an invisible boundary fence. It was the one thing guaranteed to send her – or any of the other girls that tried to flee – crawling back. Clawing at their arms. Itching at invisible insects beneath their skin. Sweating. Feverish. Desperate.

The policeman knew he couldn't risk Torre de los Boliches again. He knew, too, he couldn't return to the Segovia Palace either. Once

Tatiana vanished, answers would be demanded. Recordings would be watched. He'd be identified. There was gambling at the Palace, too – that meant the potential presence of sophisticated equipment. Eyes in the sky. The kind of Vegas-style face-recognition software employed to cut out card counters. Fletcher couldn't beat equipment like that. No matter how good his disguise was.

That's why he'd had Rivera checked out in the first place. The construction worker had come to his attention a couple of months before. He'd been a fleeting figure who'd seemed happily ensconced with his lady friend. But then she'd departed, and he'd begun venturing out more frequently. People had talked about the T2. The guy seemed like an oddity – that was fine by Fletcher. The get-up the officer sported to appear like a rental car manager meant he didn't fit in either.

He'd seen something in him from a distance: a quality. Something about the way he carried himself. Fletcher had made a living noticing things. And he noticed things about Rivera – things that flip-flops and hippie beads couldn't hide.

That's why he'd started digging.

He'd made inquiries. On one occasion, he'd seen Rivera walking up the hill with his shirt off and had slowed down to offer him a lift. The other man had declined. But, as he'd done so, he'd leaned towards Fletcher's open window and thanked him. The policeman noticed the tattoos – a badly inked Fulham badge, and a logo emblazoned on his left shoulder - as well as the taut, lean, battle-marked physique they adorned. It had only taken a few minutes online to learn the logo was that of the US hard-core band Black Flag. With that piece of information, he'd been able to enlist the help of colleagues back in the UK to search the database of the passport agency. His discovery had then led to him trawling military archives.

He'd been pleased by what had been unearthed.

* * * * *

Fletcher frowned at his paper once more. He cursed silently; the situation was on a knife edge. If any more information leaked out, then maybe the campervan driver wasn't looking like such a sensible horse to have backed.

Chapter 48.

Rif looked up from behind his desk. He'd been looking at the newspaper. It didn't make for good reading. Amrabat – his assistant – had delivered it with a worried expression.

Amrabat had worked his way up through the Moroccan organisation until he was all but indispensable. He'd seen the best of Rif – those few moments where he was relaxed and not thinking of his next move. But, in his role, he'd far more frequently seen the very worst of his boss. Having the crystal paperweight thrown at him was, in truth, small fry; he'd seen his boss smash up entire offices in petulant tantrums while responding to perceived slights. He'd also seen him murder irritants in cold blood on occasions when it seemed he was killing just to kill.

He feared that was the side of him which was currently waiting in the wings. Amrabat knew he'd be likely to bear the brunt. He was privy to the kind of incriminating information that meant he could put his boss in jail forever. Knowing that he knew such things was his boss' best insurance policy. However, men who knew secrets like those the assistant kept also knew they could be blotted out instantly in order to preserve those secrets. For the last twenty years, it had been an arrangement that had worked very well. It was like a Costa del Sol version of *Mutually Assured Destruction*. Both parties stood to lose everything if they turned against the other person.

So they didn't.

It lent Amrabat a certain leverage. He was one of the few people who – on occasion – was permitted to question his boss' decisions.

Today was *not* such a day.

Amrabat sensed it as he stood, waiting for a response. He wore a tailored suit – just like his boss. He sported designer jewellery – just like his boss. And he smelled of expensive cologne – just like his boss. But when his boss was annoyed, Amrabat ceased to be an equal partner – he was simply another person on the payroll. He cleared his throat and spoke hesitantly. 'Everything alright, Abdellah?'

Rif held up the newspaper. 'This bothers me.'

Chapter 49.

Fletcher chewed at his nails. It was a habit he found he'd adopted once again – ever since progress started to be made. The policeman was desperate to put his plan into action; he'd spent nearly three years looking for a way into Rif's organisation. Everywhere he'd turned, he came up against walls. The set-up had seemed impregnable – he'd wasted eighteen months searching for an ersatz Moroccan he could deploy. But there was no such thing. And then he'd stumbled on his source. He knew, though, he couldn't play his hand too quickly. One slip and it would all fall apart.

He wouldn't find another Tatiana – that was for certain.

In the private room, she'd assured him she could get out. Carlos – one of the guards – was sweet on her. She told Fletcher she could do Carlos a favour, and he'd look the other way.

Fletcher didn't ask for details. All he did was set a date.

He would be waiting at a rest stop on the AP-7 at the agreed time. And she would meet him there. He'd put everything else in place: Rivera was onside; the force had a safe house; Mühren was ready to offer support, and it seemed that Rif was suddenly weakened.

The pieces of the puzzle felt like they were finally falling into place.

But then Rivera was arrested for murder.

* * * * *

The strings Fletcher pulled with Interpol granted the ex-soldier a speedy release. He'd already spoken with Mühren about bringing his compatriot on board. But the unspoken agreement was that everything would be done on the quiet. The charge didn't stick, of course – it was never going to. Fletcher's worry, though, was that his supposedly incognito recruit had suddenly put his head above the parapet. A picture in the paper would spell the end of his usefulness.

He hadn't spoken to Rivera yet; he hadn't wanted to go to the station in case anyone made a link between him and the man in the cells. The pair of them might have looked like just another couple of *guiris*, but a murder charge was still a murder charge. And people noticed things.

Fletcher had a long list of questions for the ex-soldier.

Chapter 50.

Rif frowned. He hadn't quite reached the state of apoplexy where he posed a threat to the lives of his subordinates, but he wasn't far off. He gritted his teeth at his second-in-command. 'You want to tell me what the hell went wrong here?'

'It's – er – it's complicated.' Amrabat stammered.

'No!' Rif slammed his hand down on the desk. 'It's not fucking complicated! Complicated is not being able to buy FC Castillo. Complicated is definitely *not* having a fucking guy whacked and disposed of. Especially not some bloody hippie photographer.' He eyed his employee coldly.

Silence.

'We were going to pin it on the *guiri* whose flat he was killed in,' Amrabat began, by way of apology.

Rif sighed. 'Well, that should have been easy. No?'

'We got the camera, sir,' Amrabat bridled.

'And the picture?' The boss tilted his head to one side in expectation.

Silence.

'I gave very simple instructions.' Rif used a letter opening knife to clean some dirt from a fingernail as he spoke. 'There was a camera flash.'

'Yes, sir.'

'So, there's nobody interested in photographing things on the hillside at night apart from bloody naturalists like that fucking Bob Marley lookalike I've been hearing about.' Rif itched at the bridge of his nose. 'I said kill the bastard. And you said no problem.'

Amrabat nodded.

'But instead of everything disappearing, I see that it's splashed all over the front pages of the fucking paper!' He calmed again. 'What did the picture show?'

'They used film. Sir.' Amrabat wore a pained expression.

'Film?' Rif's tone was incredulous. 'Who the fuck uses film these days?' He frowned. 'At least tell me you have the film.'

'We do not.'

Silence.

Rif sighed. His tone changed. 'The *guiri* was supposed to be dead by now.' He narrowed his eyes. 'What happened in the cells?'

'We don't know, sir,' Amrabat replied hesitantly. 'But the *guiri*'s still alive. And Antonio's in the hospital.'

Rif shook his head. 'Well, he's proven himself to be the useless prick we always knew he was, then.'

Silence.

Amrabat cleared his throat. 'And Ramos has been no use either. We wonder if the *guiri*'s getting help.'

The boss gritted his teeth. 'Well, bloody well find out. You're starting to piss me off.'

Chapter 51.

El Ysidro was a small town beyond Malaga, little more than a nondescript smudge on the map. The land around was arid; desert-like – nothing but hills blanketed with rocks, scrub, and sand from which groves of olive trees periodically rose. Below, the sea was an inviting expanse of rippling blue.

Rivera and Miguel were driving west.

The place was somewhere Ishaq had mentioned only a few times, but it was all they had to go on. None of the men on the site knew exactly where the kid came from - only that it was a long way for him to travel each day. But he'd definitely talked about El Ysidro. And he'd told them about his cousins working in the greenhouses of the Plastic Sea.

Miguel, Gonzalo and Rivera had asked around, but even after their questions, they didn't have much to go on. An address was mentioned. They didn't think it was where Ishaq had actually lived, but they knew that if they didn't at least go looking, they'd feel guilty. Otherwise, they feared word of the youngster's demise wouldn't get out at all. He hadn't been named in the newspaper report. Indeed, it was only when he was arrested that Rivera had learned the kid's second name. Kids like Ishaq – Miguel lamented – didn't receive monuments or remembrance services.

* * * * *

El Ysidro was only a little way inland, but it felt cut off; isolated. The streets spoke of poverty; everywhere, paint peeled from poorly tended, cheap buildings. On the road approaching it, the Renault 19 drove past several clusters of ragged people making their way along the hard shoulder – thumbs in the breeze.

'Workers, senõr,' Miguel announced. 'From the Plastic Sea.'

Rivera nodded. They looked defeated; burned and branded by the unrelenting sun as they squinted in the dust thrown up by the car's wheels.

'There's nothing here but workers,' the other man went on. 'Around here – you live; you work picking fruit and vegetables. And then you die. That's it.'

Silence fell in the car for a moment.

'Where are we headed anyway?' the ex-soldier enquired.

Miguel lifted a grimy scrap of paper from his pocket and keyed an address into his phone. Its screen was cobwebbed with cracks, but its GPS still worked.

'This way, senōr.' Miguel indicated Rivera should turn left.

* * * * *

The address they had was given to them by one of the quiet Moroccan workers on the construction crew. When asked who else lived at the property, the man had shrugged. 'Aunt, maybe? Uncle. I don't know. The house is called *Estevanico*, though – he was proud of that.'

The Renault drew to a halt outside a shabby house set back from the road. It sat behind a large gate bearing its name. The house was in a row of similar dwellings, all with windows shuttered against the heat. They were small – like little boxes - each separated from the one next to it by a small patch of rough ground. Once upon a time, they'd doubtless been buoyed up by a sense of civic pride. Now, though, many of them had fallen into varying states of disrepair. *Estevanico* wasn't the worst house on the street, but it certainly wasn't the best.

'You want to tell them?' Rivera enquired as the two men stood on the porch.

'What if nobody's in?' Miguel asked.

'Then we stick around,' the ex-soldier shrugged. 'Anyway, there's a car out front.' He rang the bell. From within, there was the sound of shuffling footfalls.

'Maybe it would be better coming from you?' Miguel frowned. 'The news – I mean.'

The ex-soldier shrugged. 'Really?'

'You found him. Didn't you?'

Silence.

The door was opened by an unshaven young man sporting a puzzled expression. He looked Rivera up and down before satisfying himself he wasn't dealing with a police officer. He didn't say as much, but there was a flicker – it was all the ex-soldier needed to see. Then the other man's eyes passed to Miguel. Rivera stared at him. He'd knocked on enough doors to know when someone didn't fit: expensive jewellery; new clothes; designer trainers. Such things didn't speak of the street they were on.

Drug money.

'¿*Qué*?' he demanded, his eyes narrowing.

'You know Ishaq?' Rivera asked in Spanish.

The man frowned, paused, and then nodded.

'I'm sorry,' Rivera said.

Chapter 52.

Rif knew the record seizure for hashish captured in transit between Morocco and Gibraltar had an estimated street value of $65 million. But that had been a few years ago. And that was only what the authorities had managed to recover.

Like any smuggler, Rif knew more than the authorities: hauls with total values much closer to $100 million had escaped detection several times. He also knew, as did anyone in his business, that it was a numbers game. For every win - and there were many - there were defeats. Runners ruefully referred to such seizures as operating losses; personnel lost to them through incarceration counted as collateral damage – they knew the lips of their operatives would remain sealed, but it didn't stop their profits from being dented. The record raid hadn't involved Rif. But he wasn't the only show in town when it came to powering narcotics across the Straits of Gibraltar.

Funding his super casino would take ready cash. Even more than he already had. And so he'd planned an enormous shipment. A gargantuan haul nearly four times the size of any known movement attempted before. It was ridiculous – he knew that much. But he was Abdellah Rif. And he fancied one last hurrah. After that, he vowed he'd go straight. Finally, become a member of the establishment. The proceeds would be washed in the normal way, and emerge clean, whereupon his pinstriped lawyers would make bank transfers and sign contracts that would establish him as the foremost property magnate in Almería.

Organising the shipment had mainly been delegated to Amrabat.

'I swear you'd sooner jack off over a spreadsheet than use a jazz mag these days,' the boss had jibed.

'Print media – it's a bit old hat, don't you think?' the assistant had shot back.

'Alright then – whatever porn website the guys up on the hill upload all the footage to then,' Rif had shrugged. 'Anyway, how are all those columns adding up?'

'We're looking good, boss.'

'How long until you get an answer?'

'An hour. Maybe two.' Amrabat reached for a set of car keys.

'Off you go then,' Rif said dismissively.

'Yes, sir.'

Whenever Amrabat ran any errands, he did so in person. Abdellah Rif used his phone to check the football results. Everything else was done face-to-face.

Chapter 53.

Miguel and Rivera sat on the back porch of Arraf's small house, watching a crow as it pecked repeatedly at a lizard that had died and dried in the sun. Miguel threw a stone to scare it away. They sipped at cans of cola. At first, Ishaq's cousin had been disbelieving. Then he'd cried, and after that, he'd grown angry, blaming the bearers for the news they'd conveyed. He'd kicked at the wooden uprights of his rear balcony, breaking some of the slats.

'Why?' he'd demanded.

'We don't know,' Rivera had replied. 'Nor do the police. As far as we can tell, he was in the wrong place at the wrong time, but that's all.'

'*Mierde*!' Arraf spat. 'They're not going to break a sweat looking for his killer, are they? That's not how things fucking work around here.'

'I'm sorry,' Rivera repeated for what seemed like the umpteenth time. Such words felt a lot like empty gestures.

'Well... sorry's not going to fucking bring him back, is it?' Arraf's voice was laced with bitterness.

Rivera shook his head slowly. 'Is there anything we can do? To help, I mean.'

Arraf sighed. 'You can take that car of yours up into the Plastic Sea and find my other cousins. Tell them.'

Silence.

'Can't you call them?' Miguel asked. 'I mean...'

'...no phones,' Arraf interrupted. 'They live in El Barranquete,' he continued. He paused, noticing his visitors' lack of comprehension. 'It's a shantytown. They work in the fields. In the greenhouses. Ask for the overseer. His name is...' he paused, thinking. '...Julio. Ask around – you'll find them.'

Rivera cleared his throat. 'Wouldn't the news be better coming from you? I mean...'

Arraf looked at his watch. 'I need to leave in ten minutes. Long trip. My truck...' his voice trailed off. 'It's not my truck - I can't drive it up there. Not today, I mean.' He paused. 'It's complicated, but the people I'm driving for – they're not the kind of people you keep waiting. If they found out I'd been fucking about in the Plastic Sea, you'd have another body on your hands. You get me?'

Miguel nodded.

'What are their names – your cousins?' Rivera asked.

'Saïd. And Nour,' Arraf announced.

Chapter 54.

Twilight was approaching when Miguel and Rivera located El Barranquete. Rivera was glad Fletcher wasn't expecting much upkeep on his loan car. The Renault 19 had been punished by dirt tracks and gravel roads; its suspension groaned. Dents and scratches had been layered on existing dents and scratches, and strange creaking noises had developed that hadn't been noticeable before.

But it was still going.

Almost everyone they asked had been unhelpful. It wasn't a surprise – most of the workers were illegal. The only *guiris* who tended to ask questions were looking to deport people. Rivera's accented Spanish made him even more suspicious. And Ishaq was a common name among the workers. Years before, the ex-soldier had been instructed in Arabic by the military as a side-line. He switched to asking stilted questions with the vocabulary he could remember, hoping it would win the confidence of some of the workers.

It only made them more suspicious.

So Rivera gave up. He let Miguel do the talking; they shifted, centring the search squarely on Julio. They reasoned a Spanish overseer wasn't the kind of figure that sailors on the Plastic Sea would feel protective towards.

Plenty of people knew Julio. But the Plastic Sea was a maze. The main paths were well-marked; they were the ones used by trucks taking produce to market. But navigating elsewhere saw the Renault nosing up dead ends and down blind alleys. The ex-soldier was amazed at the scope of the place; it was like an entire sub-civilization hiding almost in plain sight. Rivera felt like a section of Steinbeck's Depression-era Salinas Valley had been peeled off and placed in Almería. It was – he knew – a place most people would never know existed.

What Miguel and Rivera were searching for wasn't the sort of place people drove to unless they knew exactly where they were going. The shantytown was a location mainly accessed on foot.

But they found it eventually.

Julio was standoffish at first. He clearly had little concern for his workers or for the deceased young man the visitors were focused on. The overseer had assumed the men would cause him problems. But once the picking shift finished, and after repeated reassurances from Miguel, he climbed into the back of the Renault, and started giving the pair directions. He'd been hesitant at first until Miguel slipped him a couple of packs of cigarettes and reminded him they had nothing to do with the law.

* * * * *

A shack was located next to a perimeter fence. The structure had an open hatch on its front. A bored-looking man stood, obscured in the shadows, and behind him, there were two large, illuminated fridges that looked strangely incongruous with the rustic poverty surrounding them. A list of prices was chalked on the rear side of one of the shutters. The man nodded at Julio. Julio waved, and then turned to Rivera, pointing. 'Over there, senõr.' He indicated a squalid patch of ground in the distance. In front of it was a large pit over which crows circled. Beyond that, Rivera could see a higgledy collection of makeshift shelters. The smoke from a few fires was climbing into the night, and gatherings of dark shadows were clustered.

Rivera looked back at Julio, shaking his head in disgust. 'You really let people live like that?'

Julio shrugged. 'It's not my problem, senõr. I just do my job.'

Silence.

Julio looked into the distance. 'If you want to find who you're looking for, you need to go over there.' He pointed towards the settlement.

Rivera nodded grimly and set off. Miguel started to follow, but Julio grabbed his arm. 'Not you, compañero.' He shook his head, his face earnest.

'Why?' Miguel frowned, narrowing his eyes.

'Spaniards aren't welcome in El Barranquete...'

Silence.

'What will they do to him, though?' Miguel enquired, nodding towards where Rivera was traversing the ground.

Juilo shrugged. 'He's a *guiri* – things are different.'

Chapter 55.

On the odd occasions when Rif opted for more than a catnap, he slept hard. One of his ex-wives had joked that, when he crashed out, she could blow a trumpet into his ear when he was asleep and he wouldn't stir. He'd thought that disrespectful; she wasn't around any more. These days, she was an integral part of the foundations of a luxury condominium in Marbella. When their relationship neared the end of the road, she'd begun to make noises about a divorce settlement.

That wasn't how Abdellah Rif operated. Things worked out his way. Always.

The Moroccan opened his eyes. He'd been dreaming. He rarely did, but this one had been vivid. It was centred around a memory from long ago - one so clear it was like he'd actually been back in the past.

* * * * *

After Khalil became Rif, he travelled south, putting distance between himself and the fruit orchards. He knew there wouldn't be anyone on his trail. As a migrant worker, he was invisible; he was just another one of the horde of his compatriots that congregated at bus stations or slept beneath railway bridges. He was certain that - even if the corpse were to be found – nobody would be able to identify it. And even if they did, it was just another Moroccan.

Who would care about that?

But he'd headed south all the same. Rif felt safe enough, but saw no point in taking unnecessary risks.

Tarifa.

One day, perched in the hills above the town, Rif looked out across the Straits of Gibraltar. He'd stared out at Morocco looming in the distance.

Home.

The landmass seemed to reach out to him. There was something comforting about its familiarity. It seemed to speak to him: to offer him a lifeline.

There would be no shame in going back – he knew that much. Plenty before him had done the same. He was hungry. He'd run out of money. It would, as he well knew, be much easier to simply catch a ferry and cross back to Africa. There were plenty of hustles in Tangiers; he was sure he'd be able to ingratiate himself.

Pondering, he picked through the bag he'd stolen from the dead man. A switchblade. A magazine he'd found discarded on the bench of a bus station in Valladolid. A compass. A half-empty pack of sticking plasters. Two cigarettes - he'd smoked them and stubbed them out many times. But there was still enough tobacco in each for a nicotine hit or two. An apple long past its best.

He idly picked at a hole in the lining, pulling at the rough stitching. The bag was beaten, battered, and misshapen from where he'd been using it as a pillow. Reaching within, he felt a slim object which had been located beneath stiff leather and a brass buckle before - it had become detached.

The item was Abdellah Rif's passport. To find any such a document was a significant victory. It was a meal ticket that could be bartered. It was the kind of thing that would fetch a reasonable price on the black market.

But it was a Spanish passport. Sitting on the rocky outcrop of land, he felt an incredible sense of freedom. All thoughts of returning to Africa vanished. Not only did he have a new name – he had a new nationality.

Abdellah Rif could become anyone he wanted him to be.

Chapter 56.

Miguel and Julio waited at the perimeter as Rivera passed into the shadows, making his way into the shantytown. He picked his way around the rustling edges of the refuse pit. The pathway was bare earth, baked hard by the sun.

From experience, the ex-soldier knew there would be no point in trying to hide his presence. This wasn't a place he could sneak into. Though it looked like a collection of bivouacs, there were eyes everywhere. It reminded Rivera of some of the hamlets he'd been sent to overseas. Residents spotted things long before visitors thought they saw them. Such places weren't constructed conventionally. There were rat-runs and blind alleys; they frequently favoured the defender.

Whistles sounded out as he plodded on, more vulnerable now that he was alone and not in a vehicle.

So Rivera set his shoulders back and walked upright. Open. Confident. Strong. But obvious enough not to be a threat.

He hoped.

The ex-soldier headed into the centre of the encampment. As his eyes adjusted to the dimness, he saw the place was organised along a few mini-thoroughfares that all met at a central point. It was like a low-rise version of Seven Dials in the era of Victorian rookeries. Just as expected, a welcoming committee began to form. The meanest. The strongest.

Rivera came to a standstill about fifteen feet away from a hastily assembled semi-circle of men. He looked directly at each of them, working his eyes along the line. His expression was neutral; he needed assistance, not violence. They were tough, wiry men. Strong from hauling heavy crates all day long. Lean from hunger and hard work. Still young. Not the kind of men that Rivera wished to fight.

Not if he could help it.

* * * * *

'You're a long way from home, senōr,' one of the men announced in Spanish. The leader, Rivera assumed. He eyed the newcomer impassively. His companions said nothing; their eyes bored into him.

'I'm looking for someone,' the ex-soldier called out in the same language.

'They're not here,' the voice came back. Cold. A few more onlookers had been drawn into the fray. They approached, intrigued.

'I'm only here to talk,' Rivera announced. His tone was hopeful – he hoped it didn't sound desperate.

'Yeah – but nobody wants to listen.' It was another voice that piped up this time. A few of the men laughed. It was a laughter borne of bitterness – the kind of laughter that arises when the dispossessed suddenly feel power.

'I told you,' the ex-soldier protested. 'I'm here to talk.'

'Yeah?' The man switched to Arabic. 'Circle around the back in case he tries to run.'

'I wouldn't do that if I were you,' Rivera called out, speaking Arabic himself. 'I'm not that easy to stop.'

The circle fell silent. A slightly older man stepped out of the shadows and approached Rivera. At least he *looked* older. His shoulders were more hunched than those of the others. As the firelight caught his face, Rivera saw it was deeply lined. But, where the eyes of those around him gleamed with menace, his seemed curious – sympathetic, even.

'¿Hablas inglés?' The man asked.

'I do,' Rivera nodded.

'Who are you looking for, senōr?'

'Two people,' Rivera replied. 'But the reason I'm here - it's about someone else.'

The other man frowned, tilting his head slightly. 'Well, if we don't know a name, we can't help you. Can we?'

'Ishaq En-Nesyri' Rivera announced.

Silence fell.

'What about him?' the other man enquired eventually, frowning.

The ex-soldier lowered his voice. 'He's dead.' He paused. 'I'm looking for his family. One of them is called Saïd. And the other one is Nour. That's all I know.'

'I'm Saïd,' the stooped man announced sadly. His voice was little more than a croak. It seemed the news had made his stoop even more pronounced.

'Nour.' A woman's voice called out from the darkness.

'I'm sorry for your loss,' Rivera said quietly.

Chapter 57.

Back when Rif arrived, Tarifa had a strong Moroccan community; the freshly-minted Spanish citizen felt himself drawn to it. One of its representatives approached the newcomer soon after his arrival, telling him he ran a hostel – he provided food and lodging. Rif had been suspicious, keeping his hand on the switchblade as the man led him through a maze of streets.

But the offer was genuine. For the first time in weeks, Rif had slept indoors with a full belly. In the evening, the man spent time discussing current affairs with his guests before leading them in games of Ronda and Tute.

Living at the hostel was easy – he was fed and watered each day; he made friends with some of the other vagrants and street kids who passed through the doors. Most of them were hustlers; quick-talkers; braggarts. Rif, though, kept his mouth shut. He was always wary. Always a watcher. He saw the way they operated: on the first day, they'd stay in the grounds of the house. Nervous. Timid. New arrivals, scared of the outside world. On the second day, they'd venture out into the street. If someone had a football, they'd play with it. On the third day, they'd change tack. They'd be out foraging. Robbing people.

Rif became one of them.

* * * * *

But he swiftly learned Tarifa wasn't a big enough place for him to remain out of trouble. While the other residents followed each other into situations, unthinking, Rif stood back and observed. His plan was simple: he wanted to figure out how to take what he needed from them before he moved on. He realised he needed somewhere with a transient population. Somewhere with moneyed tourists and larger nefarious opportunities. A place where the blame wouldn't always be laid at his door.

Soon after his arrival, the police raided the hostel. They lined all the boys up in the yard and demanded identification documents.

None were forthcoming.

The boys stared sullenly back at the officers, kicking idly at the dusty ground, and playing straight into the hands of the law. Knowing they could easily link the street rats to a whole slew of robberies, the police began loading them into their vans. For most of the boys, it would be the first rung on a ladder. Once processed, they became persons of note. When that happened, the police would simply come knocking time and again, keen to link them to anything unsolved. Some of them were several steps up the ladder already.

Incarceration didn't suit Rif's intentions, though, so he rolled the dice. As the lead officer approached him, ready to shackle him in handcuffs, he held up his new Spanish passport. He used his new name for the first time.

Glaring at him, the officer tore the document from his hands. He scrutinised it, looking hard at the youngster before him and then back at the photograph. The likeness wasn't perfect, but the resemblance was clear enough to be convincing.

Then, the officer called over one of his colleagues. The two of them studied the passport, tilting it up to the light to check the various stamps and watermarks until they were satisfied it was genuine. Neither of them wanted to be convinced by what they saw, but the evidence was irrefutable.

By the time they were done, Rif was the only one who hadn't been loaded into one of the waiting vans. The lead officer looked at him, a hateful expression on his face. He opened his mouth to speak and then changed his mind.

He threw the passport onto the ground at Rif's feet and turned away.

Chapter 58.

The exits at Torre de los Boliches were kept locked – Rif's orders. It wasn't the kind of place the Fire Department came to check. The Kbir had ways of making irritating problems of that sort vanish. Zoning laws and local ordnances didn't affect them. There was always someone for sale. Besides, the Fire Chief was a regular passenger on the coach from the Segovia Palace. It wasn't in his interest to make trouble – not with the kind of preferential rates he was given with the girls.

So the doors remained locked.

But Carlos had kept his word. Of course, he'd subjected Tatiana to the kind of indignities which a man in his position considered to be his right. But she'd suffered much worse in the past. In fact, she'd been surprised he hadn't wanted to go further. Afterwards, he'd shrugged and let her head out of the fire escape.

'Sixty minutes, *muñequita*,' he'd called out behind her. 'Don't be late!'

* * * * *

From time to time, the girls were let out. Not officially, of course. But sometimes they persuaded their captors to relent – if only momentarily. Rif would have been puce with rage had he known, but the place operated on privileges. For much of the time, they were miniscule, but there was an element of bartering, nonetheless.

There were two reasons for the girls leaving the site.

The first was church. Some of them – fallen women though they were – still believed. Tatiana sometimes wondered if it was because of the profession they'd found themselves in that their faith was still so strong. They needed church to beg forgiveness; to make confession; to ask for absolution. The irony of being able to attend church was not lost on them. In order to circumvent the guards, they had to grant them their various demands. Agnieska – a recent arrival – told Tatiana she would have needed to go to confession three times a day to undo the sins Carlos had foisted upon her in return for the chance to be face-to-face with a priest.

A small church was located half a mile down the road. Some of the guards had talked to the priest; he therefore took confession at unorthodox times. The man of the cloth wasn't in the employ of the Kbir, but he certainly didn't turn his nose up at the large denominations of currency that miraculously made their way into the untended collection bowl on a regular basis.

The second reason for leaving was using a phone. Telephones were strictly off limits in Torre de los Boliches. The guards had radios to communicate with each other, and Rif wanted the girls kept in complete isolation. However, on occasions like family birthdays and Christmas, they would ask to walk down the hill; a bank of public phones sat by the roadside close to the nearest bus stop. The guards permitted such excursions – sulky call girls were bad for business. They were never happy – even after their daily doses of dope. But if they were denied occasional family contact, they were more down than usual. It was seen as harmless; the families were – in most cases – well over a thousand miles away, and mired in poverty. None of the girls wanted to worry their kin, so they played the parts of dutiful daughters, making light of their situation. The guards made it clear that the Kbir tapped the calls. It wasn't true, but the nightingales knew what kind of punishments were doled out for minor infractions – they didn't dare risk further wrath from their overseers for bad-mouthing them.

So a kind of détente was established. The guards could be bribed to look the other way. Visits to the payphones or to the church never lasted more than an hour, anyway.

That was the rule.

Chapter 59.

Rif departed Tarifa on a bus bound for Marbella. He reasoned the policeman must have thought arresting him wasn't worth the hassle. Processing Moroccan migrants was one thing – it was an easy win. There was no need for court approval, and they could easily be fitted up for whichever crimes were required.

A Spanish citizen, though, would require paperwork. Hence, Rif remained free. The look in the policeman's eye remained with him; it said that - whatever the passport claimed - in the mind of the officer, Rif would never be a real citizen. It was this which had driven the boss ever since: a desire to be valid. To be vindicated.

He knew the places in the hostel where the other boys hid their belongings. He also knew how ruthless they were, which is why he'd steered clear of stealing their loot before. Now, though, he was free to peruse their stolen goods at his leisure. Anything of value went into a couple of extra rucksacks he'd pilfered.

After the raid, the owner of the hostel had made himself scarce; he didn't want to have to answer the kind of questions the police were likely to ask. He certainly didn't want to be framed as a Fagin-like figure. So Rif made his way through the owner's quarters too, like a magpie, taking anything of value. Any cash. Any jewellery. Anything he could pawn.

It was a start.

* * * * *

When he arrived in Marbella, he'd scouted around. The marina and the waterfront were too wealthy for his purposes. It was the kind of place where he – a street kid – would be too noticeable. He'd be moved on. So he decided to extricate himself before that happened; he caught another bus along the coast to Fuengirola. Once there, he knew he'd found the place he'd been looking for. His Valhalla. Thousands of tourists flocked into town each week and then left again. They carried vast quantities of cash with them. At first, Rif had robbed a few of them at knifepoint. But then he realised there was no need.

He simply waited until the early hours of the morning. Blind drunk tourists would pass out on the sand like burned-to-a-crisp beached whales, and he'd help himself to whatever they had upon their persons, combing their pockets for wallets; travellers' cheques, and loose change. Soon, he had enough money to rent an apartment. And, once he had a foundation, he began building.

A year after arriving in town, Rif had a gang working for him. During the summer season, they patrolled the beaches from midnight until sunrise. It was easy work - most of the time; the police didn't put too much energy into investigating tourists who'd been robbed.

Anyway, tourists were rarely in town more than a week. And then the problems they'd reported disappeared. Of course, the police made occasional arrests, but Rif simply saw any such losses as collateral damage – any of his boys who were pinched knew better than to blab.

During the afternoon, Rif had his boys selling trinkets on the beach. They'd walk endlessly backwards and forwards. As they did, they were casing people – looking for marks. If there were wealthy-looking tourists, they bore them in mind for further investigation. Sometimes, they'd even follow them back to their hotels. Holidaymakers seemed to have tunnel vision; they had eyes only for happy hour hijinks and cut-price cocktails. Street kids were simply background scenery.

The Moroccan bought a stake in a bamboo-built beach hut that served giant quantities of chicken, chips, San Miguel and Sangria to sunburned *guiris*, along with a selection of local seafood. From an office at the rear of the shack, thick with the scent of barbecuing sardines, he ran the rental of sunbeds on the beach. It wasn't an official set-up. Resort hotels placed loungers and straw parasols as permanent fixtures during the season for the complimentary use of their guests. The de facto boss just decided they ought to pay for the privilege of them being gratis. All the money came back to Rif, who, minus a healthy commission, would then pay his boys a wage. He fed them, housed them, and sorted out any of the issues they had with other workers. Then, in winter, he hired them out as a work crew on construction sites that continually sprung up along the coastline. He did deals with foremen, undercutting Spanish workers' wages by almost a third; he then split the proceeds with people whose palms needed crossing with silver.

In turn, Rif became a foreman himself.

But the Moroccan wanted more.

He *always* wanted more.

Chapter 60.

Rivera sat close to the campfire with Saïd and Nour. Various residents of the shanty milled around, eyeing them suspiciously. Darkness had drawn in. The greenhouses glinted in the moonlight, looking like a sheen of water pouring down the hillside. Both cousins were morose; they'd accepted the news with a quiet stoicism, but were now brooding on it.

'Your English is excellent,' Rivera announced.

Saïd shrugged. 'I was a student – a long time ago. A lifetime.'

Silence.

'So...' Saïd began. 'I guess you'd better tell us the details.'

Rivera sighed. 'I wish I could...'

* * * * *

'How did you find us?' Nour asked.

'Arraf,' Rivera replied.

Silence.

'He was in my apartment,' the ex-soldier went on. 'He'd stayed over going to some monster trucks thing. I've never seen anyone so excited about bloody cars – he was like a kid.'

Nour smiled sadly, then frowned. 'Why do you think he was murdered?'

Rivera grimaced. 'Honestly, I don't know. He was too innocent to be mixed up in any gangland stuff, I'd have thought.'

'Yes,' Nour nodded. 'Far too innocent.' She paused. 'So – you have no idea?'

'I have my suspicions,' the ex-soldier answered.

'Such as?' Saïd enquired.

'He looked like a photographer – a friend of mine.'

Nour frowned. 'Is that enough to get someone killed where you live?'

'No.' Rivera shook his head. 'But this photographer sets up camera traps – he's on the search for the Iberian lynx.'

'Go on,' Saïd pressed, frowning.

'My theory is that one of his traps was triggered and photographed something it shouldn't have.'

'A person?' Nour questioned.

'Maybe.'

'Someone doing something they shouldn't have?' Saïd frowned.

'Possibly,' Rivera nodded. 'It would have been a one-in-a-million chance, but I can't think of anything else.' 'And if that's the case, then Ishaq was a tragic waste. He was just in the wrong place at the wrong time.' He cleared his throat. 'I'm sorry, but I think they came looking for Pancho – the photographer. He stays at my apartment sometimes.'

'I don't follow,' Nour frowned.

The ex-soldier sighed. 'They – whoever they are – were looking for a skinny guy with dreadlocks. When they broke in, they took the camera. I guess they thought that was it – the evidence. And their orders were to kill the photographer – Pancho.'

'But instead of Pancho, they found Ishaq?' Saïd enquired.

'Yes,' Rivera nodded. 'I'm sorry,' he said once more. 'But that's what I think.'

Chapter 61.

Tatiana didn't feel nervous until she was waiting for the bus. The nightingale fanned herself distractedly. She'd studied the timetable during the pretence of a previous phone call, and knew exactly when the number 351 was supposed to arrive. But she was aware she was vulnerable every moment that she was out in the open. Every passing car was a threat. Every person, a predator.

Descending the fire escape, she'd been expecting someone to shout. She had the same feeling as she crossed the scrubland towards the fence. Upon reaching it, she pulled aside a rolled back panel of chain-link sheeting. The makeshift exit was an open secret between the guards and the girls. Once again, she expected to be challenged. But there was nothing. She'd worn flat shoes to make the walk easier; they had poor grip, so she scrambled down the rough ground of the slope towards the pavement, slipping and sliding on the scree.

Having lived by moonlight for so long, the feeling of the sun beating down on her bare arms was strange; uncomfortable. A few cars passed as she waited. She toyed with the idea of sticking her thumb out and flagging them down. They would – she reasoned – stop for her; a reasonably young, still-pretty, platinum blonde with very few clothes on. But she feared they might be vehicles associated with the Kbir. Instead, she pulled a baseball cap low down on her forehead, and tried to blend in, certain the eyes of any passing motorists were boring into her, nonetheless.

Then, the bus arrived.

* * * * *

As she boarded, Tatiana was terrified someone would spot her; shout at her; drag her out and march her back to the Kbir. But nothing happened. She simply stepped on, paid for a ticket with small change lifted from a punter, and took a seat near the front. Aside from the driver, there was an elderly couple; a harried looking middle-aged lady, and a teenage boy with headphones and a skateboard.

None of them paid her any attention.

They continued to ignore her as the bus threaded its way down the narrow roads of the hillside. She checked her watch anxiously, measuring the bus' progress. If all went according to the timetable, she would reach the rest stop on the AP-7 five minutes before the hour was up. From there, Fletcher would spirit her away.

If he was there.

Chapter 62.

The flames crackled and fizzed as they chewed at the fence post Saïd had added to the bonfire. Rivera drank the last dregs of the tea Nour gave him – it was sweetly scented. The fire was for cooking and light – the warmth of the evening wrapped itself around the trio like a blanket.

'I need to go,' Rivera announced eventually. 'My friend is waiting.'

Saïd nodded.

Silence fell.

'You know, Nour began – if there's anything bad here, it's usually to do with the bogeymen. The Cucuy.'

'Hush!' Saïd's eyes widened white in the firelight as he hissed at his sister.

'Don't talk to me like that!' She raised her voice indignantly, looking at him with disdain.

'You don't know what you're talking about!'

'Oh, and you do, brother?' She shook her head. 'You don't know anything. And what you *do* know, you're too scared to say.' Nour pursed her lips.

Saïd glared at her.

'How did he die, anyway?' Nour asked, turning to Rivera.

The ex-soldier grimaced. 'I think it was chloroform.'

Saïd looked hard at Rivera. 'That's not an everyday chemical.'

Silence.

Nour's eyes were dark in the glow of the fire. 'Kbir?'

'We don't know that,' Saïd protested.

'No... but we know it's a possibility,' she insisted.

Saïd paused. 'Alright,' he nodded, a defeated expression on his face. 'It's a possibility. I agree.'

'So, are we just going to let them get away with this?' Nour enquired angrily. 'They murdered him – our own flesh and blood.'

'What choice do we have?' her brother replied. 'They're a huge organisation. It's what they do. They torture people. Kill people...'

'But you want revenge, right?' Rivera interrupted, sensing the frustration growing in the other man.

'Of course.' Saïd's jaw was set. His eyes blazed. 'But I wouldn't know where to start. I'm not a fighter – I'm a thinker.'

'But the pen is mightier than the sword,' Nour argued.

Her brother eyed her with incredulity. 'Yes, sister. It is – until you're looking down the barrel of a shotgun. Or until there's a knife at your throat. The Kbir don't go in for writing too much, from what I hear.'

'But they're to blame,' Nour argued.

'We don't know it was them for sure, though.' Saïd spoke morosely.

'But we might be able to find out,' Rivera suggested.

Saïd raised his eyebrows. 'Proof, you mean?'

'Call it a hunch,' Rivera replied. 'I should know in a few days. It might be nothing. But...'

'...it might be everything,' Nour broke in. 'And if it is, it'll be like the Hydra. You keep cutting off the heads until you're left with the last one. Then you cut that one off too.'

'Since when did you turn into a bloody vigilante?' Saïd shook his head. 'We'd never get near – you know that.'

'So, take the job. Work with Arraf,' Nour shrugged. 'That way you'll get closer than you ever would living here.' She sniffed. 'Otherwise you can just go back to work tomorrow and pick tomatoes, safe in the knowledge Ishaq will never be avenged.'

Saïd paused. He looked hard at Rivera, switching back to English. 'Who are you exactly, senōr?' he asked.

'What do you mean?' Rivera frowned.

'There can't be many *guiri* construction workers who speak Arabic as well as Spanish,' Saïd replied. 'There must be even fewer who'd be able to track down Arraf. Let alone find us – here, of all places.'

'I guess I just got lucky,' the ex-soldier replied.

Silence fell around the campfire once more. The siblings cast glances at one another.

'Are you a policeman?' Saïd enquired. 'Because that's all I can think of. The only other people who'd have the information you have are Kbir. But I know you're not with them – not with the skin you have. So, are you?' he pressed.

'No.'

'Before?'

'Not exactly.'

Saïd sighed, frustrated. 'If I ask you a question, will you answer honestly?'

Rivera nodded. 'I'll try.'

'Are you going after Rif?'

'Kind of,' the ex-soldier shrugged.

Saïd nodded. 'Can I help?'

'Maybe. Next question?'

'Can I?' Nour cut in.

'Sure,' Rivera nodded, puffing out his cheeks. 'Why not? Anyway, what was question two?'

'Do you have a plan?' Saïd continued.

'Yes,' the ex-soldier nodded. 'Sort of.'

The trio fell silent for a moment, and then Nour spoke. 'So, if you had an inside man – I mean, someone driving for Rif... would it help?'

Rivera shrugged. 'We've got another angle we're working. But having someone on the inside is always going to help. Any information is good information.'

The siblings looked at one another for a silent moment.

'So, there you go, brother...' Nour announced. 'You'll never get a better opportunity than this.'

Saïd sighed. 'Very well.'

Chapter 63.

Rif's voice was icy. 'What the fuck do you mean, gone?'

Amrabat inhaled sharply through his nose, ready to face the other man's wrath. 'It's what Carlos told me, boss.'

Rif nodded, regarding his subordinate as much with disappointment as with anger; it always irritated him when those under his command passed the buck. Once a finger was levelled, they would do anything they could to avoid the blame, shifting responsibility in desperate bids for self-preservation. 'Carlos?' he frowned.

'The pimp – one of the pimps. He's the one on the door. The fat fucker – from Cadiz.'

Silence.

Rif's eventual reply was measured; soft almost. 'And what exactly is being done to recover the bitch?'

'The usual, boss.'

'The usual?' Rif's face grew into a frown once more. His crow's feet puckered; his nose scrunched, as if scenting something foul. He fixed his assistant with a laser-like glare.

Amrabat swallowed nervously, realising his mistake. Before, his team had always succeeded in hushing up any absconders. The girls had always returned. And if not, they were replaced. Rif had no reason to be informed. That's how Amrabat had perceived it. As long as Torre de los Boliches was functioning and the girls were ready to service his guests, he had no need to know.

But the girls that escaped before were never Tatiana.

They weren't the boss' favourite. They weren't the one he liked to have on hand to accompany him to dinners or parties. They weren't the one he paraded around on his arm from time-to-time like a trophy wife.

Her running away wasn't part of the bargain.

Chapter 64.

The Renault pulled up in front of Arraf's house. Rivera engaged the handbrake with a sharp grinding sound. For a moment, the passengers sat in silence. Miguel had joined them once Saïd and Nour had agreed to leave the shanty.

'You know he's not here, right?' the ex-soldier frowned at Saïd.

The passenger produced a key hanging around his neck on a length of string. 'He always hoped that one day I'd changed my mind – that's why he gave me this.'

'You're coming in, right, senōr?' Nour asked.

'Give me a minute,' the ex-soldier replied.

Saïd and Nour stepped out of the car and made their way to the unlit house. Rivera turned to face Miguel, who regarded him pensively.

Rivera chewed his lip. 'Listen, my friend,' he began in a heavy tone. 'I'm not just a construction worker.'

'No kidding!' Miguel laughed.

The ex-soldier frowned. 'What? I'm not convincing enough on the site?'

The other man chuckled. 'Oh, you're convincing, alright. At least when it comes to pouring concrete, but you're a *guiri*. You speak Spanish. You speak Arabic.' He shrugged. 'Most of your countrymen can barely speak English.'

Rivera grinned.

Silence.

'Military?' Miguel enquired.

'Long ago.'

'Police?'

'Not exactly.'

'Spy?'

Rivera shook his head.

Miguel held up his hands, showing his palms. 'Look, *amigo*. What you do – that's your thing. And...'

The ex-soldier handed his friend the car keys. 'Listen. Take the car. It's yours for now. Tell Cesar I'm sick.'

'He'll never believe that – you're as tough as old boots!'

Rivera shrugged. 'So, tell him I've gone to see an old girlfriend or something.'

The other man nodded. 'Is this about Ishaq?'

'Kind of,' Rivera nodded.

Silence.

'You need help?' Miguel's voice was little more than a whisper.

The ex-soldier patted his friend's leg. 'No, but thanks for asking.'

Sniffing, the Spaniard fidgeted with the key ring the ex-soldier had given him and then looked up. 'You've done this kind of thing before, no?'

Rivera nodded and then proffered his hand. 'Drive safe, *amigo*.'

Chapter 65.

As the door shut, Rif sank down on his office sofa, grimacing. He'd dismissed Amrabat before he became tempted to pull out a pistol and spatter his brains all over the room. The boss knew his assistant wasn't to blame. But when wronged, his revenge often had to be instant – he'd lash out at the closest person, irrespective of their level of guilt.

Tatiana was gone. That worried him. Of course, she'd return. She'd have to. Surely? The dope the nightingales were kept on was a deliberate ploy; it kept them tethered. Kept them loyal to Torre de los Boliches. He ensured their veins were filled twice a day with the finest, purest heroin his people could source. That was why they didn't escape – at least that's why they'd never escaped before.

Amrabat's slip, though, gave him pause for thought. Not for the first time in the last few days, he wondered whether ruling by fear and surrounding himself with yes-men had distorted his view of things.

If his most senior lieutenant was capable of untruths, what other lies might he have been fed?

* * * * *

Rif rarely thought about feelings. Ultimately, he was motivated by two things: power and revenge. Everything else, he saw as an indulgence. So the sensation tugging at his heartstrings was an oddity to him. He couldn't work out why Tatiana's vanishing act was bothering him so much: ever since he'd arrived in Fuengirola, he'd had easy access to women. He'd started out with street walkers and worked his way up through increasingly glamorous girls until he'd ended up married.

That marriage hadn't lasted long.

Nor had any of the others.

It hadn't mattered, of course. For men like Rif, there were always other choices. He'd made it a habit to marry isolated beauties with few family ties. Frequently, by the time he'd grown bored with them, they had fewer family members left than when the couple had tied the knot, anyway.

Often, there were none left at all.

None of the marriages were relationships; they were exercises in ownership. Rif gave orders, and those orders were followed. His wives had been little more than mistresses – they'd just been better paid. And he'd controlled them completely.

Tatiana was a hooker, and so other people had her all the time. But she remained his property. The idea she'd decided to abscond was – more than anything – disrespectful. She wasn't allowed to think for herself. These days, she had no voice; she simply followed orders – those were his rules.

Rif demanded little. Just complete, unquestioning obedience.

He sighed and lit a cigar. Whores were ten-a-penny. But whores who could keep other whores in line were not. They were worth hanging on to – until they outlived their usefulness, at least.

Tatiana had been his favourite. But now she was just another score he'd have to settle.

Chapter 66.

Saïd handed Rivera a glass of water as the ex-soldier joined him and Nour at the table. The ex-soldier sipped it – it remained tepid, but neither Saïd or Nour seemed to notice, and at least it was clear. A dim lamp hung above them; a fly flew lazy loops around it.

'So what's the plan, senōr?' Saïd enquired.

Rivera narrowed his eyes and looked hard at the other man. 'Arraf offered you a job before, right?'

'Yes,' replied Saïd. 'But it came with conditions. He never said as much, but it did. It still does. That's how these things go. Always.'

'What conditions?' the ex-soldier enquired, his brow furrowing.

'Nour,' Saïd whispered.

'What about her?'

Saïd sighed. 'In the eyes of the Kbir, there are two types of women: mothers and hookers.' He paused. 'And Nour is too young to be a mother...'

Rivera nodded grimly. 'Couldn't Arraf say something, though? He's in with them, right?'

'Yeah,' Saïd chuckled drily. 'He can say something, but they won't give a shit. Remember, he's just a driver. He has cash and jewellery and a house, but you take that away from him, and he has no more power than those who live in El Barranquete. He has to follow orders. It's all the same.' He paused. 'But if you know some place Nour can disappear to for a while, then maybe I can work with Arraf and feed some information back to you.' He looked hard at the other man. 'I've got nothing to lose but her...'

Rivera nodded. 'I know a place.'

* * * * *

Next morning, the trio sat on the back porch of Arraf's house as they went over their idea. It was a long-shot. But so was Fletcher's plan. At least they had a common goal. Nour had been in favour from the outset; Saïd had slowly come around.

The time had come.

Nour and Saïd embraced, and then she and Rivera departed. For the plan to work, they needed to separate.

The ex-soldier and Nour would ride the bus to Malaga, then she'd catch a connection towards Fuengirola. They'd share the same bus on the first leg of the journey. But they'd sit in different sections. Strangers. After that, Rivera would disappear. He hadn't told the pair about Fletcher – there was no need to burden them with too much unnecessary knowledge. All he'd said was that he was getting help; that he had back-up. He didn't give them the details. He hadn't told them he'd be visiting Pancho's friend in Malaga to collect the developed photographs either. There was no need.

Rivera gave Nour the key to his apartment in Latinaja. At first light, he'd hiked to a nearby gas station and purchased each of the siblings a burner phone. Nour's job to begin with was simple: she was told to buy food and then stay put.

Saïd, meanwhile, would wait at Arraf's house. He'd tell him Nour had gone to nurse a friend in the Plastic Sea who'd been injured. He didn't think his cousin would believe him. But he also doubted he'd press the issue too much. For now, he'd have what he wanted: Saïd as a driver. He'd simply follow Arraf's lead and do what he was told. As he did, he'd keep his eyes and ears open and see what he could discover. There were no guarantees he'd find anything useful, but there were no guarantees any of them would succeed in what they were attempting, anyway.

* * * * *

At the bus station in Malaga, Rivera and Nour parted ways. He waited until she was out of sight before heading off in the opposite direction. She'd stepped off the bus nervously, no doubt finding it strange to be surrounded by so many people. But she'd adjusted quickly, realising she looked much the same as most of the other passengers. En route, the ex-soldier had called Fletcher, filling him in on developments. The policeman was somewhat appeased – he hadn't forgiven Rivera for his front-page fandango, but he conceded that the other man was at least moving things in the right direction.

Before heading off from Arraf's house, the ex-soldier had handed Nour an additional twenty euro note. 'What's this for?' she'd frowned. 'I have cash for food – I already told you that.'

Rivera spoke bluntly. 'My cat's name is Rosie. Her favourite brand is *Criadores. Pollo y conejo*. Understand?'

She nodded, smiling a little.

'Good.' His countenance darkened. 'Remember: don't talk to anyone. And once you're there, don't leave the apartment. Got it?'

'Yes.' She rolled her eyes. 'We've been through this – it's easy.'

'OK,' Rivera sighed. 'One more thing: there's a gardener – an old man named Pablo. He won't bother you – he'll just keep an eye on any comings and goings. Other than that...' He paused. 'You'll be sharing the apartment with my photographer friend. For now, he can't go outside either. That's why you need to stock up on food.'

'What's his name?' Nour frowned, taken by surprise at the ex-soldier's latest revelation.

'Pancho.'

'But how will I know it's him? I mean - for definite. What if the Kbir...?'

Rivera grimaced. 'He looks like your cousin.'

Chapter 67.

Fletcher had been waiting for Tatiana at the rest stop, as promised. She'd assumed he'd worn the same style of luridly luminous shirt as the night she'd met him for ease of recognition – she didn't know it was his usual attire. Once ensconced in the safe house, she'd said little. She was nervous. Nervous the Kbir would find her. Nervous the policeman would sell her out. And nervous, because she knew how men tended to treat her.

Deep down, she suspected Fletcher would be no different.

The policeman had been at pains to portray his professional intentions. He'd shown Tatiana to a room and indicated the lock on the inside of the door. He'd handed her a burner phone – for contacting family, he'd said. But he'd told her it would still be better if she ran any phone calls past him before making them. For about an hour, he'd referred to her as 'young lady' before she'd informed him he sounded like a creepy schoolteacher when he did.

'You're not a prisoner, Tatiana,' he explained. 'You're free to go at any time. But if you do, then you're likely to be in great danger. I won't be able to protect you outside of the house. And if you do go, then the plan I've been putting together won't work.' Fletcher paused. 'It won't be forever, but for now, I need you to keep a low profile.'

She nodded, unsure.

'We can stop Rif,' Fletcher continued, his tone passionate. 'We can take down his whole organisation. If he thinks you've disappeared, then he won't consider you a threat. That's when you'll be most dangerous to him.'

She'd nodded once more, and he'd shown her out to the sun deck at the rear of the residence. The property had been a police safe house ever since the 1980s. After the murder of Chas Edwards, buyers didn't have any hunger for the macabre villa, so the price had plummeted.

The force had stepped in. They'd needed a safe house, and the place had been built like a fortress.

* * * * *

For the purposes they required, the property was perfect – it was only accessible by one road, save for the spot Edwards' killer had known about where a narrow path clung to the edge of a perimeter wall. Over the years, the dry earth of the access path had crumbled into the canyon, so it was no longer a path – more a tightrope. The house was surrounded by a bricked barrier topped with barbed wire and broken bottles, and three sides of it jutted out into the canyon, which fell away steeply. The roadside front was guarded by another wall and a bank of security cameras.

It was quiet.

Really quiet.

'Help yourself, Tatiana.' Fletcher gestured at the fridge as they moved through the kitchen. 'Anything you want. I stocked up on fruit. Vegetables. Everything. There's a barbecue out on the deck too. Let me know, and I'll fire it up for you any time.'

She smiled weakly.

The police officer stood, ill at ease. The nightingale was still dressed for Torre de los Boliches; still attired as she was when he'd collected her. The policeman wished she'd cover up – whenever he tried to avert his eyes, he feared he might still come across as lewd. 'Er – any questions?'

Tatiana looked at him hard. Her face was drawn; heroin chic; pronounced cheekbones and heavily made-up eyes. Her skin was pale. She grimaced, uncomfortable, itching a little at her sleeve. 'Methadone?'

'Already?' Fletcher frowned.

She shook her head. 'Not until the shakes set in. I want to quit. But if I'm going to work with you, then I'll need help.'

'Will it be enough?' Fletcher asked. He pointed at the sideboard where what he'd procured currently sat.

'It's never enough,' she shrugged. 'That's why I need to quit.' She paused. 'You need to lock it away, too.' Shaking her head, she smiled sadly. 'Otherwise I won't be able to help myself.'

He nodded.

'This place,' she continued. 'It's nice. Is it yours?'

'I wish!' Fletcher grinned. 'No – this is a safe house.'

She frowned. 'A *safe* house? How can a house be safe?'

The policeman shrugged. 'We hope... it's a safe house. It belongs to the police.'

She nodded and lit a cigarette.

'I'll – er – leave you to it, then,' he said uncomfortably. Fletcher walked right through the house muttering to himself until he was standing in the front room, staring through the blinds. They were closed tightly enough to make him invisible, but the gap was sufficient to allow him a view of the street outside. He rocked back and forth on the balls of his bare feet. The marble floor felt pleasantly cold against his skin. He worried he was feeling too relaxed – the plan was almost going *too* well so far.

Outside, it was quiet. The sun beat down on the melting tarmac, and mounds of dried, browned pine needles were heaped up against the kerbs. His eyes roved further upwards, over the hillsides, towards Torreblanca. Turning away, he walked over to the cabinet in the front room. Opening it, he revealed a steel lock box from which he withdrew a Beretta 81 that he tucked into the rear of his waistband. The cabinet's racks were filled with assortments of weapons and ammunition.

Another lock box was secreted in the basement.

* * * * *

Rumour had it the basement hadn't been discovered until nearly a decade after the police had taken over the house. There were many tall stories surrounding the Edwards property, however. Into one of the plug sockets a switch was built, which made a bookcase slide along a pair of runners to reveal a staircase. Within the secure, thick walls of the subterranean level was a panic room. Some of the guns in the lock box there dated back to the Edwards era. A few of them had no serial numbers. Others had been made completely untraceable by other means. There had been some debate about whether to destroy the firearms. But someone had made the less than scrupulous decision that they might still be of use.

Plants.

Hits.

The possibilities were many.

Keith Michaels – the officer who'd preceded Fletcher as the supposed proprietor of Carvajal Rental Cars had filled the newcomer in. In Fletcher's opinion, he'd been a better care rental operator than a police officer. Any pride he took in his work seemed superseded by the pride he had at still having a full head of hair. His lustrous grey locks were greased back in an approximation of a Teddy Boy coiffure. Undercover police work relied on blending in, but Michaels' haircut marked him out. Fletcher's own get-up was ridiculous, but men dressed like him on the Costa were ten-a-penny. Before he'd departed for his sabbatical, Michaels reminded Fletcher of what he was dealing with. 'They're even worse, this lot,' he'd explained through a cloud of halitosis.

'Worse?' Fletcher frowned.

'Yeah – worse than the last lot.' He grinned ruefully. 'And they had their moments, didn't they?'

'I know – I was fucking here too, back in the day. Back in the eighties. Remember?'

Michaels had shrugged. His bonus-sized paunch made him look like Fletcher's extra-overweight older brother. 'You were young then. Don't forget that.' The older man shook his head. 'Without me, you wouldn't have known which side of the fucking bed to get out of in the morning.' He paused. 'Look after yourself, yeah?'

'Roger that.'

Chapter 68.

Carlos went into hiding shortly after Tatiana's disappearance. Girls at Torre de los Boliches had never vanished before. They'd departed through misadventure. They'd expired through beatings being administered too vigorously. The usual stuff. Then, there were the suicides. On occasion, nightingales turned tricks during their supposed church visits. They'd then return with extra medicine. And sometimes, they simply supplemented their dose until it transported them into oblivion. But none of them had ever slipped away completely – not until now. Carlos knew what the repercussions would be, so running was really his only option.

Life in the hills, though, had made him complacent. When it came to moving quickly, he was out of practice; unprepared. Most of the guards were the same. They'd lost the street hustler's lean, wiry ability to roll with punches. They were sated; under-worked; overfed, and bored. On the streets, they'd been myriad personalities within the same day; shape-shifting chameleons who adapted to different circumstances continually. In the hills, their days were mundane and slow, punctuated only by sex and drugs. Carlos, like the rest of them, had become sloth-like. He took one of the cars parked in the lot at the rear of Torre de los Boliches. After the leaving the site, he drove the vehicle to a deserted property he knew in the hills. It was on the edge of a small urbanisation a few miles outside of Mijas. The property had been one he'd earmarked early in his tenure, before comfortable living had lessened his worries about needing such a bolt hole.

* * * * *

Had Carlos taken one of the older cars, he might have got away – for a few days at least. But he panicked. Before the alarm was raised, the doorman simply climbed into the first vehicle he encountered in the parking lot: a sleek, black BMW.

The car was one of Rif's work fleet that he'd driven many times before. Towards the rear of the lot, there were dozens of other cars he could have chosen instead - older Peugeots and Seats. But he was worried enough not to think things through. He simply thought about the speed of the getaway.

All of the cars had keys in their ignitions. It wasn't as if anyone would dare to steal from the Kbir. So Carlos could have had any of them. He knew that much. His only obstacle was an ancient guard positioned at the gate. His presence was a mystery to everyone, but he retained his position on Rif's insistence. The man sat, half-blind, spending all day in a little hut where he pressed a button to raise and lower a red and white striped barrier whenever anyone drove in or drove out. But he was too decrepit to recognise who was passing him.

The camera positioned on the roof of his hut was far sharper, though.

And any cars the organisation had purchased in the last five years were fitted with GPS trackers.

Carlos didn't know that.

Chapter 69.

Pancho's friend, Luis, lived on *Calle de la Horedada*. It was a street filled with cream-coloured apartment blocks built in the 1970s. They all had six or seven storeys; all had narrow balconies on the side that faced the street, and all had awnings deployed against the sun. Successive decades of summer temperatures had faded the once-fashionable orange and brown patterns to blurs of pale pastel. Behind them, people were rising from the slumber of siestas, and beginning to emerge onto pavements. Doors of cafés were being thrown wide; the grilles of storefronts were sliding up, and there was a general chatter of voices echoing through the air. The district was near the hospital and close to the university as well. It was known as a student area, but it still retained a working class population which had preceded the arrival of its scholars.

The pavements were wide and patterned with large, shiny pearl-coloured flagstones into which smaller, glittering tiles had been set to make intricate patterns. Towards one side of the street, there was a small park. The slides and swings were untroubled by children at this hour; to touch them would have had a similar effect to plunging flesh into boiling lava. At the perimeter of the park were lines of established palm trees. Beneath them, elderly residents sat, talking in groups. Some of them played cards, while others snoozed on benches. Out of the shade, the heat was relentless. Rivera was used to such temperatures; months of working construction under the searing Spanish summer had acclimatised him. But street-level still felt like an oven.

Luis' shop wasn't a shop as such. To reach it, Rivera had to cut down a narrow access road. He crossed a small parking area hemmed in by two apartment blocks. The loading bay of a convenience store called *El Figaro* opened onto it, too. Old work vans and dilapidated hatchbacks were parked in the various spaces. A row of lock-ups sat at the foot of the apartment block, and on one of them, a small handwritten sign announced that *LUIS TEVEZ: PHOTOGRAPHER*, operated from within. A phone number was written beneath the name.

Rivera rattled at the grille, but it was locked. He wasn't surprised: the temperature within would likely have pushed the mercury to a thermometer's limits. Getting no answer, he called the number instead.

'*Si*,' the voice at the other end of the phone answered after a couple of rings.

'My name is Rivera. Pancho said that...'

'*Si, senōr*,' the other man cut in. 'Apartment twenty-nine.' The noise of a buzzer rang out.

Rivera held the door open and looked up. The building's rear was more drab than its street-side frontage. He couldn't imagine anyone would have trailed him, but he tried never to make such assumptions.

Remaining vigilant, he looked around, scanning for possible exits. Then he stepped inside.

Chapter 70.

Rif's men arrived in the late afternoon.

Tracking their quarry had been easy.

As Carlos ate the cold contents of a tin of kidney beans, he imagined himself as an off-grid fugitive who'd simply vanished. He was blissfully unaware of the truth: he was denoted as a blinking dot on a number of computer screens several miles away. The screens were overseen by the obese IT technician who monitored the security cameras at Torre de los Boliches. When the man had first learned about the nightingale absconding, he'd been worried, lest he be blamed. But once he realised Carlos was in the frame, he reverted to being his usual, cocky self. A squad was sent out to the location he'd pinpointed, and he turned his attention back to playing video games.

The property Rif's men encountered was a tumbledown villa whose grounds were overgrown. The visitors fanned out on the hillside as they approached. At the back of the building, they encountered the stolen BMW. It was parked beside a plunge pool whose water had taken on the dark, green tint of neglect.

The vehicle's keys were still in the ignition, so they removed them.

* * * * *

The first figures he saw emerging from the undergrowth had taken Carlos by surprise. He wasn't expecting visitors, so he knew the arrivals would be hostile. Reasoning it was a case of kill-or-be-killed, the escapee managed to squeeze off a couple of helpless pistol shots from behind the half-broken shutters that covered the windows. But, over longer ranges, his Raven .25 was grossly ineffective; an errant couple of rounds thudded into the earth of the hillside and another bullet ricocheted off the wall at the front of the property. Then, as Carlos aimed and pulled the trigger once more, the gun jammed. He grimaced as he tried to remove the dud bullet from the chamber. Pulling at the hammer had no effect; wrenching at the magazine release did nothing either – it simply made the sweat from his brow drip down his face more rapidly.

Carlos knew the only ace up his sleeve was that those pursuing him still believed he had a working firearm. He also knew the deception wouldn't last long. So a standoff ensued; the runaway hunkered down next to the window while those outside took cover and waited.

From outside, he heard whistles and shouts, and then the sound of running feet. Raising his head above the windowsill, he risked a glance. A bullet smashed through the rotten wood of the shutter, embedding itself in the brickwork behind him. He cursed once more. Had he bothered, he could have learned about guns – there were enough people in Rif's crew willing to teach him. But he hadn't. Instead, he'd simply availed himself of the girls at Torre de los Boliches and reasoned he'd only ever have to use the pistol as a theatrical prop. As of now, that was all his palm-sized firearm really was. He held the impotent weapon half-heartedly as he pressed himself harder against the wall.

Outside, two figures crossed paths – one running from the left of the window, and one running from the right. Carlos was no tactician, but he knew enough to understand they were trying to draw his aim. He also guessed that, when he failed to fire, they'd realise it was because he couldn't.

After that, overpowering him would only be a matter of time.

Carlos wasn't surprised when a voice sounded from behind him: 'Drop the gun, señor.' As he turned, he did as ordered, placing the pistol on the ground and raising his hands. Rising slowly to his feet, he turned and found himself staring down the barrel of a Glock 19.

The youngster holding it was clearly uncomfortable; the last time Carlos had seen the kid, he'd paid him for cleaning all the vehicles in the motor pool. The gunman's eyes were darting wildly, but his hand was steady. And Carlos knew the weapon he held would be in working order.

'Don't worry, *chiquito*,' Carlos sighed heavily. 'I'm not gonna run.' He paused. 'What are you going to do to me, anyway?'

'Not me, *compañero*.' The kid shook his head, his eyes still wide. 'Rif.'

Carlos pursed his lips and nodded his head. 'So... we wait for the boss,' he said sadly.

* * * * *

Rif eventually arrived with Amrabat driving. Once they knew Carlos had been captured, they detoured to the Segovia Palace to eat, reasoning they'd give the traitor a chance to sweat.

As he entered the kitchen, Rif saw Carlos tied to a chair. His face was bloodied. The doorman stared at the ground, looking utterly defeated. He'd pissed himself. Possibly worse.

'Well?' Rif demanded, sneering. 'Where the fuck is she?'

'I don't know, boss.' Carlos' voice was little more than a whimper.

Rif frowned. 'Don't fucking lie to me. Where are you meeting the little bitch?'

Carlos shook his head. 'I'm not lying, Mr Rif. She said she wanted to call her mother. So I let her out for an hour. We do that for the girls sometimes. Just to keep them sweet.'

Rif turned to Amrabat, glaring, and then looked back at Carlos, his expression softening. 'Listen – I believe you. Girls like that can't fucking help themselves.' He spoke calmly. 'It's not you I'm angry with – it's her. So, think, man. Where the hell would she have gone?'

The man in the chair shrugged sadly. 'I don't know, boss. She said she was coming back.'

Silence.

Rif's anger exploded at the same time as the butt of his pistol smashed onto the top of Carlos' skull. 'And you fucking believed her?' he shouted in disdain. 'Then you're as fucking worthless as she is.' He raised his Desert Eagle, levelling it at the captive. Speaking through gritted teeth, his words were all but indecipherable. 'Useless piece of shit,' he slurred, cocking the weapon.

'Boss?' Amrabat's voice hissed.

'What?' Rif demanded, speaking through gritted teeth. His eyes were narrowed to snake-like slits as they burned at Carlos.

'There are houses around here, Abdellah.' Amrabat spoke more softly.

'So?' The boss' tone was combative. 'What? Do you think I'm a pussy now or something? What the fuck's your problem?'

Amrabat sighed and spoke calmly. 'Someone might call the police. And if they arrive, we might not have time to get rid of the evidence. So, we'll end up adding to the body count.'

On hearing this, Carlos began to wail, pleading for his life.

Rif ignored him. He nodded at Amrabat instead and slowly lowered the weapon. 'How do you do things these days, then?' he demanded. 'When you've not got me doing the heavy lifting, I mean?' He paused. 'What did you use on that fucking Bob Marley lookalike?'

'Chloroform.'

'Yeah?' Rif raised his eyebrows.

'Yeah.'

'Got any with you?' Rif enquired.

Amrabat nodded, and then gestured to one of the other men.

Chapter 71.

Before Luis opened the door, Rivera noted the way the peephole darkened. He also saw how, when he'd slid back the chain, Pancho's friend cast a quick look in either direction down the corridor, to make sure the ex-soldier was alone. He was a skinny, gangly youth with thick glasses who looked about twelve. Luis scratched nervously at the skin on his arms. It was pale, and where it wasn't, it was covered with a mosaic of tattooed designs. His hair was long and centre-parted. He wore a Dead Kennedys T-shirt.

'Come in, *senõr*.'

The apartment was small and plain. It was darkened against the heat. The blinds had been almost entirely lowered, so the sun only entered through the mini-slats between them. Nevertheless, the reflection from the white floor tiles was enough to cast a dim light throughout. Photographs hung everywhere on string washing lines that criss-crossed the room. Beneath them were tables covered in slop trays of solutions and chemicals.

'So... people still like film then?' Rivera asked.

'You'd be surprised,' Luis answered. 'And there's not many of us who develop it these days. So business is good.' He grinned. 'I mean – I won't be retiring anytime soon, but I'm eating at least.'

Rivera nodded. 'Pancho...?'

'The photograph has been developed.' His tone was nervous. 'I wish I'd never set eyes on it.'

'Can I see it?'

* * * * *

The photographer picked up an envelope from a sideboard. 'I don't know who the guys are in the picture, senõr. But if they killed that person, they're not going to want this getting out.' He paused. 'It's fucked up!'

'I'll take care of it. Is this the only copy?'

Luis shook his head. 'I digitised it too – I've sent a copy to Pancho and there's one stored securely in the cloud. I've taken precautions, in case...' He hesitated. 'Just in case... If they're willing to do that, then...'

The ex-soldier reached for the envelope. 'Don't worry. They won't be able to trace you.'

The photographer nodded, unconvinced.

Rivera looked harder at the photograph, holding it up to the light from the shuttered blinds. It was grainy, but the location was clearly identifiable. A streetlight cast an orange glow over the image. But it wasn't the place that was significant; it was the person. The camera trap had captured a figure holding a handgun. The muzzle flash was visible, as was the darkened figure of another man, being pitched forward from a kneeling position by the blast. It was an execution. The stills scene looked like something from a pogrom.

'Damn!' Rivera exclaimed.

'It's a little pixelated,' Luis explained. 'You think it's enough to nail him? The killer?'

The ex-soldier shrugged. 'You can't see his face. It's too much in the shadows. Can you do anything about that?'

'That's as good as it gets, I'm afraid.'

Rivera nodded. 'This is still a hell of a find. It's date and time-stamped. We can see the guy's clothes. And if anyone wants to start breaking up bits of concrete around that trench, we know what they'll find.'

'Yes. Will they – break it up, I mean?'

'Not sure. There's a large section of wall there now with window frames awaiting glaziers.' Rivera paused. 'The people who work on that site will do what the foreman tells them, and I'm guessing the foreman does what Rif tells him.'

Luis nodded. 'But can you use it to get rid of him? I don't want a fucking guy like that on the loose – especially not when I'm the one who developed his photograph.'

Rivera nodded. 'We'll get him. We'll nail the bastard. Don't worry.' He reached into his pocket. 'How much?'

'No charge.'

'What? Come on,' he insisted. 'Pancho can pay me back.'

Luis shook his head. 'Bad karma señor.'

Rivera nodded, smiled wryly, and shook Luis' hand. 'Thanks for your help, *amigo*.'

Chapter 72.

Carlos' corpse lay on a tarpaulin sheet spread over the floor of the kitchen. Blood pooled in the folds of the material. One of the younger men in the group was combing the cracks between the tiles. He had a cloth and a bottle of bleach; he was looking for any traces of blood that might have escaped. Before his younger employee had returned with the chloroform, Rif had grown impatient; he'd dispatched the traitor with repeated blows from the butt of his pistol. Amrabat had simply looked on, watching the murder play out.

Two of the other men were standing beside the corpse, set to move it.

'Er – boss,' one of them began.

'What?' Rif frowned.

'What now?'

Rif looked down at Carlos for a moment. A malevolent smile crossed his face. 'You have knives in the car?'

The man nodded, frowning.

'Good,' Rif said. 'You have a saw?'

'Yes, sir.'

'Right,' Rif nodded. 'So take this fat, fucking bloated sack of shit out to the edge of the canyon.' His tone was cold; emotionless. 'Then undress the fucker and butcher him. Carve him up like a pig.'

The man nodded, paling a little. 'And then, sir?'

Rif shrugged. 'I figure the local wildlife can heat hearty tonight – let's do our bit for the environment, shall we? Feed him to the wild dogs.' He paused and looked hard at the other man. 'They still have them around here, right?'

'They do,' the man replied. 'But... will it work, sir?'

'Of course.' Rif shrugged and turned to his lieutenant. 'Amrabat? Remember?'

'It works,' the lieutenant nodded, slowly.

'But, what if...?' the man protested feebly.

Rif sighed. 'Too many bloody questions, kid. Do what you're fucking told. If not, then you'll make yourself sound like a pussy. This is how we did things back in the day. It'll still fucking work – believe me. It's simple: the dogs eat the meat and the bones and then rats, mice and ants vacuum up the blood and any other fragments.' He narrowed his eyes. 'Do I need to draw you a fucking diagram?'

'N-n-no... sir.'

Rif chuckled, turning to Amrabat. 'Fucking kids, hey?' He shook his head.

His lieutenant nodded, grinning. Their shared glance fizzled; for a silent moment, it contained all the decades they'd been together. Amrabat held his boss' gaze, his eyes smiling until the other man looked away.

Sauntering towards the door, Rif beckoned his lieutenant over before addressing him in a low voice. 'Take plenty of pictures.'

'Abdellah – are you sure?'

'Yeah,' Rif nodded. 'You're going to show them to the guards up on the hill.' He paused. 'They may be a bunch of useless, brainless bastards up there, but they're not so fucking dumb they can't learn a lesson or two. Especially not with some decent – er – evidence...' He looked hard at the other man. 'Make sure they know exactly how any further carelessness will be punished. Understand?'

Amrabat nodded.

'The girls will no longer sneak out.' Rif's order was blunt. 'I don't care how many fucking favours they grant in return. Are we clear?'

'Crystal, boss.'

Chapter 73.

'What are you so fucking happy about?' Rivera asked, seeing Fletcher smiling as he climbed into the car. The policeman picked the ex-soldier up outside a café on the campus of Malaga University. He'd wanted to go somewhere busy after Luis' apartment – somewhere he could lose himself in a crowd.

'You're a bit old to be hanging out with students, aren't you?' the policeman grinned. 'Not sure I approve of such behaviour!'

'Piss off,' Rivera growled.

'I think you'll be better off staying with me for a bit,' Fletcher announced as he drove through the suburbs. 'I've got plenty of space, and I think it'll make Tatiana feel a bit more comfortable if someone else is there all the time.' He grinned ruefully. 'She's got that much flesh on display I don't know where to look without coming across like an old perv.' He sighed. 'I've never looked someone in the eye so much before.'

Rivera nodded. 'How are things going with the police?' he asked. 'Ramos and company – I mean. Have they dropped it yet?'

Fletcher drummed lightly on the steering wheel. 'Well, the apartment's not a crime scene any more, so there won't be any surprise visits.' Fletcher squinted in his wing mirror as he changed lanes. 'Your photographer – Pancho - he's at Latinaja right now. Correct?'

'Yes – and Saïd's sister is there too. Nour.'

'Cosy!'

'Fuck off - what other option did I have?'

'OK. Well, I *definitely* don't think you should go back there – three's a crowd... it'll make people more likely to ask questions.' The driver looked sidelong at the passenger. 'Do you think we can trust her? Nour?'

Rivera shrugged. 'You think you can trust Tatiana?'

'Fair point.' Fletcher fidgeted with the controls a little to get a clearer radio signal. 'What about this Saïd, then? Do we honestly think he can get anywhere close?'

'Who knows? He's clever – and he's motivated. But there's no telling. It's not like he's got much time, is it?'

'No. What about the photo?'

'Not sure,' Rivera replied, pursing his lips. 'It would work in connection to other things. But on its own… you'd need a very sympathetic judge – put it that way.'

'Well, any jury where Rif's involved will be shitting itself.'

'Exactly.'

The two drove on in silence for a while.

'Listen,' Rivera began. 'I've been meaning to ask what your plan actually is.' He paused. 'I mean – you have the Russian girl who'll testify against Rif pimping out prostitutes in the hills. We've got the photo – we can dig up a corpse if need be, but whether or not we can prove it was Rif is another matter.'

'What's your point?' Fletcher frowned.

'I'm just saying… if we're going to put this guy away, I'm not quite sure how we're going to do it with what we've got. And, like I said, if he gets a courtroom he owns – which will almost certainly be the case…'

'…Interpol is on side,' Fletcher shrugged. 'It'll be alright.'

'Even so, I've been in this game a long time. On and off, I mean. And I can't see how you're going to do it.'

'We're like the Rebel Alliance,' the policeman replied. 'And they're the Evil Empire.'

'Star Wars?' Rivera scoffed. 'You've got to be fucking joking me!'

'What?' Fletcher shrugged. 'There are plenty of similarities: a small, under resourced force outwitting a major power.' He paused. 'You know George Lucas based them on the Viet Cong, right?'

'I don't need a bloody history lesson. I asked you about a plan…'

'My plan's evolving. But it's still a plan.' He paused. 'Rif doesn't play by the rules, so nor will we.'

Rivera frowned. 'A dirty war?'

'Maybe,' he replied enigmatically.

'Are we talking about a fit-up job?'

'Well,' the officer shrugged. 'If we *do* go down that route, then it's no different to how we used to do things back in the day.' He paused. 'Let's just say I've been feeling nostalgic.'

Chapter 74.

In Rif's drug smuggling heyday, moving hashish across the Straits of Gibraltar from North Africa had felt easy. There was plenty of confusion about which Navies had jurisdiction over particular stretches of water, so the smugglers had simply powered through, taking advantage of officials' indecision. Every time the authorities had adapted their approaches, the smugglers had done the same.

Since those early days, things had simply grown. Rif had done deals with other operators. But, ultimately, his approach hadn't changed - he just had interests elsewhere too. But his narcotics operation was still blossoming. His employees and hauliers had been used to open up markets in places far away from Fuengirola. Rif knew the authorities suspected him. But he also knew they could never link anything to him.

He was always one step ahead of them.

Hence Playa de Las Tres.

* * * * *

The authorities may well have been a step behind, but when they started catching up, they were able to bring back-up in huge numbers. Rif still favoured guerrilla tactics for landing cargo. Light and fast could carry the day against numerical superiority – frequently the flotillas employed against smugglers' vessels were slower and more cumbersome.

Back in the 1980s, he'd used fast boats to cover the distance across the Straits of Gibraltar. The boats' produce would be unloaded in the dead of the night and then whisked away without trace. Being intercepted was merely bad luck – the authorities would have to pick the right beach at the right time, and hold their nerve. It was like throwing a dart at a board when blindfolded and trying to predict the score.

In recent times, though, things had become more complex: patrol boats; radar-equipped planes; the cooperation of the Moroccan coastguard. There was more cargo than ever, but more of it was being impounded all the time. Rif was realistic enough to know he'd always lose some of his wares. But it would be a cold day in hell if he was going to lose any of the next shipment.

Not this time.

He'd invested heavily in the latest haul of hashish.

Too heavily.

If it paid off, though, it would fund most of the construction of his super casino – at least until more sponsorship from the establishment could be secured. All Ibanez's money was tied up in FC Castillo – he would be powerless to prevent the Moroccan's next move. With the windfall the shipment would bring, Rif knew he could bury his rival.

Until then, it was a gamble.

But what wasn't?

Chapter 75.

'So, what do you want to know?' Tatiana had accepted one of Rivera's hand-rolled cigarettes. Fletcher poured them each a glass of water from a jug. The ex-soldier was concerned. Not so much because of the danger Fletcher's plan put him in, but more by the stirring in his loins. Tatiana was stunning in a kind of trashy, sleazy, Sunset-Strip-West-Hollywood-circa-the-mid-1980s manner. He didn't know how much her dark eyeliner was there to mask the gaunt hollows of her junkie's visage. He didn't care – she was hot. Ever since leaving the military, Rivera worried he had a sex addiction. He'd even read about it, but he wasn't certain enough to make a self-diagnosis. For long periods, he could go without; the issue was that, when it was on his mind, it was the *only* thing on his mind. It was all-consuming – the kind of thing that could destroy an operation.

Fletcher eyed Rivera warily, his hand still on the other man's glass. 'I might add some fucking bromide to yours,' he said quietly.

'What?' Tatiana asked.

'Nothing,' Fletcher smiled sweetly. 'Anyway, we know all about the brothel in the hills. Anything to add?'

She shrugged. 'None of the girls who ever left there, left there by choice.'

'So, Rif killed them?' the policeman pressed.

Tatiana nodded. 'I believe he sold some to his clients, too.'

'Anything more?' Rivera enquired.

'The super casino.' Tatiana spoke quietly, exhaling smoke as she did. She looked hard at the ex-soldier. He couldn't work out if it was a look of disdain or one of intrigue.

'Is that real?' frowned Fletcher. 'I thought it was just a rumour – smoke and mirrors.'

Tatiana sighed. 'He's a strange man,' she explained. 'A psycho, I think.' She paused. 'He used to hire me out to people. And he used to get me to watch the girls – to keep an eye on them. But, at other times, he used to treat me almost like his girlfriend. As if he even liked me or something.'

'You think he loved you?' Fletcher asked.

'I doubt it.' She smiled wryly. 'I don't think Rif ever loved anything. Maybe himself. Maybe money. But not me. I think he just used to like telling me things. How do you say – captive audience?'

'Why, though?' Rivera enquired. 'Why tell you?'

'Power, I guess,' she replied. 'He knew I couldn't get away. *Thought* I couldn't get away. And he knew that I'd have to make all the right noises. You know – I'd tell him how impressed I was. Stuff like that. I think it made him feel like a bigger man. He has to hear praise all the time – it feeds his ego.' She sighed.

'So, the super casino?' Fletcher pressed.

'On the coast. He just bought the Hotel Sol.'

'Really?' Fletcher frowned.

'Yeah – he was boasting about how he'd done it in secret. But he's done the same with a batch of other hotels. His plan is to knock them all down. That's what he said. And then build the biggest casino in... I can't remember what he said – Spain; Europe; the world. Who gives a shit, right?'

* * * * *

Rivera turned to the policeman. 'You think it's possible to build something like that?'

Fletcher narrowed his eyes. 'Well... yes and no. I just didn't think it was true – until now. I'm going to have to tell Mühren.'

Tatiana continued. 'The way he was talking, it's going to be the biggest building on the coast.'

Rivera nodded. 'Is he worth that much, though? I mean... hookers; buildings. That's the usual stuff. But building something like that – how? I mean – you'd have to have an insane amount of cash.'

'He must have been plotting for years,' Fletcher announced, lighting a cigarette. 'Land down at the front now – it's got to be pretty much priceless. Most expensive seats in the theatre. Right?'

Rivera nodded.

'There's something else, too,' Tatiana explained.

'Really?' Fletcher raised his eyebrows. 'Doesn't the man ever fucking sleep? What is it this time?'

'Drugs, I think,' Tatiana continued. 'There have been lots of people coming and going. Many meetings. I think he's doing something big.'

'So he's still involved in narcotics?' Rivera said. 'I thought he was more legitimate than that. Surely there's too much for him to lose these days?'

'He's always been involved in drug running,' Fletcher explained. 'Hashish. Ever since... well, ever since anyone can remember. But nobody's ever been able to pin anything on him. He's a wily little fucker, that's for sure.'

'So what makes you think he's angling for something drugs-related now?' Rivera asked. He held the woman's gaze until she looked away, exhaling a lungful of smoke.

Tatiana shrugged. 'I hear things. See things. He thinks he's so clever. But he's not really – he's just ruthless. Everyone's terrified of him, so nobody ever speaks out. That's why his methods are never questioned. And that's why he makes mistakes - sometimes.'

'So... do you know where? When?' the ex-soldier pressed.

She shook her head. 'Only that it's going to be big. Huge.'

Fletcher pursed his lips, nodding. He looked at Rivera. 'Saïd?'

'Maybe,' the other man shrugged. 'If he gets taken on, he might be able to confirm it.' He paused. 'And if he *does* get taken on, then they must *really* need drivers. That'll tell us something at least.'

The officer nodded. 'Right. Well, Tatiana has to stay here – for now. And I have my suspicions Rif's people will have watched the films back by now. If they stumble on the footage of me at the Palace, someone will probably be figuring out I'm a person they'd like to talk to.'

'So – you're going to lie low too?'

'I am.'

Rivera frowned. 'What about the car hire place?'

Fletcher shrugged. 'It's a front – remember. It doesn't matter if it makes money or loses it. Not really. The force picks up the bill. And Manuel – the mechanic - has taken some time off to visit his family, so it's not like there's anyone in the workshop, anyway.'

Tatiana yawned and stretched; her body was lean, lithe, and clearly visible through the thin material of the tight clothes she was wearing. 'I'm going for a lie down,' she announced, her voice low.

As the nightingale stood up and sashayed away across the sun deck, Fletcher glared at Rivera. 'Don't even fucking think about it, soldier,' he growled.

'What?' he protested, shifting in his seat.

'Don't give me that bullshit! I can read your mind.'

'I was thinking about the mission.' Rivera shrugged.

'Missionary position, more like,' Fletcher glowered. 'You want my advice – you won't go anywhere near her. For starters, the number of cocks that have gone off in her face would be simply indescribable – who knows what you'd catch? But, more importantly, you fuck her and you risk fucking everything up.' He pointed his finger to emphasise his words. 'So take a fucking cold shower or think about some ugly, old, fat bird. But do *not*, whatever you do, get into that. Understand?'

Rivera nodded, his face solemn.

Chapter 76.

Rif felt an old familiar tingle running down his neck as he stood on the beach looking at the Gulf of Cadiz. No matter how far he rose, or how wealthy he became, it was this which excited him: the thrill of the chase; the joy of the hustle. The idea of getting something over on people who wanted to stop him – of going one better.

Over the years, the authorities had forced his operations further afield. It had been a gradual process that made it necessary for him to shift, cove by cove, along the coast. He could have gone the other way; higher up towards the Costa Blanca. But beaches were busier there, and shipping was monitored even more closely. Escape wasn't always as easy.

So, he'd opted to move west.

Playa de Las Tres was a known landing spot. It was accessible by road, and – at night - its waters were heavily patrolled. By day, though, the police presence all but vanished. It was a tourist haven. Having squads of armed soldiers on the sands would be bad for business. So, the mayor had petitioned the coastguard, and politicians had waded in. Once Rif found out, he made it a target.

The more the authorities tried to foil his plans, the more Rif saw it as a challenge. He considered himself above them all, anyway. That they had the audacity to try and stop him was insulting.

Disrespectful.

So, he decided to get his own back, and do something outlandish. Those pursuing him – he knew – would find it unbelievable.

* * * * *

Not only did Rif intend to land the largest haul of hashish ever smuggled between Africa and Spain. It would arrive on the beach. And it would happen in broad daylight. The fast transport boat would simply be gunned through the water right up to the shoreline. Once it beached, it would be hauled straight onto a lifeboat trailer which his employees would have waiting on the sand.

From there, the trailer would be driven up the beach where – along with the boat – it would be dragged into the rear of an articulated lorry. The measurements had already been made. People who needed to be bribed had fat little nest eggs sitting in hidden accounts, or bundles of cash secreted beneath floorboards.

The whole thing would be done in under five minutes.

After that, the empty trailer would disappear.

* * * * *

Rif knew the tourists wouldn't interfere. As long as their skins were covered in bronzer and their bellies were full of booze, they didn't tend to move from their sun loungers. They would probably consider it a curiosity – but they certainly wouldn't get involved. Many of them would still be grotesquely hungover from the previous night's excesses. The worst they would do would be to film it. And if they did, Rif didn't care.

By the time any footage was viewed, the cargo would have vanished. His men would have ghosted away like phantoms.

At an industrial estate on the outskirts of Cadiz, the fully-loaded articulated lorry would be driven into an enormous warehouse where the produce would be unloaded and divided between a fleet of panel vans bought new for the purpose. Rif's gang of drivers was insufficient for such a task, so he'd drafted in extra men that could be vouched for. Amrabat had worried about their loyalty, but Rif knew time was ticking – he was impatient to move forward.

From there, the vans would simply drive away. The produce would be sold, and the articulated lorry would be junked, becoming something that never was. Within three days, almost all aspects would be utterly untraceable.

Rif squinted at the horizon. Then he turned to Amrabat. 'How long until the tides are right for us?'

'Three days, boss.'

Chapter 77.

'Do you trust her?' Rivera asked when Tatiana had left the sun deck.

'Not really. But I think she trusts me,' the policeman replied.

'She doesn't look well.' The ex-soldier paused. 'I mean – she's easy on the eye, but there's no flesh on her bones.'

'She's an addict, remember? She's not well. A lie down isn't what you're thinking it is, sunshine. It's a euphemism – methadone.'

Rivera nodded. 'So...' he pressed. 'What now?'

Fletcher smiled. 'You, my old son,' he announced, 'are going to go and have a knees-up at the Segovia Palace tomorrow night.' He paused. 'With everyone else having to keep a low profile, you're the man now.'

'I am?' Rivera frowned.

'Yeah – it's time for you to fucking step up. Rif's men won't recognise you, will they?'

Rivera shrugged. 'I guess not – are any guys from the construction site likely to hang out there?'

Fletcher grinned and shook his head as he refilled his glass from the jug. 'Extremely unlikely. The drinks are eye-wateringly expensive. And it's a school night too. Remember?'

Silence. Rivera ran his hand over the condensation that had gathered on the sides of the jug. 'What about Ramos?'

'He's on shift. I've checked.'

'Won't I look odd, though?' The ex-soldier frowned. 'I mean, being alone and all?'

'Negative. Loads of old perverts go up there.'

'None taken.'

Fletcher chuckled. 'Hey, I've seen you eyeing up Tatiana, you dirty dog.' He paused. 'I don't like to cast aspersions, but she's considerably younger than you. Anyway, there's a coach that takes the Viagara crowd over to Torre de los Boliches every night.'

'Where's that?'

'It's the knocking shop in the hills.'

Rivera frowned. 'I'm not sure I like where this is going...'

'Don't worry – you're not going to be an active participant. Your dick's going to stay in your trousers. You're not going there for pleasures of the flesh.'

* * * * *

Fletcher looked hard at the other man. 'You've got something of a reputation, you know? When I was digging around, I ended up speaking to a British police officer called Christie. She told me you were a bastard, but in the best possible way – she said you're very competent. She trusts you. High praise.'

Rivera pursed his lips. 'So, what do you want me to do?'

'I want you to give Rif and his boys something to think about.'

The ex-soldier nodded, chewing his lip.

Silence.

'Tatiana will explain the layout of the place in the hills,' Fletcher said. 'And you're going to get in there and fuck things up.'

'Extraction plan?'

'I love you military blokes.' Fletcher chuckled. 'You all sound the same.' He nodded. 'There's an abandoned cottage a mile down the hill. You'll have to hike to it off-road, but it'll be easy enough to find. I'll be waiting. That's where we'll rendezvous.' The policeman glanced at his phone as it pinged out, then looked back at the other man.

'Just so we're clear... when you say give them something to think about, what do you mean?'

The policeman smiled. 'Have some fun. Express yourself. Do what you're good at.'

Rivera raised his eyebrows. 'Sounds intriguing. Go on.'

'Have you worn a wire before?'

'What?'

'You know – an earpiece?'

Rivera nodded. 'Once or twice, but it was a long time ago.'

'Good,' Fletcher continued. 'I'm going to have you wear a camera, too. It'll stream to my laptop at the cottage. That way I can talk you through who you're seeing. What to do. Where to go. Stuff like that. I've checked the internet coverage – it's good, and there are a couple of other networks I can piggyback off if need be.'

'One issue, though...'

'Go on.'

'If I go up to the place in the hills, then I'll be off limits after that, too. You risk running out of people on your side who can be seen in public. And that means they won't be able to go back to this Boliches place – that'll be a problem, right?'

'No – I don't think so.' Fletcher shook his head. 'Not quite.'

'How so?'

'Because you're going to burn the bastard down. Light it up like a Christmas tree. The fucking Kbir get away with things because the entire place has always been off limits.' He paused. 'Nobody will be able to turn a blind eye when you're done, though. The pyre will be visible from Morocco. And there's an IT guy there - you're going to get him to wipe all the footage too, so you can still be out and about – free and easy.'

Rivera nodded. 'We're pretty much as far off the books as we can get now, aren't we?'

'We are,' Fletcher replied. 'No authority in the world would sanction what you're going to do. Even Mühren will take some pacifying after this.' He laughed drily. 'But I'm sick of playing by the fucking rules.' He looked hard at the other man. 'You just need to make sure that – when the fun bus departs – you're on board. The rest of the plan will evolve from there. You'll be fine!'

Chapter 78.

'Is this the guy?' the boss in charge of the drivers demanded, pointing at Saïd.

'Yes sir,' Arraf nodded. In the presence of the other man, he'd shed his cocky persona. Instead, he resembled a nervous pupil in the presence of a strict teacher.

The man's name was Ziyad. He had broad shoulders and a thick neck. Arraf described him on the drive to the depot; he'd been on an Olympic wrestling squad years before. His enormous bulk stretched the seams of his T-shirt. His arms hung down limply. He looked less like a man and more like a Soviet-era statue carved out of rock to celebrate strength through industry.

'Name?' Ziyad spoke in Arabic. He regarded Saïd from beneath his hooded eyes. His large forehead seemed almost too heavy for his face. Scars stretched across it, running down from his shaved head, and giving him a look of perpetual anger.

'Saïd. Sir.'

'Can you drive?'

Saïd nodded.

'You have a licence?'

'No... I mean – yes – in Morocco. But not in Spain.'

Ziyad sighed and then shook his head dismissively. 'No matter. We can sort that.' He strutted towards the new man, stepping lightly on the balls of his feet. Leaning into Saïd, he spoke again. 'Arraf has vouched for you.' He paused. 'Tell me - why do you want this job?'

'So I can pay my rent,' Saïd shrugged.

'Fair enough,' Ziyad nodded. 'But drivers are dime-a-dozen. Why should I choose you? How do I know you're not going to fuck up?'

Saïd raised his voice slightly, looking the boss directly in the eye. 'Listen... Ziyad. For what feels like forever, I've been living in El Barranquete. At the edge of the Plastic Sea. My home has been a shelter made of wooden crates and plastic tarps. All weathers. My days have been fourteen hours long. Fourteen hours of vicious heat and breathing in the kind of chemicals whose containers have skull and crossbones flags pasted on the side. I've had all my humanity stripped away.' He paused. 'You can choose to give me this job. Or you can choose to kick me out. But I'm past caring. There's nothing you can do to me that hasn't been done in the hills. So make you choice quickly. And if you're *not* going to employ me, then quit wasting my time.' He paused. 'Oh, and if you want someone to grovel, then you're looking at the wrong fucking man.'

Arraf breathed in sharply. Ziyad tilted his head back and regarded the new man imperiously. 'You've got balls. I'll give you that. There's not too many people who'd dare talk back to me like that.' He turned to Arraf. 'I like him...'

'So?' Saïd interrupted. 'Sir?'

Ziyad nodded and then addressed Arraf. 'Take him up to the office. Clean him up a bit – he looks like a bum right now. Get him photographed for his licence.'

The boss then faced Saïd once again, proffering his hand. As he shook it, he exerted slightly too much pressure. A warning. 'There's only one rule here.' He paused. 'Don't fuck up. Otherwise, I'll tear your fucking head from your body with my bare hands.' He crunched Saïd's knuckles a little further. The new man stifled a wince. 'Understand?'

'Yes... sir.'

Ziyad nodded, turned, and swiftly made his way across the concrete floor of the warehouse, disappearing behind a stack of pallets where he could be heard shouting instructions at some of the other workers.

Arraf widened his eyes as he turned and looked at his cousin. 'What the hell was that about?' he hissed. 'I thought he was going to break you in half! What did I tell you? Act scared of him. Otherwise, it pisses him off.'

Saïd shrugged. 'Yeah, but I don't think he wanted that.' His tone was a little sheepish. 'Sometimes you have to change things up once in a while, cousin. Stop things getting stale.'

'Yeah – and sometimes Ziyad rips people's heads off...'

'Idiot,' smiled Saïd. 'He was bluffing – it was obvious!'

'Psycho!' laughed Arraf, clapping him on the shoulder.

Laughing, the two men made their way towards the office.

Chapter 79.

Cicadas chorused around the back deck of the Edwards property. Rivera emerged from the small pool where he'd been cooling off. He stretched and then looked over at Fletcher. 'Is that a Millwall badge in the tiling?' he asked.

'Yeah,' the policeman nodded. 'No accounting for taste, hey?' He grinned. 'I guess whoever did it was pretty shit – it looks more like a kid's drawing of a bear than a lion!'

The two men laughed. Rivera sat down on a plastic chair, still dripping. The moon shone down, lending the canyon beyond a ghostly glow.

'So... what are you thinking then, Rambo?' Fletcher asked, looking again at the rough plan of Torre de los Boliches Tatiana had drawn. 'Any bright ideas?'

'Well...' the ex-soldier looked up from studying the page. 'If I get in, I'll be in a pretty good position, I should think. And if I ride with them from the Segovia Palace, I should be able to get in, right?'

'Absolutely. And the wire means I'll be able to point you in all the right directions. I'll tell you who to talk to.' The officer's smile spread across his face. 'That way, you'll be able to send old Abdellah a message he can't ignore.'

Rivera nodded. His expression grew serious. 'You know, we're going to end up starting a war if we're not careful.'

'Maybe.' Fletcher shrugged.

'Won't that just make Rif go to ground?'

'Negative,' the policeman shook his head. 'He's the kind of bloke who wears his balls outside his boxers. He'll be straight back out – spoiling for a fight.'

'You sure we can wipe the footage? I don't want any of them trying to track me down.' Rivera looked hard at the policeman. 'I'm just a hippie who lives in a Silverfish, remember?'

'Then you'd better ditch your fucking peace and love for a bit; think hate and war instead. The way I see it, if you beat them all up badly enough, they won't be able to name names or remember faces, anyway.' Fletcher raised his eyebrows. 'Catch my drift?'

'Well… I do like a challenge.' Rivera chewed his lip and dabbed the towel at his face.

'Now you're talking my kind of language,' Fletcher chuckled. 'I knew I'd find the right man. It's like when Brian Clough went to Derby and bought Dave Mackay – it made everything else come together.'

The ex-soldier shook his head and looked disdainfully at the other man. 'That's the dumbest analogy I've ever heard. There's only a handful of people in England who would understand it – let alone Spain!'

'But you're one of them.' Fletcher grinned. He patted Rivera's forearm. 'Not bad for a Fulham fan! Come on,' he stood up. 'I have something to show you.'

Chapter 80.

The team of drivers assembled on the concrete floor of the depot. They hung around in twos and threes, smoking and talking. Some conversed in Arabic, others in Spanish. They'd all been issued with new sets of uniform – identical but for the badges of the companies they supposedly drove for. Behind them, a pair of fork lift trucks moved backwards and forwards, transferring loads and stacking pallets on top of each other; their wheels made squeaking noises on the smooth concrete. Saïd stood close to Arraf.

'Right ladies,' Ziyad announced brusquely as he walked in. 'Listen up.'

'This isn't how things normally happen,' Arraf leaned in and spoke to his cousin through the side of his mouth, frowning.

'How so?'

'Usually we just get given a truck and a list of destinations,' his cousin explained. 'They give us the uniforms and the paperwork all matches, but we're normally sent off in ones and twos. This is something different.'

'Something big?' Saïd questioned.

'Maybe,' Arraf shrugged.

* * * * *

The men clustered around Ziyad. He read instructions from a clipboard. 'We're waiting on a call. So, back here in an hour, boys. There's food next door. Make the most of it – you're not going to be stopping long enough to eat much once this thing gets going.'

A few groans arose.

'Shut up,' Ziyad growled. 'This is a major piece of fucking driving, so you need to clear your diaries. We're looking at seventy-two hours before you're back here. Minimum.'

More muttering.

'And before you all start bitching, know this: the boss man is paying double time,' Ziyad announced. 'All the time. As of...' He looked at his watch. 'Now.'

The mood lightened. A ripple of acceptance passed through the group.

'What are we driving?' Saïd piped up before Arraf dug an elbow into his cousin's ribs.

Ziyad frowned. His countenance clouded. 'You're new, so I'm going to let that one go.' His eyes narrowed, viper-like. 'There's a rule around here when it comes to cargo.' He looked around expectantly. 'Which is...?'

'No fucking questions,' the group chorused.

'But since newbie here is wondering, I'm going to give you the lowdown.' Ziyad looked at his clipboard once more. 'You'll leave your mobiles here – standard procedure. You'll be given a work phone for the duration. A burner. We'll then be heading to another location.' He looked straight at Saïd, raising his eyebrows. 'Curious?' He paused. 'You don't need to know where right now. But once you're there, you're each going to be given a van.' He waited for the information to sink in. 'You'll then be given a list of directions. And that's fucking that. Should be an easy few days, ladies. A nice little earner. You've just got to drive where you're told to fucking drive.' He paused. 'And don't fuck anything up.'

Ziyad looked around the room. 'Any questions?'

Chapter 81.

'Where the hell did you get this?' Rivera's eyes widened as he looked at the package Fletcher had deposited on the table. He'd waited until after Tatiana had gone to take her methadone dose before revealing the item.

'Don't ask!' Fletcher shook his head.

'No – I mean it. Where?' the ex-soldier pressed.

'What?' The policeman shrugged. 'You were in the military. This sort of stuff's your bread and butter. No?'

'I was a sniper,' Rivera sighed. 'This is bloody Semtex!' He shook his head at the package of plastic explosive. 'It's not like you can get this on the DIY aisle down at the supermarket! And they don't sell it on eBay!' He frowned. 'Is it traceable?'

'Doubt it,' Fletcher shrugged. It was found down in the basement with the rest of Edwards' guns. He was probably planning on using it to blow his way into a bank vault – before they bumped him off, I mean. It's the best part of thirty years old.' He grinned. 'It's perfect.'

* * * * *

Rivera chewed his lip and frowned. 'When are we doing this?'

Fletcher leaned back, lacing his fingers behind his head. 'Tomorrow night.'

'You're sure about that? I mean – don't we need a dry run or something?'

'No can do, mate. We get one shot at this. You know – before Rif gets too suspicious about one of his girls absconding.'

Rivera nodded. 'So, why the Semtex?'

Fletcher leaned forward and pointed to the rough map Tatiana had drawn. 'Here, here and here.' He jabbed his finger at the piece of paper. 'Propane tanks. They feed into each of the main blocks – that's my guess. They'll still be connected because the kitchens are in working order.' His eyes twinkled. 'I said you were going to fuck things up, right? Well, you torch them, and you'll have every fire fighter in Almería on the scene.'

'And the buildings?'

'They only use one of them, really. That's what she reckons. The rest are vacant.' He scratched at his stubble. 'It's not about the buildings, though. It's about putting a dent in their operation. It's about pissing Rif off – if the police are on the scene, they'll close the place down. At least for a while. He'll have to work his contacts on the force to get things moving again. And that won't happen overnight.'

'So this is a smokescreen?'

'Literally,' Fletcher chuckled. 'I want him to take his eye off the ball. If he's distracted, there might be other chinks in his armour which come to light.'

'And then the fit-up happens, right?'

The policeman nodded. 'I have a plan, but if your lad Saïd can give us something good, we might be able to work a different angle, too.'

'Too many ifs for my liking.'

'Yeah, but this is an organisation, mate. It's not some tin-pot-two-bank robbers-and-a-getaway-driver kind of thing, is it? We've got to be flexible. Once we get a way in, then we exploit it. That's how this plays.'

'I still don't like the odds.' Rivera shook his head. 'There's too many of them, and too few of us.'

'So they're slow,' the policeman shrugged. 'We're fast. We're hidden, and they're exposed. Viet Cong. Remember?'

'You've been rehearsing that little speech, right?'

'A little.' Fletcher nodded, the hint of a smile crossing his countenance. 'Why? Did it sound rushed?'

The ex-soldier shook his head. 'Not too bad - just a little like a movie script.'

'Exactly!' Fletcher grinned. 'Bit of glamour. Hollywood-style. Trust me.' He patted the other man's arm. 'It'll all be fine.'

The ex-soldier sighed. 'Do we even know if the Semtex works?'

'No.'

'No?'

'No, so we need to wake up bright and early tomorrow morning.'

'Why?' Rivera's brow furrowed.

Fletcher's face lit up. 'We're going fishing!'

Chapter 82.

'See you outside for a smoke,' Arraf said to Saïd as the crowd of drivers dispersed. 'I need to take a leak.'

Saïd nodded. Once on the forecourt, he looked around. The smokers hugged the shade at the edge of the warehouse. Many of them were absent-mindedly scrolling on their phones. Saïd removed the mobile Rivera had given him from his pocket. There were only two numbers stored in it: the ex-soldier's, and his sister's. He typed quickly, selected Rivera's name, and pressed send.

JOB HAPPENING. 2DAY/TMRW
VANS – APPROX. 20? LOCATION?
NO PHONES – ORDERS FROM BOSS.

Chapter 83.

Halfway through the drive, Rivera's phone buzzed. He looked at it, hoping for a message from Betsy; with every day that passed without a call, he had more of a sinking feeling. The tone of her texts had slowly shifted from romantic to merely amicable. Though he was loath to acknowledge it, he was worried their relationship had run its course.

'Who is it? Your lady friend?' Fletcher enquired.

'No – Saïd. He's got the job. He's a driver.'

'There you go then, mate!' The policeman thumped the steering wheel in celebration. 'Things are looking up. It's a good news day!'

'Yeah – pretty cryptic, though – his message.'

'Go on...'

'Twenty vans. Today or tomorrow.'

Fletcher whistled. 'That's an operation, my son. A big one.' He looked sidelong. 'Can he keep us posted?'

'Negative – looks like they're going to confiscate phones.'

The policeman nodded. 'Gut feeling?'

Rivera shrugged. 'Drug shipment?'

'Yeah, I agree. A big fucking drug shipment.'

'So? Change of plan?'

'No – I think we press on,' Fletcher replied. 'If the Semtex works, we're good to go. And who knows? If Saïd gets lucky and comes through, we might get something useful at his end, too. We might even be able to hit the bastard with a two-pronged attack. A pincer movement.'

'Very well,' Rivera nodded. 'So this is your idea of an evolving plan – incorrectly applying military metaphors?'

'Roger that,' Fletcher shrugged, grinning. 'One step at a time. Anyway, look on the bright side. It's a perfect day to be on the water. No point wasting a good opportunity.' He paused. 'I should've packed a picnic...'

* * * * *

'You know this is madness, don't you?' Rivera announced, absent-mindedly trailing his hand in the water. The boat was a little motor launch Fletcher had borrowed. The officer had piloted it nearly a mile offshore into the calm blue of the Mediterranean and into an area devoid of other vessels.

'What?' he grinned as Rivera regarded him doubtfully. 'My grandfather used to fish like this. He had a load of gizmos left over from the war.' As he spoke, he looped a fuse through a small amount of Semtex fastened to a lead fishing weight. He stood, one foot poised on the prow of the boat. The sunlight sparkled on the rippling surface of the sea. 'I'm going to give this three seconds. Should be enough...'

'How does it pan out now, anyway? This plan of yours?' Rivera demanded. 'Have you even got one?'

The officer looked up, scratching his head. 'Want me to level with you?' He paused. 'I don't exactly know yet. But in an ideal world, I reckon there are a few possibilities.' He grinned. 'You're going to blow up Torre de los Boliches. Rif's going to take his eye off the prize. Tatiana's going to go on record. Then your mate Saïd is going to drive a truck full of hash to us. I'll plant it so Rif can't dodge it or weasel his way out from being charged. And then, while he's having to pay off lawyers left, right and centre, his super casino will be dead in the water.' He drew breath. 'And then, while all that's happening, we can bring the rest of his crew in for questioning and really start investigating. Someone'll roll over – if we offer them a good enough deal and some time in Witness Protection. And then we've got him.' He squinted at the contraption he had in his hands and then raised his voice a little. 'Cover your ears!'

The next moment, the Semtex-laden weight splashed into the water. A heartbeat later, both men were covered in sea spray as the charge exploded. The small vessel rocked on the waves, and plumes of water rose up in the air.

Fletcher laughed and whooped. 'Well, I reckon we're in fucking business, my son!'

'Back to the plan,' Rivera continued once the surface had settled. 'It's a hell of a lot of dominoes that all have to fall at the right time.' His tone was doubtful. 'But you say we're in business?'

'I'm talking about life as a trawler man!' Fletcher smiled. He cast his arm out, indicating dozens of stunned fish now lying on the surface. He lifted a net out from the hull of the boat and began scooping them up. 'Look on the bright side,' Fletcher continued. 'Fresh sea bass for lunch *and* dinner. I'll do it on the barbecue. Feed old Tatiana up with some decent nosh.' He smiled. 'How does that saying go again? Give a man a fish and you feed him for a day; teach a man to fish and you feed him for a fucking lifetime.' The policeman laughed. 'But give him some Semtex and he'll be done fishing by breakfast time... which gives him the rest of the day for plotting the downfall of an international super criminal.' He smiled. 'What's not to like?'

Chapter 84.

'Right then, ladies!' Ziyad's shout rang out as he entered the warehouse once more. Bright sunlight spilled in through the space where the sliding doors had been opened. Everywhere else seemed pitch black in comparison. 'You know the drill.' He pointed at another man. 'Nadim will take your phones.' He paused. 'No fucking ifs. No fucking buts.'

The men moved towards Nadim and the bucket he held out for them. One by one, they deposited their phones into it. Some placed them carefully; others threw them dismissively.

'There are three minivans out front,' Ziyad went on. 'The journey shouldn't take more than a couple of hours.'

'What then, boss?' A voice asked.

Ziyad narrowed his eyes. 'It's all taken care of – leave the thinking to me.'

The big man turned and frowned at a trio of drivers who were laughing loudly with Nadim. They grew silent as they became aware of his eyes boring into them.

'Get a fucking move on!' Ziyad's tone was one of annoyance.

The drivers began trooping out towards the waiting vehicles.

Chapter 85.

As the afternoon wore on and Rivera's departure time for the Segovia Palace approached, Fletcher's tone changed. Gone was the jokey demeanour, and – in its place – his countenance grew serious. He checked and re-checked everything multiple times. As the pair ran through the plan again, the policeman fitted the ex-soldier with an earpiece. Fletcher rigorously tested the audio, making Rivera walk out to the edges of the property so he could monitor the device's effectiveness.

'State-of-the art this,' he explained, before pausing. 'Don't ask...'

Tatiana looked on.

'Mission control is going to be in the abandoned cottage I mentioned.' Fletcher indicated its position on the map once again. 'That's your extraction point, so any problems – go there. I'll have a car ready.' He paused. 'And a rifle.'

'Understood,' Rivera nodded. 'Can you definitely get reception there? Internet – I mean?'

'Absolutely,' he nodded in reply. 'It's all been checked. I'll have three hot spots running simultaneously. Short of satellites being shot down, we're all good.'

* * * * *

'So, what's all this?' Rivera enquired, looking at the various items assembled on the table.

'These are your charges,' Fletcher explained. He held up the various components as he made his explanation. 'Semtex,' he began. 'Great for fishing, but even better for lighting up Torre de los Boliches.' The plastic explosive was in three rectangular blocks. 'Next up, a mobile burner for each batch of explosive.'

'And these are the triggers?'

'Right. The fuse connects to the phone, and once the number gets called, it completes the circuit. Then it's goodnight Saigon. I'll tape each phone to a block of explosive.' He looked hard at Rivera. 'At the moment, it's not live. You arm it like this.' He indicated a tiny switch on the side. 'They're magnetic; if they're normal propane tanks, they'll stick to them. But if not, you can just leave them beneath. As long as the charges are out of sight, it doesn't matter. They won't be there for long. But the closer they are, the better.'

'And that's it?'

'That's it.'

Rivera frowned. 'You seem very knowledgeable about all of this stuff – for a policeman, I mean.'

Fletcher grinned. 'This stuff was all the rage back in my heyday. I was trained for a while in bomb disposal – this is just a case of flipping things round. I started off working for the Met. Then I was shipped out to Ulster on assignment.' He paused. 'I learned my lessons pretty fast out there – I had to. Questions?'

'Yeah – how do I get it all there? I mean – I'm supposed to be a regular punter, right?'

'Don't worry - I've made you a kind of harness. I'll give you one of my shirts. It'll be a little bulky, but it should hide everything. It won't be comfortable, but it'll get the job done.'

'So I'm going there in the guise of a suicide bomber?' the ex-soldier asked.

'Yeah – but the charges won't be armed.' The policeman shrugged, nonchalant.

'What if I get searched?'

'Never happened to me,' Fletcher replied. 'And I've never heard of anyone else getting searched at the Palace. They don't want to piss people off.' He turned to Tatiana. 'What about at Torre de los Boliches?'

She shook her head. 'No – it's just fat old men who want sex. No searches.'

'There you go then,' the officer nodded. 'Anyway, I'm going to give you my crappiest, brightest orange Hawaiian shirt.'

'Why?' Rivera frowned, a pained expression crossing his face.

'Well… if you were intending on blowing a place up, you'd wear drab threads, wouldn't you? You'd try to blend into the background. Right?'

'I guess,' the ex-soldier shrugged.

'Of course you would,' Fletcher nodded. 'So, this way, you'll just look like a tourist with too much money to burn; no class; no idea. Nobody will suspect anything.' He paused. 'Once you're done there, just head to the cottage. Then I'll dial the numbers and blow the whole thing sky high. Easy!'

'Casualties?' Rivera pressed.

Fletcher shrugged. 'Well, if there's collateral damage to any of Rif's guys, then I'm not going to lose any fucking sleep.' He looked at the map. 'Tatiana has indicated that all the – er – working rooms are on this side of the block.' He pointed. 'Having a few walls in between should be enough to shield the girls from the blast. The worst of it at least.'

'What about Oksana?' Tatiana demanded.

'Yes,' Fletcher grimaced. 'She's a problem.' He turned to Rivera. 'Tatiana thinks she'll likely be working at the bar. Odds on she'll have filled the vacant Madam position, so she'll be the one who's most vulnerable.' He indicated another point on the map. 'So… can you shift her out into the grounds? I mean, before the charges are placed.'

Rivera shrugged. 'I can try. If she gets found wandering around before the police get there, someone's going to smell a rat, though. Surely?'

The officer nodded grimly. 'You're just going to have to improvise. Keep your fingers crossed.' He looked at Rivera. 'Bring her with you if you can – let's remove her from the equation.'

'She'll slow me down,' the ex-soldier warned. 'I hadn't banked on escorting anyone – especially not cross-country. Once those charges are armed, we don't want any delays, do we?'

'Better being a bit slow than a bit dead, no?' Fletcher replied. 'Anyway,' he went on, 'we should be alright. Nothing'll happen until the charges are triggered.' He smiled, thinly. 'Providing nobody randomly calls any of the numbers trying to sell us double-glazing!' The policeman's laugh was hollow.

* * * * *

'Here's a new mobile for you.' Fletcher slid a smartphone across the table. 'They'll take it from you up in the hills, of course. It's completely clean. Untraceable. I've put real apps on there in your fake name – Joe Taylor. There's a load of genuine numbers too. Not that anyone'll check. And these,' he continued, passing the ex-soldier a pair of glasses, 'are your new specs.'

'Really?' Rivera frowned.

'Yeah. State-of-the art. They've even got a backup radio. But, more importantly, a live camera stream. This way I can be your ears *and* your eyes.' Fletcher grinned. 'The voice of your conscience. They're a fucking miracle!'

Rivera nodded. He then paused, pensive. 'Look – I know you want to seize the day, but is there any particular reason we're doing this tonight, Fletcher? I mean – wouldn't it make sense to plan a little more?'

'Negative, hombre. Tonight's the night.'

'Why?'

Fletcher cleared his throat. 'Remember Ramos?'

'The Comisario?'

'Yeah.'

'What about him?'

'He's bent – Mühren's got proof; that's why Ramos was so pissed off when Interpol stepped in and bailed you out.'

Rivera nodded. 'The figures.'

'Yeah. Anyway - this evening he's being entertained by Igor Miletski – a Russian gangster from Tatiana's past. He's looking to muscle in on Rif's trade.'

'Brave man!'

'Uh-huh – Mühren has him tapped. Ramos will be offshore in Miletski's yacht at exactly the time you strike. He'd normally hush up anything Rif's involved in. He monitors the switchboards pretty closely – he runs interference on anything that originates up in the hills. But he won't be able to this time. Phone reception offshore is pretty patchy at best, but the beauty of it is that – since he won't be on dry land – they won't be able to put him in charge of operations.'

'That's it?'

'Pretty much,' Fletcher nodded. 'But Mühren's also going to use some of his stooges to leak some information about Miletski, too. If Rif buys it, he'll likely believe that it was the Russian who was behind the firebombing.' He grinned at the ex-soldier. 'Like it?'

Rivera sighed. 'I think liked things more when I was living on campsites in my T2. And spending my days reading books...'

The officer laughed. 'Yeah, but you can do that shit anywhere. This way you get to play James Bond for a night. Everyone needs a bit of excitement once in a while!'

Chapter 86.

'So, Ishaq was your brother?' Pancho's words were tentative; hesitant. Nour looked hard at him. The new flatmates were seated at the table; an uncomfortable silence between them. They hadn't said much since the Moroccan had moved in. The photographer was usually a talker – an extrovert. But the mixture of guilt and fear he was experiencing had made him clam up. Nour, meanwhile, was still trying to process recent events; she was still adjusting to her change in location.

'Cousin,' Nour replied.

'I'm sorry,' Pancho sighed.

Nour shrugged.

Silence.

Pancho had cooked some rice and vegetables. Neither of the pair had done any more than pick at the food.

'Did Rivera give you any idea of time?' Pancho enquired. He trusted the ex-soldier, but hadn't been made privy to any of his plans.

'No.' She shook her head.

'He'll sort things out, you know,' the photographer continued after a period of quiet. He spoke in a tone of forced confidence.

Nour shrugged. 'Talk is easy. Cheap. We're talking about Abdellah Rif here. He's untouchable. He doesn't care about talk – he just kills people.'

'Did Rivera tell you why he thought Ishaq had died?'

'Because he looked like you.' She narrowed her eyes and looked hard at the man opposite her.

'Yeah.' The photographer grimaced, uncomfortable.

Chapter 87.

'This is the beauty of Carvajal Rental Cars,' Fletcher announced as they drove through the darkness. 'New motors on tap. Bloody love it!'

'Nobody saw you take it off the lot?' Rivera enquired.

'No, mate.' Fletcher shook his head. 'I moved this baby into the villa's garage weeks ago. All part of the plan.'

'So, tell me – you acting like a chauffeur.' He paused. 'Do people often get dropped off at the Palace this way? I mean, it's a bit ostentatious, isn't it?'

'People arrive like this fairly often,' the policeman replied. 'Usually, by the time they come back from Torre de los Boliches, they're drunk as lords, so it's chauffeurs or taxis all the way.'

'We could quite easily be walking into a trap here, couldn't we? I mean – Tatiana's very nice and all, but all it would take is one phone call. One tip off. And we're toast. It's not like Rif can't afford to make it worth her while.'

'I know,' Fletcher sighed. 'There's nothing we can do, though. Every plan has a weak point...'

'Yeah – your plan's got fucking loads of them!'

The policeman pursed his lips. 'That first night I met her, she told me a story about Rif.' He paused. 'It was one of the worst things I've ever heard. The things he made her do...' his voice trailed off.

'And you don't think she was spinning you a yarn?'

'Negative. I think she wants him dead. *Really* wants it. I've heard some pretty bad fucking stories in my time – none of them came close.'

'And if not... what if there's a welcoming committee at the Palace? Or one up in the hills?'

'Mühren's in the loop. Interpol knows what's going on – up to a point. Any issues, and they'll bring in their people. Cars; armour; choppers. The full works.'

Rivera nodded.

Fletcher turned into a well-lit junction. A long driveway curved its way upwards through illuminated, well-tended gardens. At the top of the hill sat the Palace itself – a magnificent, opulent structure. As the driver approached the entrance, a valet approached. Fletcher waved him away, proceeding slowly. 'Nothing happens here until after ten. It's early doors at the moment, so go in and get yourself a meal. You've got all that cash I gave you, so tip heavy. Tip bloody everyone. The quicker they think you're a high-roller, the more likely they'll be to approach you about after-hours activities. It won't happen straight away, though. And I'll be online as your eyes and ears in twenty minutes. Remember, you're Joe Taylor.' He handed over a driving licence with the ex-soldier's likeness. 'Stick that in your pocket. They're unlikely to ask for it, but you never know.'

Rivera reached for the handle of the door. As he did, Fletcher grabbed his arm lightly. 'Good luck, mate.'

Chapter 88.

'So, everything's fine?' Rif demanded. He was unsmiling.

'Yes, Abdellah.' Amrabat replied, relieved to be able to answer positively. 'We received word from Asilah. Everything's on schedule.'

Rif, seated behind his desk, nodded. He glanced at the scorpion sat in amber for a moment, running his finger over the smooth edge of the ornament. 'Then it is so,' he announced. 'All the pieces are in place. Once the shipment is sold, the casino building gets underway. And from there, old friend, the sky is the limit.'

Amrabat nodded. His boss' ability to switch from apoplectic to amicable within the blink of an eye was – he knew – the sign of someone who was deeply unhinged. Such shifts never failed to take him by surprise. Whenever he was friendly, the assistant trod on egg shells, ever wary that something might disrupt his equilibrium just as swiftly as it had been created.

A frown crossed the boss' face. 'Any news on Tatiana?'

The other man grimaced a little, shaking his head. 'There are a few leads we're chasing up. A couple of sightings.' He paused. 'We'll get her, though – I'm sure of it.'

Rif nodded. 'Let me know the moment you find her. We'll take her back – treat her right.'

Amrabat frowned. 'You're sure about that, boss?'

The other man laughed. 'Don't you worry! I'm going to teach that girl a lesson, but I don't want the other nightingales getting spooked. Not until afterwards. Then she'll become a fucking cautionary tale. Understand?'

Amrabat nodded.

Chapter 89.

'Good evening, sir.' The doorman's greeting was fawning as he addressed Rivera. He was bedecked in Segovia livery and a maroon brush coat with gold-embroidered epaulets. The top hat would have looked strange in London's West End in the middle of winter; in the midst of the Costa del Sol in summer, it was bordering on ludicrous.

The ex-soldier nodded and slipped a fifty euro note into the man's pocket, noting his employee name tag: Lars.

As he moved a couple of steps towards the open doors, the man called out after him, obsequiously, his voice betraying the merest hint of a German accent. 'Much obliged, Mr...'

'...Taylor.' Rivera turned and smiled.

The doorman nodded. 'If you'd like to dine, sir, I'd recommend the filet steak. It's outstanding – our chef is Michelin-starred.'

Rivera nodded, smiling. 'Sounds delicious.'

'And if - Mr Taylor - you'd care for any – er - extra entertainment, then do let me know. I can always pass the word on.' The doorman held Rivera's gaze for a moment, smiling.

The ex-soldier nodded again. 'That sounds most appealing. Thank you, Lars.' As he shook hands with the doorman, he pressed another fifty into his palm. The doorman's eyes twinkled.

'You have a great evening, sir.'

Rivera smiled again, moving into the glittering entrance hall. A large staircase stretched upward and huge portraits of matadors lined one edge of the vestibule. They were interspersed with the heads of bulls – their glass eyes regarding the room with expressions of perpetual anger. Enormous marble pillars rose up to the ceiling on the other side.

The ex-soldier moved towards the restaurant.

Chapter 90.

Given her previous silence, it came as a surprise to Pancho when Nour stood suddenly and declared she was going out. In a heartbeat, she switched from demure to demonstrative.

'No!' he hissed. 'You can't.'

'But Rivera's not here now,' she argued. 'How do we even know he's still alive? If we stay here, we're targets. We'll be victims.'

'He's alive,' Pancho insisted.

'You don't know that!' she scoffed. 'It's just wishful thinking.' An angry tear ran down her cheek. 'For all we know, he's dead in a ditch somewhere. And Rif's men are heading here to finish us off.'

* * * * *

Nour stood by the kitchen counter, her arms folded defiantly. Pancho's protestations had only half-succeeded in placating her.

'Until we know he's dead, we stick with the plan,' Pancho implored. 'Think about it – he's the best chance we've got. And if he's given us a plan, it's our job to follow it. He might even need us to help him out.'

Nour laughed drily and sank down, putting her head in her hands for a moment. As she did, Pancho moved past her, standing in front of the door.

'I want to be out there,' Nour went on. 'Doing something. Anything. I want to bring that bastard down. Even Saïd is doing something. But I'm sitting around here, doing fuck all.' She spat her words out angrily.

'We're fighting a guerrilla war here, though – you know that. Rivera will be able to move quickly – under their radar. But the moment any of us get caught, they'll use us for bait. Or worse...'

Nour straightened up, sniffing.

'Give it one more day,' Pancho pleaded. 'For me.'

'I'm not doing any of this for you, idiot.' She smiled bitterly and then frowned. A look of vague amusement crossed her face. 'I notice you're trying to bar the door.' She paused. 'Do you think you could stop me?'

Pancho puffed out his chest. 'Yeah.' He continued, unconvincingly. 'Probably. So if you want to get out, then you've got to come through me.'

'I may well be stir crazy,' she smiled. 'But let me assure you, Mister Photographer, that if I wanted to get out, I'd walk right through you.'

'I'd like to see you try,' Pancho bridled, a little hurt.

Silence.

'You want to have a beer or something?' Pancho asked suddenly. 'There are some cold ones in the fridge.'

'It's against my religion.' Nour shook her head.

The photographer nodded and shrugged. 'It's the only suggestion I have. Call it a peace offering. Got any better ideas?'

'No.' She shook her head.

'Balcony?'

'Yeah. Go on then. Why not?'

Chapter 91.

Rivera ate the filet steak with sautéed vegetables. It was served in the same way he'd seen fancy dishes presented on television – it seemed to him the more someone paid for a meal, the less food they got. He passed on dessert and drank nothing but iced mineral water. As he chewed, he cast his eyes around the room, feeling out of place in such moneyed surroundings. He worried his shirt would make him stand out, but realised he wasn't in a high fashion hotbed. There were plenty of people dressed in similarly garish styles. The message was clear: if your money was good, the Segovia Palace didn't care what you were wearing.

The ex-soldier's earpiece crackled slightly. It was minute; unobtrusive. And it was made completely invisible by the ex-soldier's shoulder-length locks of hair.

'Well played earlier, Rivera,' Fletcher rasped. 'Very smooth – you'll be like Sean bloody Connery by the end of the evening.' He paused. 'I know it's obvious, but don't ever answer me unless it's an emergency. Your earpiece acts as a two-way microphone, as do the specs. And don't touch your ear. The eyes-in-the-sky for their casino operation will detect things like that. It'll trigger their algorithms. If you need me to repeat myself, then just cough a couple of times.' He paused. 'And good lad for staying off the sauce – keep it that way.' Fletcher chuckled. 'Oh, and I see what you see, remember? So I saw you checking out the waitress' arse. I approve – she's a tidy package. But keep your mind on the fucking job!'

* * * * *

Finishing his meal, Rivera wiped at his mouth with a napkin and laid a few banknotes on the table as a tip.

'Right. Time for you to take a walk, old son,' Fletcher announced. 'Watching you eat has made me hungry. Let's get you away from the table and have you do something useful, shall we?'

The ex-soldier rose.

'I'm just going to give you a few suggestions about where to go,' Fletcher said. 'We won't bother with the casino. If it's hi-tech enough, they might even have some kind of sensor that jams our signal.' He paused. 'Just keep on going straight across the hallway to the bar. Last time I was here, they rounded up the after hours crew in there.'

* * * * *

'Good evening, sir.' The woman on the door gave a glittering grin. As she did, she proffered a glass of champagne borne aloft on a silver tray. Rivera took it, leaving a fifty euro note in its place. The woman bowed graciously. 'Have a pleasant evening, Mr...'

'...Taylor.' Rivera finished her sentence and walked through the door.

Entering the bar, he placed the glass of champagne down on a dark table. He then made his way towards the serving area.

'Well, good evening, sir.' One of the staff greeted him as soon as he sat down, instantly producing a decorative mat and a pot of salted snacks. His dark hair was slicked back, and he wore a collar with a bow tie beneath the glittering sequins of his burgundy waistcoat. 'And would sir like a table tonight?'

'I thought I might sit belly-up,' Rivera shrugged.

'A wise choice, Mr...'

'...Taylor.'

'Very good, Mr Taylor,' the barman beamed. 'And might I ask what your beverage of choice is?'

The ex-soldier smiled. 'Old-fashioned. With a twist.'

The barman nodded. Rivera watched as he placed the sugar, bitters and water into a tumbler, mixing them until the sugar dissolved. While he did, he kept up a constant stream of empty chatter designed to ingratiate himself with the guest. He filled another glass with ice and stirred in the whiskey, adding a splash of soda water. Before sliding the cocktail across the bar, he garnished it with orange and a cherry. It was – the ex-soldier had to admit – an excellent-looking drink. It almost seemed a shame he had no intention of consuming it.

Rivera laid down a fifty.

'Er – you pay the tab at the end, sir,' the barman announced, a little uncomfortably.

'I know,' the ex-soldier nodded. 'But that's for you. I appreciate a job well done.'

'Very kind of you, sir.' The barman gave a slight bow.

Rivera nodded. 'I didn't catch your name...'

'Diego, sir.'

The ex-soldier leaned in. 'Tell me, Diego,' he began, sliding another fifty across the bar and lowering his voice. 'What might a guy do for action around here?'

The barman frowned. 'I'm not sure I follow. I...' As he placed his hand on the banknote, Rivera kept hold of it.

'...after- hours, I mean,' the ex-soldier interrupted. 'Lars on the door mentioned something. Who might I speak to – if I'm interested, I mean?'

Diego paused. 'Stick around here, sir. I can have a word with someone if you like?'

'I'd like that very much, Diego,' Rivera grinned, releasing his hold on the banknote and patting the back of the barman's hand. 'I'm in no hurry.'

As the barman departed, the earpiece crackled once again. 'Well done, son,' Fletcher rasped. 'Just leave off the cocktail. It looks strong enough to stun a fucking elephant!'

Unseen, Rivera carefully, and with a tinge of regret, upended his glass. He slowly poured the cocktail onto the deeply carpeted floor beneath his bar stool.

* * * * *

'This is your man.' Fletcher's voice crackled once more in Rivera's ear as another employee walked towards him. 'Butter him up. Play nice.'

'Mr Taylor.' The new arrival approached Rivera with a smile. The ex-soldier shook his hand, palming off another banknote in the process. 'Some of our more – er – trusted guests will be making their way to an after party.'

'Go on.'

'It's very exclusive. By invitation only.' He paused. 'But Lars and Diego said you might be interested and...'

'...will there be girls there?' Rivera interrupted, affecting a drunken slur.

'Oh yes, sir,' the new man grinned, nodding earnestly. He leaned in and spoke quietly. 'Many, many girls.'

'Then name your price!' the ex-soldier beamed, swaying.

'We like our most esteemed guests to go to the members' lounge before we depart. Of course, we organise the transport.' He looked hard at Rivera and spoke in a low voice. 'Five hundred upfront. The girls negotiate their own fees.' The man paused. 'Am I counting you in, sir?'

The ex-soldier nodded.

'Er, might I...?'

Rivera nodded. He made a show of squinting at the man's name badge before speaking in a slurred voice. 'You know, I like you Alfonso. You're my kind of guy.' He reached into his pocket, withdrew a wad of notes, and counted off six hundred. 'One for luck, old bean,' he belched, handing the extra note over as a tip. 'Now then. Show me the way to this members' lounge,' he demanded, slapping at the other man's shoulder.

'Well played Rivera,' Fletcher's voice crackled as the ex-soldier followed Alfonso out of the bar. 'A thoroughly convincing performance... old bean.'

* * * * *

'Jesus!' Fletcher sighed through the earpiece as the ex-soldier entered the members' lounge. 'This place is filled with the same old faces that were here when I passed through before... they must be here virtually every night. Like desperate fucking regulars.' He paused. 'Anyway, be nice...'

Rivera nodded his thanks to a waitress who provided him with another glass of champagne. He then seated himself on a Chesterfield sofa.

Alone.

'You'll be here for about forty-five minutes,' Fletcher explained. 'Long enough for them to bill you for a couple of vastly overpriced drinks. Everything here's designed to fleece you. But just stick around and keep your mouth shut.'

The ex-soldier reached over and used a little of his drink to water the plants in a nearby pot. He settled back into the sofa, listening idly to the bragging, braying voices filling the room.

'Want me to play I-Spy with you?' Fletcher's laughter cackled. He paused. 'Only joking – I'm going to keep quiet for a bit now.'

Chapter 92.

The coach journey to Torre de los Boliches passed without incident.

It was only at the point of boarding that Rivera felt truly out of place. He couldn't help thinking that the group of men – of which he was the youngest by at least a decade – resembled retired tourists on a package holiday. The driver even carried a clipboard as he worked his way down the line, bowing, and graciously accepting tips. It was as if he was about to unveil the itinerary for a cultural day trip.

But the other men seemed to accept it as the usual order of things: they had plenty of money. Therefore, the job of the world was to bend to their will. They'd all formed the opinion that anything preventing them from doing exactly what they wanted to was an imposition. Therefore, receiving what they'd paid for was – to their minds – the natural order of things.

* * * * *

Once they reached the hills, the men were unloaded from the coach and shown into a vestibule. From there, they took a staircase to a lounge area on the next floor. The décor was pleasant – clean and recently decorated. Large prints of classical paintings hung on the walls in a vain attempt to make the place seem less seedy. Some of the older men struggled with the stairs, wheezing and sweating their way upwards.

'Head to the bar.' Fletcher's voice crackled in the earpiece. 'That's Oksana serving the drinks. Tell her you know Tatiana and grab a beer. During the next ten minutes, this whole place will turn into a meat-market, so you're best off out of it. When it empties out, you should hopefully get the chance to start being a bit more proactive.'

Rivera made his way to the bar. As he did, he dodged a series of scantily-clad women bearing raffle ticket numbers. They stroked at him, fluttering their lashes, grabbing at his groin. On the sofas behind, their colleagues draped themselves over the new arrivals, proffering drinks and regarding the men with doe-eyed expressions.

The ex-soldier seated himself at the bar. Oksana - the barmaid looked at him, impassive. Rivera leaned in to make himself heard above the noise of Euro Pop piping into the room. She frowned and bent her head towards him to hear better.

* * * * *

'What would you like to drink, sir?'

'Tatiana says hello.' Rivera spoke in a low voice.

The woman froze for an instant before lifting a cloth and wiping at the bar's surface. She didn't look at him as she spoke. 'And you don't want to tell my boss?'

'No, it's your boss I helped her escape from.'

Oksana frowned, watching as a couple of giggling girls led men out into the corridor. The doorman held out a tray, relieving them of their phones as they went. 'How do I know you're for real?' she demanded.

The ex-soldier shrugged. 'Ask me a question.'

'Yes, fire away, mate,' Fletcher announced. 'Tatiana's listening in.'

'Where's she from - Tatiana?'

There was a brief delay before Rivera relayed the answer given. 'Yakutsk.'

'Her husband's name?'

Rivera once again spoke the answer proffered over the earpiece. 'Dmitri.'

'Mother's name?'

'Yulya,' the ex-soldier replied after a short pause.

'Very well,' she nodded, sliding a beer across the bar to him. 'I believe you.' She frowned, casting a quick glance around the room. 'But what are you doing here?'

'Don't worry,' Rivera reassured her. 'You don't need to do anything. Just act normal. I'm going to try to get you out of here.'

'And the others?' Oksana narrowed her eyes.

'Them too. Later on.'

She nodded, uncertain. 'Can I help?'

He leaned in a little further. 'The surveillance.' He paused as a further group of men lined up by the doorway with their chosen women. 'Do you know if they have a room or some place where they monitor the cameras and things like that?'

Oksana thought for a moment. 'There's a room downstairs at the end of the corridor. It's filled with screens. A fat guy spends his days there eating potato chips and jacking off.'

'Yeah,' Rivera nodded. 'Sounds about right. That'll be it.' He looked hard at her. 'I'm going to try and get rid of this doorman guy first, though.'

Oksana nodded and then straightened back up. Rivera watched in the mirrored glass behind the bar as the doorman approached. The ex-soldier was now the only customer left in the room.

* * * * *

'¿Que pasa?' the doorman wheezed as he sat down. He was a bulky, heavy-set man with body odour. His beer gut protruded from where his shirt rode up over a hairy mass of sweating paunch. Around his neck, he had a large, golden medallion that glittered where his top buttons were unfastened.

Rivera smiled weakly.

'You don't want to get some action, senōr?' he enquired, nudging the guest.

'Careful!' Fletcher's voice warned in the earpiece. 'Play it cool.'

Rivera cleared his throat, tucking a fifty euro note into the breast pocket of the doorman's shirt. 'Is there some place I can get some fresh air first, please? I had a little too much champagne earlier. If I can stand outside for five minutes, I'll be ready to have a crack at the ladies.' He grinned uncomfortably. 'Do you know what I mean?'

The doorman laughed. 'Yeah, there's a fire escape,' he nodded. 'But I'll have to stand there with you.' He paused. 'Company policy. It'll cost you too, I'm afraid.'

Rivera nodded and stood, ready to follow the doorman. As they moved towards the door, the other man bent down and picked up the phone tray, holding it out and smiling apologetically. 'House rules, senōr. Same for everyone.'

The ex-soldier deposited the phone Fletcher had given him into the tray. He was led down to the end of the corridor and then a bar was pressed on a fire door. The other man swung it open and the two men stepped out onto a metal fire escape. It overlooked scrubland and, beneath it, an unlit concrete path ran around the rear of the block.

The doorman offered Rivera a cigarette and lit one for himself. He then turned his back on the ex-soldier. 'She's a tiger – that Oksana,' he laughed. 'Breathe deep on fresh air – that's my advice. You'll have your work cut out for you. She'll fuck you six ways to Sunday – she'll make your nose bleed.' He looked back at Rivera, who laughed heartily in fake response. The doorman turned again to look out into the darkness. 'Don't worry – I took care of her earlier,' he leered. 'Slipped her a length. Warmed her up for you.'

Silence.

Rivera's movement was so quick the doorman didn't even have time to emit a noise. One moment, he was standing, contentedly inhaling cigarette smoke, and the next, he was plummeting through the air. The last thought that crossed his mind was one of puzzlement: he wondered how come the world had turned upside down, and why the ground seemed to be rushing up towards him.

The ex-soldier had simply reached down and grabbed both of the man's ankles, wrenching them upwards with such force that one of the man's shoes came off in his hand. It had been too fast a motion for the doorman to grab at the fire escape's guard rail. And so, with his bulk suspended in the air, gravity had done the rest. The man had fallen like a stone. Head-first onto the ground below. Which he hit with a thud.

A sickening crunch echoed across the scrubland. Movies love the notion of heroic death – the idea that people expire very publically in blazes of glory. The reality is usually far from that: one moment, people are alive; the next, they're not. And, most of the time, nobody notices – not until much later.

Rivera listened for a moment.

Silence.

He wedged the fire exit open with the doorman's shoe.

Descending the steps, he reached the ground ten seconds later; he saw that blood was seeping out of the doorman's shattered head. His neck seemed to have concertinaed into itself. He dragged the corpse into the bushes, scattering a handful of earth over the dark liquid.

One down.

Chapter 93.

'Get some rest,' Ziyad ordered to the assembled group of men. He puffed at a cheroot as he spoke. 'There are camp beds set up next door. Once you get going, you won't be sleeping for a while. And we don't want any accidents – especially not this time. No fuck ups.' He narrowed his eyes. 'I mean it – this is the big one. You play your cards right and there'll be decent bonuses at the end of it all.'

'Can you tell us the plan yet, boss?' one of the men asked innocently.

Ziyad sighed. 'What's with all the fucking questions?' He shook his head. 'What I can tell you is this: the goods are scheduled to arrive at midday. Once they're here, they'll be processed and split into batches. And then, you lot get on it.'

'What's being delivered?' a voice piped up.

Laughter rang out through the warehouse.

Ziyad shook his head, a smile crossing his face. 'Watch it – you bloody joker!' he grinned. 'Once the batches are sorted, they'll be loaded into vans. You'll have other things in the back too – for cover. Just like normal. Furniture. Vegetables. Shit like that.' He paused. 'The plan is that a van departs here every twenty minutes. Regular enough to be believable, but not to so close together that people will be suspicious.'

'Why vans?' a man asked. 'I mean – I'm not complaining - we all get bonus pay because of it. But why not a truck?'

Ziyad frowned. 'Not that it's any of your fucking business, Faissal, but these deliveries are going wide. *Really* wide. You'll all be given legitimate job dockets to memorise. Most of you will be crossing borders. And the boss wants this done quickly. In trucks, you have to stop every few hours and rest; you can't drive more than nine hours a day, otherwise it fucks up your paperwork. In vans... you don't.' He scanned his eyes across the assembled group. 'So get some rest. For brunch, I'll be serving black coffee and Ritalin.'

Saïd moved over to Arraf as the men made their way into the annexe. 'Is this normal?' he enquired. 'Drugging drivers and enforcing rest - it feels like a military mission or something.'

'Yeah, it's not usually like this, cousin,' Arraf replied. 'It must be something pretty big.'

'No pressure then?' Saïd puffed out his cheeks.

'Of course not!' Arraf grinned, slapping the other man on the back. 'You'll do great!'

Chapter 94.

Rivera already knew Rif's men were not as skilled as people believed. They were armed, and they postured and posed, but they didn't look trained – at least not to his eye.

But there were plenty of them.

The ex-soldier didn't like the odds. He knew it only took one stray bullet to ruin plans. And if there were plenty of people firing stray bullets, it still put the odds firmly in their favour. No matter how bad they were. A bullet was a bullet – it didn't matter if the shooter was trained or not.

He was taking no chances.

* * * * *

His job was simple. There was no need to engage the enemy unless it was absolutely necessary. So he stuck to the shadows, working his way quickly and quietly around the perimeter of Torre de los Boliches' buildings. Like any soldier, he wanted to reconnoitre the area – he was clear on the mission, but he wanted to get an accurate sense of how big a force he was likely to be facing.

'Radio silence,' Fletcher's voice hissed. He paused. 'Good luck.'

The grounds were lit sporadically. In places, overgrown sections made the going slower. But two minutes later, Rivera had encountered no opponents. He was crouched next to the first of the propane tanks. It was dimly lit by bulbs set into nearby flagstones. The ex-soldier removed the pair of wire cutters Fletcher had provided him with.

He worked slowly. Methodically. When he was finished, he held the device close to his glasses. 'You able to see that, Fletcher?' he whispered.

'Roger,' came the voice through the earpiece. 'I can enhance the picture quality at my end.'

'Well?' Rivera whispered.

'Yeah – exemplary. You're good to go with that one. Just place the charge on the underside of the tank about a third of the way from the end with the connection.'

The ex-soldier did as instructed.

Fletcher whistled. 'That's a behemoth of a tank!' He paused. 'No bandits around, then? Tatiana reckons they mainly concern themselves with the gate and the main building, so fingers crossed you'll avoid them.'

* * * * *

The next two propane tanks were mined in exactly the same way. The second was almost a carbon copy, while the third was in an unlit area. Rivera's charge was placed in pitch darkness.

'Yes, my son!' Fletcher encouraged him. 'I can still make out what you're doing. Twist the ends and it's job done. Easy!'

It was only as Rivera was standing up from the third tank that the dynamic changed.

'Freeze!' a voice hissed.

Chapter 95.

Rivera raised himself slowly, scooping up a handful of gravel and then holding his arms up in surrender. There were no lights or windows around for him to catch a reflection of the threat he faced.

He turned.

An armed man approached, holding a revolver in front of him in a firing stance. The ex-soldier took in the weapon, and – even in the darkness - noticed the man's hands were shaking. He was young. Scared.

'He looks like a right fucking cowboy!' Fletcher muttered, sounding more irritated than worried.

'Who the hell are you?' The guard demanded, approaching warily. His feet crunched on the gravel of the path and he almost tripped. He pulled his leg in irritation, disentangling his foot from a creeper that had grabbed at it.

'Maintenance,' Rivera replied, tonelessly. 'Who are you?'

'But it's the middle of the night!' the youngster insisted, ignoring Rivera's question. 'There's no maintenance work after dark.'

'Emergency,' the ex-soldier shrugged.

'Are you a *guiri*?' The other man squinted at him in the darkness.

'They needed an expert,' Rivera shrugged. 'I'm the best there is.' He spoke nonchalantly. Then he paused. 'But it's proving a little tricky. I don't suppose you have a torch I can borrow?' He smiled ingratiatingly.

The guard shook his head, confused. 'I need to check with my boss.'

'This kid's fucking useless,' Fletcher announced. 'Get rid of him.'

* * * * *

'Have you not got a camera on you? A phone?' Rivera asked. 'You can show your boss what I'm doing if you like.' His tone was open; friendly.

'No senōr.' The man shook his head.

'Radio?'

'I – er...'

'Get a fucking move on, will you?' Fletcher cleared his throat. 'We haven't got all night!'

'I'm calling my boss.' The other man announced, reaching into his pocket.

Rivera grinned affably and nodded.

As he dialled, the youngster turned away slightly and pressed the phone to his ear.

It was all the opportunity the ex-soldier needed. He flung the handful of gravel and then sprinted at the other man, driving his fist between his adversary's eyes with the full force of his acceleration.

He crumpled.

Unconscious.

* * * * *

'Nice!' Fletcher chuckled. 'You're not going to put him out of action permanently?'

'Negative.' Rivera spoke softly. 'He's just a kid.'

The ex-soldier checked the casualty's call hadn't connected, and then shouldered his inert mass, carrying him round the side of the buildings to where he'd ditched the doorman. On the way, he picked up a discarded length of hosepipe he'd seen on the path, and used it to bind the man's hands.

'You're a bloody humanitarian, you are,' Fletcher scoffed at the other end of the line. 'Next thing, you'll be visiting him in jail and sending cards at Christmas.'

'Piss off,' Rivera hissed as he took the man's revolver and slipped it into his pocket. 'Right. Radio silence. I'm going back in.'

As he climbed the fire escape, he looked around and listened carefully. There were giggles and a few rasps emanating from some of the windows.

Rivera edged through the open doorway. The corridor was deserted. He made his way through the deserted lounge room to where Oksana stood, polishing glasses. In terms of hair colour, build and attire, she was a carbon copy of Tatiana - Rif plainly had a type. Approaching the bar, Rivera leaned over, peering at her footwear. The heels were precipitously high.

'You have a pair of flat shoes anywhere?' he enquired.

She nodded.

'Right. Get them and meet me back here in three minutes.'

The ex-soldier moved towards the door. He knew speed was of the essence – he'd been surprised at how easy things had been so far; he was certain he'd encounter more opposition before he was done.

* * * * *

Rivera left the lounge.

He moved swiftly, silently descending the stairs to the vestibule. Following Oksana's instructions, he moved down to the far end of the corridor and drew close to an open door. Leaning through it, he saw a bank of screens. An enormous man sat, munching on the contents of a giant pack of crisps. It looked as if he'd been poured into his seat; rolls of flab overhung the arms of the chair. One of his hands was thrust down the front of his trousers.

Rivera closed the door behind him. At first, the ex-soldier wondered if the other man was watching the action taking place in the rooms upstairs. But, as he drew closer, he saw he was engaged in half-heartedly playing a video game on a smaller console screen before him while a porn movie was playing on the screen of his phone at the same time.

The ex-soldier pressed the confiscated revolver – a Ruger Security Six - into the back of the fat man's head. As he did, the man froze, wincing. He then shook his head angrily, trying to free himself from the pressure of the barrel.

'I want you to wipe all the camera footage that exists tonight.' The ex-soldier spoke slowly, in a measured tone.

'Rif will kill me if I do,' the man replied.

'I'll kill you if I don't. And I'm the one with the fucking gun. So, do yourself a favour and play nice. Then you won't get hurt.'

'You're bluffing,' the fat man wheezed.

'Listen,' Rivera continued, pressing the barrel of the gun harder against the other man's head. 'I won't lose any sleep if I have to blow your brains all over these screens. I promise you that much. So you have a choice: either do what you're fucking told, or suffer the consequences.'

'You can't erase the footage without me,' the fat man announced smugly, twisting around in his chair to regard the newcomer. 'And I'm under Rif's protection.' He paused. 'Anyway, how would you know if I'd done what you asked?'

The ex-soldier sighed. 'I'm a quick learner. I'm good at figuring out whether people are lying. And I'm in a hurry.' He paused. 'There are two things that I know. Number one: the footage will be wiped in the next three minutes. Number two: you still currently have a choice over whether you live or die.' He sighed. 'I don't know what Rif's paying you, but surely it's not so much that you want to risk losing your life for it? Is it?'

'You don't fucking scare me,' the fat man announced, sneering.

Rivera placed the revolver back in his pocket.

* * * * *

What happened next happened extremely quickly. Rivera grabbed the fat man's arm, twisting it behind him. His head smashed involuntarily into the console in front of him. He fell forward, tumbling out of his seat and onto the floor as the ex-soldier twisted his hand further. Rivera then locked his legs around the other man, rendering him immobile. With his free hand, he reached into his back pocket and removed the wire cutters Fletcher had given him.

The ex-soldier made one deft motion.

He removed the man's smallest finger below the first knuckle.

The clipping sound was followed by a short delay. Then the man howled in agony as blood spurted out of the open wound. His free hand tried to scrabble on the floor for the severed digit.

Rivera retrieved the gun from his pocket and hit the fat man directly above his eye, drawing blood. The IT operative looked from Rivera to the section severed from his finger in disbelief, his mouth struggling to form stuttering words.

'I told you I was in a hurry,' the ex-soldier explained calmly. 'I'm *still* in that same hurry.' He paused. 'So here's what's going to happen. You're going to wipe the footage and prove that you've wiped it. Otherwise, I'm going to remove a finger – a full finger – every thirty seconds until you either pass out, or I'm satisfied the job's done.' He looked hard at the other man. 'So... what are you waiting for?'

The fat man hauled himself back into his desk chair and began urgently tapping at keys. A whole series of menus flashed up onto the screen. Breathing in rapid, halting inhalations, he manipulated a mouse to select files and clicked to make them disappear. Then he turned to face Rivera, looking up at him expectantly.

'Where are they backed up?'

'The cloud,' the man replied. 'But I've erased them – look.' He gestured back at the empty screen, desperate. His eyes widened as he panicked once more. Then, as he turned back to face the computer, the ex-soldier whipped him with the butt of the revolver, knocking him unconscious against the desk.

'You know, maybe I was a little fucking hasty describing you as humanitarian!' Fletcher chuckled. 'Right – extraction time.'

Chapter 96.

After descending the steps of the fire escape, Rivera and Oksana - now wearing what looked like running shoes - made their way across the grounds of Torre de los Boliches. It was uneventful. Beyond the main concourse, the gardens were shrouded in darkness; no guards appeared. As the ex-soldier moved further away from the buildings, he paused, reorienting himself.

'This way,' Oksana hissed, negotiating a path through the scrub. The ex-soldier frowned – the woman seemed far more au fait with the layout of the gardens than he'd expected her to be.

As they approached the road, their way was blocked by a section of the chain-link that surrounded the entire complex. The pair hesitated, looking from side-to-side for any of Rif's goons. But the way was clear.

Nearing the fence, Rivera moved to the front. 'Alright,' he announced, whispering. 'We have two choices: climb or cut.' He removed the bloodied wire cutters from his pocket.

Oksana shook her head. Moving towards the loose fence panel Tatiana had used previously, she peeled it back, revealing the exit.

Rivera shrugged. 'Or not...'

Decorative cacti tore at their clothes as they made their way down the steep slope and onto the pavement. Once they reached it, the cicadas fell suddenly, silent. The night was eerily quiet. A dim, orange streetlight burned in the distance, but – other than a fox crossing the road beneath it – the place was deserted.

'Where now?' Oksana asked, scratching at a laceration on her calf.

'Follow me,' Rivera replied.

Chapter 97.

Twenty minutes later, the pair arrived outside the cottage. They'd been scratched and grazed by the undergrowth, and Oksana had twisted an ankle, but once they reached smoother tarmac, she'd been able to walk more easily.

Moving to the rear of the property, the pair passed the policeman's car. Otherwise, there was no sign of life. It looked – to all intents and purposes – like just another deserted villa.

Rivera knocked on the door.

It opened a moment later.

'Welcome to mission control,' Fletcher whispered from the darkness. 'Come on in.' As they passed him, he handed each of them a pair of latex gloves. He looked at Rivera's companion. 'Oksana, it's nice to meet you. Forgive the precautions,' he went on, 'but we're taking no chances.'

The trio passed through two doors and then entered a room which was brightly lit. Plastic refuse sacks had been taped to the windows to serve as blackout blinds. The policeman handed a bottle of mineral water to each of the new arrivals.

'Thirsty work?' he enquired.

'A little,' Rivera nodded. Tatiana rose from her chair and embraced Oksana. The two men averted their eyes, a little surprised by the tenderness of the moment.

'Right,' Fletcher announced. 'At risk of cutting short this rendezvous, we need to get moving.' He looked around. 'Tatiana, I need you to bag up the bottles, the food leftovers, the plates – anything on the table. Got it?' He handed her a spare refuse sack. 'Oksana – put the light on in the hallway for me, will you?' He waited a moment until the new arrival did as requested. Then, the officer switched the light off in the room. 'Rivera, take down the blackout blinds from the windows, please. Make sure you get the tape off too.' He paused.

'And give me the wire and those glasses too while you're at it – we don't want them falling into the wrong hands.'

* * * * *

'Right, soldier,' Fletcher announced. 'I'm going to recalibrate the electronic equipment out in the car. We'll wait for you outside.'

'Want me to wipe down?' the ex-soldier enquired.

'Affirmative,' the policeman replied. 'Other than the door handles, nothing outside of this room has been touched.' He paused. 'Ten minutes enough?'

Rivera nodded.

Chapter 98.

'No headlights for now,' Fletcher instructed as Rivera closed the door of the car.

'You really do have a flair for the dramatic, don't you?' the ex-soldier snorted. 'They're not going to see us down here, surely? We're a valley away!'

'Yeah... but I don't want anyone pinpointing where we've been later on. I don't know how thorough the Kbir will be with their investigations. These are false plates. But even so...' He looked at the ex-soldier and raised his eyebrows. 'Shall we?'

Rivera gunned the engine, slid the car into gear, and slowly pulled off the villa's driveway and onto the road.

'Wind the windows down,' Fletcher said. 'That way, we'll hear if this thing works.' He tapped a few keys on his laptop and a series of numbers scrolled across the screen. 'Right,' he exhaled heavily, waggling his fingers nervously as they hovered in the air just above the keyboard. 'The moment of truth.' He paused. 'All three phones are hooked up to this same line. So, when I press enter, they should all blow simultaneously.' A bead of perspiration rolled down the policeman's brow.

'So what are you waiting for?' Tatiana frowned.

Fletcher sighed.

'She's right,' Rivera added. 'Just bloody do it already. If not now, then when?'

The policeman jabbed his finger at the keyboard. It seemed for an instant as if time stood still.

Then, from beyond the hillside, a noise resembling a giant thunder crack reverberated. Its echo continued to roll in a deep, sustained rumble long after the car had reached the next junction and joined the main road.

Rivera switched on the headlights.

'Well, I'd say that was pretty convincing,' Fletcher laughed, nodding. 'Good stuff, people! I think we just sent a message out to Rif.'

'What now?' Rivera enquired.

'Now...' Fletcher pulled another window up onto his screen. 'I have a series of pre-recorded messages. Tip offs for the police. They're scheduled to report the blast at intervals of ten seconds. That should start the ball rolling. After that, the lines should get clogged up pretty quickly with genuine callers.' He pressed another couple of keys. 'Fingers crossed it'll make this a major incident straight off the bat. And if that's the case, they'll have to move without Ramos being present.' He cleared his throat. 'And now, we head back to Chas Edwards' place. Lie low.' He paused. 'After that, we'll just have to wait and see.'

Chapter 99.

Captain Weir – senior pilot for Iberian Express-Air - was fastening his shirt buttons when the blast hit. He was in his usual room. With his usual girl. On this occasion, it was a longer layover, so he'd managed a full evening at the Segovia Palace before indulging in Torre de los Boliches' pleasantries. He'd been looking at himself in the mirror; noting the map of ruptured capillaries spreading across his face. The evening hadn't been a success – success was more and more infrequent these days. Despite a handful of elephant-strength blue pills, he hadn't been able to perform. Instead, the nightingale had simply joined him in polishing off a bottle of scotch.

Previously, his visits to the hills were simply benefits afforded by the nature of his job. Now, though, he couldn't help thinking it was the other way round: it felt as if he simply worked to fund his nocturnal exploits. After three divorces and numerous promotion denials, the visits merely staved off the misery of his existence. He didn't consider himself an alcoholic. But the hangovers were growing worse; the blackouts more frequent. And when he hadn't had a drink, the shakes came sooner. His impotence simply added insult to injury.

When the blast came, it nearly threw him off his feet. He tensed, feeling the building sway. Moments later, he heard the shimmering of broken glass falling like water through the air. The girl – Olga – drew the sheets of the bed around her naked frame; her face was suddenly a pallor so pale that her visage almost blended in with the material. She'd been asleep, but – now she was awake – her eyes looked enormous. Fearful.

Frowning, Weir moved towards the door. The pilot had to wrench it open – the force of the blast had damaged the frame. Feeling his heart thudding in his chest, he stepped gingerly out into the corridor, as if in a daze. The carpet fabric was already dampening from the water sprinklers' automatic jets. Emergency lighting blinked through the haze of dust and debris; smoke was pouring through doors that had been blown open further down the corridor. A distant echo of long-ago training kicked in. He felt compelled to help; to seek out survivors.

The pilot walked on. Peering into the deserted lounge, he saw an electrical cable sparking where it had been blown out of the wall. A section of brickwork had caved in, and the red glow of fire was visible from outside. Weir heard the beeping of various alarms. The acrid smell of smoke was overwhelming.

He began descending the stairs.

* * * * *

At the bottom of the steps, Weir was faced by a panicked man brandishing an automatic weapon. The other man – a holdall slung over his shoulder - was clearly in shock. For a moment, the pilot found himself in the sights of the weapon.

Then, the gun was lowered.

'Get out of here senōr!' the gunman screamed, his ears clearly damaged by the blast. 'Get the fuck out of here! Now!'

* * * * *

As the pilot walked on, the adrenalin made him suddenly sober. Flickers of light blazed in his peripheral vision.

He rounded the corner of the main block, struggling to take in the scene.

As he walked down the pathway, he saw that the rest of the complex was aglow. Both the other blocks were ablaze, and even from the distance at which he was standing, the heat was incredible; it seared at his skin. The flames were shooting nearly a hundred feet up into the sky. In the confusion, Weir was sure he heard shots being fired.

For a moment, he stood, swaying. Light-headed. Narrowing his eyes, he squinted against the brightness. Darkened figures ran frantically between the burning buildings, silhouetted against the flames. Agitated shouts sounded out, and the shrieks of nightingales were clearly audible.

Weir was standing ten feet away from the third propane tank when it detonated. The last charge was secured to its underbelly. It hadn't fired when Fletcher placed the encrypted calls to trigger the timers. But with all the noise, damage, and smoke, none of the confused residents had considered the threat it posed.

Slowly, though, the encroaching flames began to breathe upon Rivera's handiwork. After melting the glue on the duct tape, the heat began turning the rubber casing of the wires into a semi-liquid form.

Once that happened, the temperature rose; it honed in on the wiring Fletcher had assembled earlier in the afternoon. Next, a globule of solder swelled and teetered in a bulbous silver mass, before rolling lazily along the wire and settling itself comfortably into the minute space between two frayed strands.

With the circuit complete, the last propane tank exploded.

Chapter 100.

On any other day, Ramos would have taken charge. Ordinarily, once the trickle of calls to the emergency services became a flood, the Comisario would have headed to the scene and – if it looked like being a problem for the Kbir - done his very best to suppress the story. But, today, Ramos was being entertained. He'd lost count of how many glasses of champagne had already been pressed upon him.

Igor Miletski was a businessman on the rise. He'd identified Ramos as a future ally.

The Russian had skirted around the edges of Rif's operation. But he'd quickly realised the Moroccan had things sewn up – he had a thirty-year head start on him, and so anywhere he looked in the construction world, the Russian was met with closed doors. It was the same with vice. So, he'd followed the only course he thought logical: the police. Miletski reasoned the authorities might do business with him over his North African competitors, providing the price was right.

Hence Ramos being on the Mediterranean in a luxury yacht with an embarrassment of women aboard.

When his phone rang, alerting him about an explosion in the hills, he was nearly four miles offshore. At first, he'd wondered if it had been a deliberate ploy on the part of Miletski – to have him out of the way while he tried to torpedo Rif's organisation. But, then, he realised that line of thinking made no sense.

Police procedure meant swift action was required for something of such magnitude. The force had no choice but to put Onega in charge. From Ramos' point of view, it was a disaster.

Onega – the officer who steadfastly turned down every questionable opportunity Ramos accepted.

* * * * *

Within an hour of the alarm being raised, updates were scrolling across the screens on all major channels; a corps of journalists had been despatched to the scene, and a press helicopter had been scrambled to film the carnage from above. Any hopes Ramos may have harboured that the reaction might yet be muted were quashed.

Where Onega sprang into action in a disciplined, organised fashion, the guards at Torre de los Boliches were slow and confused. The police cordon which was swiftly established around the complex meant there was no escape for the insiders unless they wanted to shoot their way out.

They didn't. So, they surrendered; the nightingales who were wandering around in various stages of undress were scooped up by the attending officers. And they were only too happy to talk.

It was easy work for Onega. It didn't take more than a glance to establish the link between the heavily made-up young women and the pot-bellied old men. Talking to a selection of shell-shocked sexagenarians simply confirmed his suspicions. In their bomb-blasted states of confusion, they readily admitted what they'd been doing, throwing themselves on the mercy of the law enforcers. They claimed ignorance, and hoped the police's focus would be on the commanders rather than the customers.

* * * * *

Once the bodies were tagged and loaded into ambulances, Onega made his decisive move: he leapfrogged Ramos and placed a call to Rattin. Like the Comisario, the Jeffe Superior was a deeply religious man. He harboured strong suspicions about Ramos, and certainly didn't want him involved.

Under Rattin, the issue became a moral one, and the Jeffe Superior was happy for the press to portray it as such. He'd risen to prominence on an anti-corruption ticket, so the opportunity Onega provided was like manna from heaven: he could show just how strong the strong arm of the law really was.

By the time Ramos reached the shoreline, he'd realised defending Rif was useless. His only hope, instead, was saving his own skin.

Chapter 101.

The next day dawned in another brilliant brushstroke of Mediterranean blue. Fletcher hadn't slept; he'd spent the early hours monitoring how the blast had played out in the media. As the sun rose, he watched it, looking out across the canyon towards the sea and working his way through a fresh packet of cigarettes. Indeterminate shapes slowly turned into trees and boulders as the half-light's sepia tones lifted.

Rivera walked out onto the sun deck with a mug of instant coffee. 'You think Chas Edwards was happy here?' he enquired.

Fletcher shrugged. 'Beats Battersea, doesn't it? But I think he'd have probably been fed up with looking over his shoulder.'

Rivera paused for a moment, taking in the view. 'How are the girls?'

'Asleep.' Fletcher furrowed his brow. 'Remember what we talked about, yeah?'

The ex-soldier shrugged. 'And the... Methadone?'

'Later. I've been talking to Mühren. Once we're done with this, he's going to have them checked into a facility. All bells and whistles. The staff there will get them clean – properly clean.'

Rivera nodded. 'So – how has the press reacted?'

'Better than I'd hoped for, actually. It's plastered all over everywhere. A huge investigation's been launched. And the beautiful thing is that Rif's name keeps getting mentioned. They're even talking about the Kbir – and that never happens.' Fletcher grinned. 'If the bastard's not going to take his eye off the ball now, then he never will.'

'So, what next?' Rivera asked, licking the gummed edge of his cigarette paper.

'I was talking with Tatiana after you went to sleep.'

'Oh yeah?' Rivera raised his eyebrows as he lit his roll-up.

'Piss off!'

'And?'

'She's agreed – we can use her as bait to smoke Rif out.'

Rivera pursed his lips. 'I don't like the idea of that very much. Sounds risky.'

'Yeah? Well, you're going to like the next bit even less.'

Silence.

'Why?' the ex-soldier asked, frowning.

'We're going to use you as well, old son.'

Chapter 102.

'I don't fucking understand!' Rif's tone wasn't angry. Not even perplexed. Just utterly disbelieving. He stared at Amrabat in complete incomprehension. 'What the hell happened there? The place doesn't even exist any more!'

Amrabat held up his hands. 'We can pretty much cover everything, boss. But sometimes...'

'...so why the hell was...'

'...we can't account for a lone wolf.' It was the first time in years Amrabat could recall interrupting his boss when he was angry. But now he was committed, he continued. 'We had everything else in place, but this guy – and it seems like it *was* just one guy - blew the tanks. And that was that. The guards were in place, but they didn't manage to stop him.'

Rif looked coldly at Amrabat. 'So... who do I need to kill?'

'We don't know,' the other man shrugged. 'The fires are still burning. Ambulances are carting away the wounded and the dead. The police have got the whole place locked down. It's like a bloody warzone. And the press...' He shook his head. 'Don't even get me started. They're swarming – there's no way we can hush this up. I'm sorry.'

'Ramos? Where's that useless prick? What about all the bloody money we pay him?' Rif spat. 'He's a fucking freeloader.'

'Yeah, well... he wasn't on the scene when the blast happened. And so the whole thing was given to another Comisario.' Amrabat looked at a note scrawled on a scrap of paper. 'Onega.'

'So fucking take care of him!'

'This guy's as clean as a whistle, boss. And, anyway, he's involved another officer – Rattin.'

'Who?' Rif frowned.

'He's the Jeffe Superior.'

Chapter 103.

'I don't like it.' Rivera shook his head.

'Now, where have I fucking heard that before?' Fletcher grinned. 'We'll tell him you've got the photograph – he's bound to go for that. That might be enough to bring him out into the open.'

Silence.

'We've got back-up,' the policeman went on, earnestly. 'Mühren will be on board.'

'Yeah, but I'm basically the sacrificial lamb here, aren't I? It's not like I can go in armed. And once they've got the picture...'

'What are you saying?'

'Mühren had better be bloody quick. Otherwise they'll have carved me up by the time help arrives. I imagine that's the way Rif operates, right? Slice first and ask questions later.'

'So you'll go through with it, then?' Fletcher enquired, raising his eyebrows.

'I didn't say that.' Rivera shook his head. 'I was speaking conditionally.'

'Ooh! Fancy grammar!' The officer chuckled. 'I like it! And...'

'...and I was pointing out the flaws in your plan.'

'Of which there are many,' the officer conceded. 'But it will evolve. They always do.' He smiled. 'I haven't let you down so far, have I?' Fletcher paused. 'You're coming round, mate! I can tell. We're holding the cards here, anyway. We've got Rif on the ropes - he doesn't realise it, which is why he won't be expecting what we do next.'

'Unless he *does*, though.' Rivera's tone was blunt. 'For all we know, he'll be on high alert – like a cornered rat. Think about all the things we've done to piss him off – he'll be bloody livid!'

'No.' Fletcher shook his head. 'He won't get that it's all linked. He'll think the job in the hills was the main thing – nobody's ever had the nerve to cross him like that before. If we go in with Tatiana and claim it's all about recovering the photograph, then he won't twig. You can be damn sure he won't think anyone's going to come in for round two. Especially not straight away like this.'

'So?'

'So – your mate Saïd is pretty key now.'

'Really?' Rivera said doubtfully.

'Yeah – if he's involved in trucking this load of hash Tatiana's been talking about, then he's worth his weight in gold.'

'How so?' Rivera frowned.

Fletcher pursed his lips. 'Saïd'll call it in, right?'

'Yes.'

'So, once he does, we'll get Mühren's guys to pull him.'

'Him, or the whole lot of them?'

'Just him,' the policeman replied.

'OK...' The ex-soldier frowned. 'But how does that help?'

'He'll go into Witness Protection, for starters. After that, his gear's out of commission, so they'll turn a blind eye to me borrowing it.'

'What? Are you breaking into the drugs trade now or something?'

'No!' Fletcher chuckled. 'We're going to plant it in Rif's office. Interpol will be on hand – they'll uncover enough stuff to put him away for a couple of years, minimum. That's the fit-up.'

Rivera nodded slowly. 'And you think the courts will swallow that? It's not the eighties any more. Evidence obtained under duress – all of that stuff.'

'It doesn't need to be the eighties any more – there's a consensus here. People want rid of him. They're not going to ask too many questions.' He paused. 'Anyway, once he's behind bars – even for a little while - he's not untouchable any more. And that's when the wheels start coming off for him. It's the tip of the iceberg.' Fletcher grinned. 'His empire will start to fall apart. Interpol thinks it can control the vacuum – install its own people. Break the Kbir. So we'll let them. Any questions?'

'Yeah. Loads.'

'Such as?'

'Why the photo?'

'To get us an in, mate – at the Segovia. Make sense?'

'I think so,' Rivera nodded. 'But who'll get the hash inside?' The ex-soldier paused. 'You can't do it. And if I'm out of action and she's with the boss. Then...'

'...your flatmates are going to step up,' Fletcher beamed. 'Nour and Pancho – it's their time to fucking shine!'

Chapter 104.

Rif pursed his lips. 'Sometimes I wonder why I even fucking bother. I'm surrounded by incompetent fools.'

'Thanks, Abdellah.' Amrabat grinned ruefully.

'Well, it's not like you're proving me wrong,' the boss replied. 'How much do we pay for street sweeping each week?'

Amrabat frowned. 'Er – twenty grand or so. Why?'

'We send kids as young as twelve around on mopeds to put security cameras out of action.' He paused. 'Please tell me the cameras have been blanked out at Torre de los Boliches. Otherwise, the police are going to have a bloody field day.'

'Of course,' Amrabat nodded. 'But that's part of the problem.'

'How?'

'We don't have any footage of who did this,' the assistant replied. 'That fat fucker – the guy who did the computers... he's the only one who knows how to get to the back-ups. But we don't know where he is – or if he's even alive.'

'He's a fucking dead man if I ever see him again,' Rif continued, unimpressed. 'Eyewitnesses?'

'Yeah,' the other man scratched his neck in irritation. 'They reckon it was one man, like I said. But it's sketchy, and all the nightingales have been shipped away too.'

'What about the fucking doctor who doses the girls up?'

'Emil?' Amrabat paused. 'Dead. Or jail, maybe. No word, though. It's a bloody disaster.'

'So what the hell happened?' Rif sighed. 'I mean *really* happened?'

'We think it was a guy called Taylor.' Amrabat spoke quickly. 'He came to the Palace. Rode on the bus.'

'And why didn't we suspect him?'

'Usual reasons, boss.' Amrabat paused. 'He tipped heavy. Dressed loud. He looked just like the rest of the losers looking to get laid.'

'And once he got there – to the hills?'

'He just kind of disappeared.'

'Did he have help?' Rif pressed.

Silence.

Rif slammed his fist into the table. 'Find him, Amrabat. I want the fucker dead. I'll cut his fucking throat myself.'

'You sure?'

'Of course, I'm bloody sure.' He paused, the vein on his temple throbbing. 'And find out what Ramos was up to while you're at it. If I find out he's getting in bed with someone else, then his days will be fucking numbered. Understand?'

'Yes, Abdellah.'

Chapter 105.

'You're fucking joking!' Rivera shook his head. 'She's a fruit picker, and he's a photographer. You can't send people like that into battle. It's not fair. They'll crack.'

'Of course you fucking can!' Fletcher replied. 'They're perfect.' He paused. 'Nour wants a place in Witness Protection. That's fine. I get it. I'll approve it too. But she has to do something to earn it, you know? You scratch my back; I'll scratch yours.'

'What about Pancho?'

'We can *offer* it to him. You know – as a courtesy. But I think he feels guilty enough about that lad Ishaq to make him biddable, anyway. He's pretty keen to make amends.'

'And they're our only choices?'

'Spanish police, mate. You know what they're fucking like!' Fletcher shrugged. 'Mühren thinks Rif has half of them in his pocket.'

Rivera shrugged.

'Don't be like that! The last gamble paid off, didn't it?'

The ex-soldier sighed. 'In for a penny...' He chewed at his lip. 'How exactly are we going to convince Rif I'm worth talking to, though?'

'Ramos,' Fletcher announced.

Rivera sucked at his teeth. 'But he knows who I am. He knows Interpol bailed me out, too. And he'll probably guess it was me masquerading as Taylor last night.'

'Yeah,' Fletcher nodded. 'I'm going to cast you as a double agent, though.' He chuckled. 'There's the Miletski angle too. If you tell Rif that the Russian put you up to the firebombing, I think he'll go for it. Especially if it comes from Ramos. Mühren's got all sorts of dirt on him – he's bound to go telling tales to the big man. Interpol's only keeping him in place to see what he might lead them to, anyway. Building a case...'

'He's not stupid, though, is he - Rif?'

'No.' Fletcher shook his head. 'But his judgement is a little off these days. You add blind rage, the massive question mark over who's behind the blast, and unrestrained desire for revenge into the mix, and who knows? We wonder if he's been overindulging in the white stuff too – that'll destabilise him some more. Hopefully.'

The ex-soldier nodded. 'Won't he check it, though? The Comisario – if he thinks I'm a double agent.'

'Yeah. Ramos will have to.' The officer grinned. 'But the person he's going to have to verify your status as an agent with is your old mate Christie. She's back in Blighty, and she's been briefed. We've set the whole thing up. At least it means her lot will get to bask a bit in the reflected glory if this thing comes off.'

Chapter 106.

Saïd yawned, adjusted his seat belt and checked the wing mirrors of the van. He'd just passed Salamanca, and the petrol gauge was running a little low.

The destination he'd been given was an address in Pamplona. He'd looked it up on an app on his phone; it was a nondescript property on a trading estate. Arraf told him he had been tasked with taking his own goods to a warehouse somewhere in Holland.

Everything had been set up to make the journey easy. The vans were new. They were comfortable. Each was fitted with a toll tag - Saïd could drive straight through the motorway barriers without having to stop. The aim was to keep the cargos moving as fast and efficiently as possible.

The new driver had made good time. He'd been unwilling to stop before the four-hour mark, lest it aroused suspicions in whoever was monitoring the journeys. But he knew stopping for fuel or to use the bathroom would be fine. Sighting a sign for a services ahead, he indicated, moving over to the inside lane. He'd stuck rigidly to the speed limit and maintained plenty of distance from other vehicles. Before departing, Ziyad had warned him and all the others that being pulled over would be hugely problematic. And if they ended up being searched, it risked torpedoing the whole operation. He'd also reminded the assembled group that the vans were all monitored – any time the speed limit was broken, drivers would be fined.

Or so he'd claimed.

*****

As Saïd entered the services, he was met with an assortment of bored truckers; families with hyperactive young children and lonely travelling salesmen sat on high stools overlooking the parking lot. The latter demographic sat, drinking espressos and scrolling through news feeds on their phones. The driver walked over to a row of payphones. Of the four, three of them seemed to be out of order. Using such appliances had become so old-hat that Saïd wondered if anyone would even bother to fix them. He deposited a handful of coins and punched in the number Rivera had given him.

The ex-soldier answered on the second ring.

'Saïd?'

'Do you have a pen?' he asked bluntly.

'Shoot,' Rivera replied.

Saïd reeled off the van's make and its registration. 'I'm at a rest stop just north of Salamanca,' he explained. 'Destination is Pamplona.' He paused. 'If you need to intercept, then I'm probably around two hours from Burgos – it'll depend on what the traffic's like around Valladolid.'

'And the cargo?' the ex-soldier pressed.

'Fresh grown in Morocco... enough for a whole town I should think. The van has *PEDRO'S SUPERMARKET* written on the side and a picture of a vegetable basket.' He paused. 'Nour?'

'Fine. Healthy. Safe.' Rivera replied.

'I have to go,' the driver announced. He hung up the receiver and made his way back out to the van. As he did, he removed the work phone from his pocket and began typing.

PISS & PETROL. ON ROAD AGAIN NOW.

Chapter 107.

'You'd better have something fucking good for us,' Amrabat announced. Rif's insistence on face-to-face communication had been abandoned once Ramos informed them he was a marked man. All personnel were on strict deployments, and the Jeffe Superior had the department on a war footing, so any trip to meet with the Moroccans would not be sanctioned. Rif - once he was assured any phone lines were secure - begrudgingly acceded. He'd delegated the initial round of negotiations to his assistant. 'Uncle's pretty mad at you,' Amrabat announced heavily.

'Yeah, I'm not surprised,' Ramos replied from the other end of the line.

'Well?' Amrabat pressed. 'Do you have a name for us yet?'

'Rivera.'

'Who?'

'Trent Rivera. The *guiri* I arrested before. That one who was in Antonio's cell.' The Comisario sighed. 'He called me this morning. It was him that bombed Torre de los Boliches. He admitted it.'

Amrabat frowned. 'He *called* to tell you that?'

'Yeah.'

'Why?'

'It's complicated,' Ramos replied.

'Stop fucking wasting my time. Talk.'

The Comisario had wrestled with every possible permutation of truth and lie, but to clear his name with Rif, he knew he'd have to throw Miletski under the bus. For now, it was all he had. 'He'd been put up to it by a guy called Miletski.'

'¡*Hijos de puta*!' Amrabat's voice was venomous. 'The Russian guy, right?'

'Correct.'

'So?'

'So this guy Rivera – he says he wants to come to the Segovia Palace this afternoon. To talk...'

'Well, he's either very brave, or very fucking stupid.' Amrabat frowned, drumming his fingers lightly on the table. 'What's his angle? There must be something - otherwise it's suicide. Why the hell does he want to meet?'

'He's a double agent.'

'For who?' Amrabat narrowed his eyes and frowned at the speakerphone.

'The British – he's the one they send out to deal with less... law-abiding types. He's balls-deep in crime out here – but, of course, he operates off the books.'

'And you can verify that – that he's one of them, I mean?'

'Already done,' the Comisario replied. 'He checks out.'

Silence.

'So, why's he helping Miletski?'

'Money, probably,' Ramos shrugged. 'Isn't that the only reason anyone helps anyone else? He sounds like a mercenary.' He paused. 'And you know how little they pay police officers? Well, they pay informants even less. He'll be chancing his arm at a double-cross.'

Amrabat sniffed. 'He won't have that arm for long if Uncle takes a dislike to him. I'll pass it on.' He paused. 'But if Uncle thinks he's for sale, he might be interested – he's not going to be very impressed, though. You should have told us all of this before.'

'Yeah,' Ramos sighed.

'Anything else I can give him? To sweeten the pill? Otherwise, he's going to hunt you down and lynch you.'

The Comisario paused. 'He's got Tatiana,' he announced, playing his trump card. 'He'll bring her too.'

'OK.' The interest of Rif's lieutenant was piqued. 'How...?'

'No clue,' Ramos replied. 'But Tatiana's Tatiana, right?'

'Yeah,' Amrabat nodded.

Silence.

'Oh, and he's got the photograph,' Ramos added, reasoning it was time to play his final Ace. 'The one from the camera trap.'

Amrabat grinned slightly. 'Yeah – that'll do it,' he replied.

Chapter 108.

'Was that Saïd?' Fletcher enquired, as Rivera hung up. The noon sun was beating down upon the canyon. Heat was shimmering above the palms. Cicadas struck up their chorus and then, all of a sudden, made a perfectly synchronised stop before starting up again.

'Yeah – he's en route to Pamplona.'

Fletcher nodded. 'Good.' He slid a notepad across the table. 'Write down everything Mühren needs to know - please. We're going to fucking roll on this.'

'He's alright with all of this, is he?' Rivera enquired. 'Your plan, I mean.'

'Yeah – he knows he'll get the evidence back when we're done. He's not got to where he is by playing a straight ball with a straight bat all the time, you know?'

'Who's going to drive up there and fetch it?'

'Nobody,' Fletcher answered, lighting a cigarette. He spoke as he exhaled. 'His chaps are going to chopper it down here. We're doing this one in style. It'll be like the *Ride of the Valkyries* scene in *Apocalypse Now*!'

Rivera shook his head. 'Not very incognito, is it?'

'Don't worry, mate. They're not coming *here*!' The policeman laughed. 'The gear will just come straight down to a private landing pad and be whisked over to Latinaja in a patrol car. Easy!'

* * * * *

Rivera passed the pad back to Fletcher. The officer looked at it, putting on a pair of glasses. He cleared his throat, wedged his cigarette in the corner of his mouth, and hummed tunelessly as he read. Once he was finished, he picked up his phone from the table.

'Mühren,' Fletcher grinned, once the connection was made. 'We're in business – our boy's come through.' He listened to the voice on the other end of the line. '...agreed.' The officer glanced at Rivera. 'Any distinguishing features? Mühren's asking?'

'What – on Saïd?'

'No, you fucking idiot! On the bloody van!'

'It's – er – painted with a sign for *PEDRO'S SUPERMARKET*.'

Fletcher nodded. 'Got that?' he enquired into the phone. 'Right you are. Fingers crossed then.' He hung up and regarded Rivera. 'Now we just need to hope Ramos comes through with setting up the meeting.'

'Feeling confident?' Rivera asked.

'Yeah – chuck Tatiana and the photo into the mix, and I reckon the going's good,' the policeman replied.

Chapter 109.

Rif and Amrabat sat, staring at the speakerphone. It sat on the polished desk surface alongside a brass ashtray. Both men were smoking; each had a glass of whiskey before them.

'So, Ramos,' Rif began, absent-mindedly playing with the thick gold bracelet he wore around his wrist. 'This line is secure, yes?'

'It is.'

Rif's eyes narrowed. 'This fucking Miletski. What do you know? What do *I* need to know?'

'I've been – er – monitoring him for a while,' the Comisario explained, uncomfortably. 'He was a nobody. And now... well, let's just say he's becoming a little more of a somebody.'

'Should I be worried?' The hint of a smile crossed Rif's face. The boss rolled his eyes at Amrabat. He then pursed his lips, extended his arm, and flipped the bird at the voice on the phone.

'Well...' the other man sighed. 'There's history – in Russia, I mean. He's ambitious. I guess he's eyeing up your operation - he wants to start off with the crumbs from your table. And from there...' His voice trailed off.

'And *now* is the time you choose to fucking tell me this?'

'He's small fry, Abdellah,' Ramos replied, dismissively. His tone had a forced cockiness. 'I didn't want to burden you with unnecessary information. That's what you said – remember?'

Amrabat spoke. 'This man. This *non-threat*, as you call him, fucking blew up half of Torre de los Boliches last night. I think the moment where he becomes someone we need to take a little more seriously has already passed, Comisario. No?'

Silence.

'Exactly,' Rif nodded. 'I want to know everything. And I want to know how we can hurt the bastard.' He paused. 'I want to know more about Miletski than his own whore of a mother does. More about him than he fucking knows about himself.'

Silence hung in the air.

'Understood. Sir,' Ramos replied.

Chapter 110.

Rivera's phone pinged. He glanced at the screen and slid it across the table to Fletcher.

'Bingo!' the officer announced, looking up from its screen. 'Late-afternoon it fucking is, then!' He picked up his own mobile and began rapidly typing.

'Does it give us enough time?'

Fletcher shrugged. 'Should do, mate. But I need to check with Mühren.' At this, the other man's phone began vibrating angrily on the table. The policeman peered at the screen. 'Speak of the devil!' he smiled. He pressed the green icon to accept the call. 'Frans!' he beamed.

*****

'Alright, good,' Fletcher nodded. 'It's a date. You bring guns... I'll bring roses.' The policeman chuckled.

Rivera rolled his eyes. The other man beamed back at him before continuing his conversation with the Interpol agent. 'Now then. What about our delivery man - any word?'

Chapter 111.

Amrabat and Rif were sitting in the same places when the next call from Ramos came through. The Comisario confirmed the British man would be venturing to the Segovia Palace.

'Rivera,' Rif spoke icily, staring at the speakerphone. 'I thought we'd sorted him out. What's happening Ramos?'

'Well, I arrested him...'

'...and you let him go?' Rif interrupted.

'I had no choice,' Ramos answered. 'He was the one Antonio was sent to deal with.'

'Well, that worked well!' Rif scoffed.

'I know,' Ramos sighed. 'But once Interpol stepped in, I had no jurisdiction.'

Rif drummed on the table in irritation. 'Yeah, well, from what I hear, it was Interpol that saved Antonio from the guiri. And not the other way round.'

'They must think he's useful to them,' Ramos replied. 'And I think Miletski is paying him, too. My guess would be it's all part of a long-term plan.'

'For what?' Rif frowned. 'For my downfall?'

Ramos sighed. 'Until today, all evidence pointed to Rivera just being an informant and Miletski being little more than a safecracker. We didn't think they were anything to worry about. No one did.'

'But now?'

'But now, it seems some of the detectives on the force might have underestimated him.'

'Who? Miletski?'

'Yes – the problem is, they think they can control him. They know if they can move you aside, there'll be a vacuum. And if they shift Miletski into position, they think they'll be able to make him their puppet. They've chosen him as their horse to back. Picked him as someone to make a deal with.'

'Why didn't they come to me for a deal?' Rif asked quietly.

'Because the problem with you, Abdellah,' Ramos replied, 'is they don't control you.'

'And they never fucking will,' Rif growled, recovering his sense of hatred.

'That's why you irritate them so much,' the Comisario went on, playing to the other man's prejudice. 'And that's why they're keen on Miletski. If they can pull his strings, they imagine they'll wrestle back control of the Costa. He'll have one arm tied behind his back; he'll do what he's told.' He paused. 'But don't worry,' Ramos blustered. 'It'll never happen. Things will settle down, and they'll go back to the good life we've always had. I promise.'

Chapter 112.

Fletcher hung up.

'Good news?' Rivera enquired.

'Yeah – Mühren's squad pulled him over just outside Burgos. Stop and search and – hey presto! – enough hash to land him in the joint on a twenty stretch.'

'No pun intended?'

'Naturally,' the officer chuckled drily. 'So, the evidence has been bagged, and it's being chopped down here as we speak. And – thanks to Nour and Pancho - that's what Rif's going to be found in possession of.'

'Has anyone told them about this yet?'

'That's our next job,' Fletcher replied. 'Well, *your* job really, old son.'

'Yeah?' the ex-soldier shrugged. 'That sounds like a bloody hospital pass.'

The policeman grinned. 'The good news is that Saïd is now in Witness Protection – at least he's in a kind of holding pattern before he gets properly admitted. We'll mention that, and it'll be an incentive to Nour. It'll show her we make good on our promises.'

'Isn't that a bit divisive?' Rivera frowned.

Fletcher shrugged. 'Yeah, well – that's how these things work. Nobody's going to dish out something for nothing.'

The ex-soldier nodded. 'Isn't Saïd still a weak point, though?'

'He's safe – I've told you. He's in custody.'

'Yeah, but what if Rif's people smell a rat? You can be damn sure they'll have people on the inside.'

'Yeah, but they won't get to him straight away, will they?' Fletcher shrugged.

'But what if they think he's sold them out? If Rif's people get spooked, word might get back to the boss.'

'Don't worry.' Fletcher patted the other man's arm. 'Mühren knows what he's doing. Not all his squad were in on it, so the whole thing looked completely legitimate. And we assume the Kbir probably have tracking devices on their vans. So, at present, Saïd's vehicle is very publically parked in a lot on the Avenida de Castilla y León.'

'Which is what exactly?'

'The headquarters of the Burgos Police.' He paused. 'Dealers lose their stash once in a while. It's a fact of life. Collateral damage. If Saïd had just dropped off the face of the earth, *then* they'd have smelled a rat. But him being pinched – it's fine. And they know he'll be out of commission now. You're forgetting how big Rif's operation is – they'll never make the connection. Besides, there are plenty of other plates he has to keep spinning right now.' He looked hard at Rivera. 'Happy?'

The ex-soldier shrugged.

'Right,' Fletcher stood. 'Next stop Latinaja. Mühren will drop some uniforms over to your flatmates later. One of his men – Thijssen - will drive them. You and I need to go on a charm offensive and explain to Pancho and Nour what they need to do for us.'

Chapter 113.

Amrabat couldn't recall seeing his boss racked with such indecision before. It seemed that – no sooner had he ended a conversation with Ramos – he was instructing his assistant to call back with new questions. His lack of stability was clear; he veered from combative steel to a self-doubt he refused to admit.

'But why the firebombing?' Rif enquired, after Amrabat had dialled the Comisario once more.

'It's a test,' Ramos sighed. 'To see if you've still got balls... sir.'

Rif smashed his hand into the table, sending the phone and the ashtray jumping into the air. 'I'll show them who's got fucking balls. I'll kill every last one of the bastards. And...'

'...I know. I get that,' Ramos interrupted. 'But they've screwed up – they've blown their cover too early.'

'You think?' Amrabat pressed.

'Yeah. Without Rivera, Interpol has nothing. Nor has Miletski. Neither side knows they're being played. The *guiri*'s only in it for the money. He's greedy, and he's arrogant enough that he wants to walk right onto your home turf.' He paused. 'You're never going to get a better chance to – er – get rid of him.' Ramos knew that, with Rivera out of the picture, Rif would turn his attention to Miletski. And, if that happened, there was a chance no one would be left to attest to his double-dealing. 'My guess is that – now he's on your radar – he'll want to see what you can offer him,' Ramos continued. 'He'll want to find out what he's worth to you. He'll tell you he can make the Russian go away, too, I should think – anything to line his pockets.'

'And what do you suggest?' Rif pressed.

Ramos sighed. 'Like I said - without Rivera, Interpol has nothing. The way I see it, Rivera being around is more of a problem than him *not* being around, no?'

'Agreed,' Rif nodded. His jaw was set firm.

'I'm still not sure it adds up...' Amrabat frowned. 'I mean...'

'You're such a fucking old lady!' Rif hissed, cutting in. 'Of course it doesn't add up – we're dealing with a fucking imbecile. He's bitten off more than he can chew. It's not going to make sense because we're trying to second guess someone who isn't working logically. He thinks he's calling the shots.' Rif paused. 'The bastard's going to have a rude awakening when I start carving him up...'

'But why the girl?' Amrabat frowned.

'Bait,' Ramos replied. 'Surely?'

'Isn't he the bait, though – along with the photograph?' Amrabat pressed.

'Yeah,' the Comisario answered. 'But he must've figured out that Tatiana was one of your favourites. He'll have done it to piss you off. To get a reaction.' He paused. 'To show he can...'

'Well, he fucking can't,' Rif grimaced, standing up.

Chapter 114.

The Segovia Palace in mid-afternoon had a sleepy atmosphere. Fletcher had lent Rivera the plushest vehicle Carvajal Rental Cars possessed – before they'd set off, he'd changed the plates in case Rif's organisation tried to run them. He'd also fitted the ex-soldier with the camera spectacles, but hadn't bothered with the earpiece or the wire.

'These glasses might not last long,' he'd explained. 'But they won't know they're bugged – even if they have sensors. An earpiece, though, would be a different matter. And a wire... they'd cut your balls off.'

'What's the emergency signal?' Rivera enquired.

'There isn't one. The moment you cross the threshold, the clock starts ticking.' He paused. 'The second you're out of sight, Mühren will roll in with Nour and Pancho – they're bright enough to know what they're doing.'

Rivera fitted the modified glasses to his face. 'Won't Mühren be recognised, though?'

'By who?'

'Well, Ramos – if he's there.'

'He won't be there.' Fletcher shook his head, grinning.

'How can you be sure?'

'Because thirty minutes ago, there was a knock on his door. Somebody made an anonymous tip-off to a man named Rattin – he holds the rank of Jeffe Superior. It's him who's overseeing the whole Torre de los Boliches investigation alongside another Comisario named Onega.'

'And?'

'Well, let's just say Mühren made the pair of them privy to the fact Ramos was being entertained by a known Russian criminal the night you blew the propane tanks. He's fucked.'

'But won't that...?'

'Don't worry. Ramos was home alone at the time of arrest. They're just going to leave him in the cells until we're done at the Palace.' Fletcher grinned. 'So there's no way he'll be able to recognise Frans. Mühren has an insider – a guy called Francisco – working for him. He's going to be on hand to show Nour and Pancho up to Rif's quarters. He can get them access.'

'And you think that'll work?'

'Yeah – they only need a tiny window of time. Then we're all sorted. An hour after we roll in, we'll be sipping cocktails. Easy!'

Rivera nodded slowly. 'And what have you got in place if it all goes wrong?'

'Nothing,' Fletcher shrugged. 'Like I said, the clock will run down from the moment you're inside. After fifteen minutes, Mühren will send in the cavalry, irrespective. They save you – if you need saving. And then they'll find the drugs and book the big man.'

* * * * *

'You OK?' Rivera asked Tatiana.

In the passenger seat, she fidgeted with a jewel-encrusted ring, and continually spun the wheel of her lighter.

'Just stay calm and do what he told you to do. It'll be easy,' the ex-soldier instructed. Nevertheless, he felt his pulse quicken. He knew it as a sign of nervousness; he'd developed the tunnel vision he almost always viewed things with when he was under duress. Tatiana was done up like a million-dollar Barbie doll, but he'd barely looked at her. His mind was set. Focused. The troglodytic part of his brain had switched to survival mode.

'You honestly think this will be enough to put him in jail?' Tatiana frowned a moment later. 'I mean... a man like Rif?'

Rivera nodded. 'Just focus on the next fifteen minutes. After that, everything will be finished. And you'll be free. I mean, *completely* free.'

She sighed, nodding, as the car eased to a stop.

'Where is he?' Tatiana frowned. She cast a nervous eye up towards the shaded portico. Ornate potted plants lined the white marble steps.

'He won't trust us completely,' Rivera explained. 'He'll be just inside - waiting and worrying there's a sniper lying in wait.'

'Wouldn't that have been a better option?' Tatiana asked, reaching for the door handle.

'Yeah, maybe.' Rivera gripped her hand for a moment. 'Remember, just nod and smile. Keep him occupied. And...'

'...I know how to keep him occupied, Mr Rivera,' she interrupted; her tone was dismissive.

They stepped out of the car.

Chapter 115.

Amrabat emerged as Rivera and Tatiana reached the top of the marble steps. Smiling, he ushered the new arrivals through the door and into the vestibule. Once they were inside, Rif appeared. At first, his face was impassive. The ex-soldier watched as his eyes darted around.

Then, Rif's face broke into a grin. 'Mr Rivera,' he beamed, striding over and shaking the ex-soldier's hand warmly. He turned. 'And dear, sweet Tatiana.' He paused as he kissed the nightingale's hand. 'I've missed you, you know.' He rubbed at her bare arm; she bridled.

As his eyes adjusted to the darkness, Rivera noted the two armed men stood at the top of the stairs, covering the vestibule with Uzi automatics.

'This is just procedure,' Rif announced apologetically, noticing the other man's gaze. 'A precautionary measure.' He paused. 'As is this...'

Amrabat approached the pair with a metal detector wand. He swept it over each of them, noting it only buzzed at the jewellery they were wearing. Satisfied, he stood back and nodded. 'They're clean.'

'Would you come with me, Tatiana?' Rif enquired. 'I'd like to talk with you... in private.' She hesitated slightly, but acceded, her high heels ringing out on the marbled floor as the boss led her away. He turned back and called out over his shoulder. 'Mr Rivera – Amrabat will accompany you to the bar. We'll talk soon.'

The pair disappeared into a side room.

* * * * *

'Mr Rivera,' Amrabat grinned. 'This way, please.' The assistant held out a hand, gesturing.

'Can't we have a drink out on the sun deck?' the ex-soldier frowned.

'I'm afraid not,' the other man replied. 'I tend to be of the belief that business is better conducted indoors.' His smile could have cut glass.

'And do I get a choice?' Rivera pressed.

Amrabat shook his head. 'Not as such.' He paused. 'You see, Mr Rif *does* want to talk to you. But not in the bar.' He clicked his fingers.

From behind the large marble pillars rising to the ceiling, three more guards stepped out. They were all armed with the same automatic weapons. Each of them was aiming directly at Rivera. They were – the ex-soldier knew – not trained. They were poseurs, posturing for his benefit. But the Uzis were real.

'So,' the ex-soldier sighed. 'It's going to be this way, is it?'

'Mr Rivera,' Amrabat tutted. 'It was always going to be this way. You have something in your possession, and Mr Rif wants it back.' He paused. 'And then there are other... issues we need to discuss.'

'I brought you the girl!' Rivera's tone was one of incredulity – he knew the longer they stalled in the vestibule, the better his chances. 'Surely that's worth something? Or are you going to go back on our deal?'

'It *is* worth something,' the other man nodded. 'Or it *will* be. But before that, there are certain things I need to make sure of.' He paused. 'And, might I remind you, Mr Rivera – we never had a deal. Ramos offered you up as a gift. He's trying to save his own skin, I imagine.' Amrabat cleared his throat. 'I'm going to give you a very simple choice: come with me now.'

'That's not a choice,' the ex-soldier protested. 'What's my other option?'

'Your other option, Mr Rivera, is that I click my fingers, and Raheem will put a bullet through your brain.'

The ex-soldier shrugged. The group moved towards the other end of the hallway.

Chapter 116.

Thijssen's radio crackled. 'That's it,' he turned to Nour and Pancho. The Interpol agent switched on the engine and pulled out of the turning where the car had been concealed. With a spinning of tyres, he drove flat out for half a mile. After that, he began to head up the driveway of the Segovia Palace. The vehicle snaked and skidded as he negotiated the tight turns through the manicured gardens.

'Remember, I'll be right outside.' He addressed his passengers with a tone of urgency, raising his voice over the roar of the engine. 'Your radios are linked up to me and my colleagues. Any problems, holler.'

'What then?' Pancho asked. 'If there's a problem – I mean?'

'Mühren will rain down hell,' Thijssen replied. 'Francisco's already in position - so your job is simple. Just get in. Get the stuff in place. And then get the hell out of there. Got it?'

The passengers nodded as the Interpol officer drew to a halt behind the car Rivera had driven.

* * * * *

The newly deputised members of the constabulary jolted swiftly into action. They climbed quickly round to the rear of the vehicle. Nour held open the trunk as Pancho reached in and grabbed both the heavy-duty bags. Each was stuffed full with tightly-packed bags of hashish liberated from Saïd's van. As the pair began hurrying up the stairs, a figure emerged.

'We are members of the Operational Support Unit,' Pancho called out, just as Thijssen had instructed him. 'You are required to give us unrestricted access to the...'

'...I'm Francisco,' the Palace employee at the top of the stairs interrupted, hissing. He waved his lanyard with an access card clipped to it. 'I know all of that stuff. Lower your damn voices, or everyone's going to know you're here.' He paused. 'Follow me. We don't have long.'

Chapter 117.

'Right boys, string him up and let him fucking swing,' Amrabat chuckled. 'We're going to teach the bastard a lesson about what happens if you get into bed with vipers.'

The journey down to the dimly lit breeze-blocked basement room had been accompanied by blunt blows from Uzi stocks, and myriad punches and kicks. The ex-soldier knew he was surrounded by ruthless men who wouldn't hesitate to open fire. But he also knew that they weren't trained; they'd make mistakes. At close quarters, they were as likely to shoot each other as they were to shoot him. He'd been biding his time, waiting for the party to reach a place where their weapons would be less useful to them.

'Have you got the strop, Raheem?' Amrabat enquired.

The small man grinned and stepped forward. This was Rivera's moment – he felt his pulse rate slow: being upended and constrained wasn't something that appealed. He sensed this was the time when his captors' confidence and complacency would peak. Two of the gunmen leaned their weapons against the wall. One tied a loop in a length of rope and threw an end around a thick pipe that ran the length of the ceiling. The other stepped forward with a pair of handcuffs, holding them before him. Three other gunmen were also crowded into the room.

'You're not so fucking clever as you think,' Amrabat chuckled, his face half hidden in shadow. 'You siding with the Russian was a mistake.' He paused and shook his head, speaking with disgust. 'Do you *honestly* think that anyone has a chance of toppling Mr Rif? He *owns* the Costa del Sol.' The man laughed again. 'He *is* the Costa del Sol. We'll be serving you up in beach barbecues by sundown: Rivera's fucking ribs!'

'I thought we were here to talk?'

'We can talk,' Amrabat announced calmly. 'After Ismail makes a few adjustments to you with the contents of his toolbox. You fucked things up in Torre de los Boliches, so we're going to fuck you up in return.' He laughed. In the corner of the room, the ex-soldier watched as the man Amrabat was referring to lowered his Uzi and plugged an electric device into the mains supply. Painstakingly, he laid an assortment of wires and crocodile clips out on a table, along with a plant mister. Amrabat looked away from him and raised his eyebrows. 'Any last requests.'

'One,' the ex-soldier nodded. He spoke in a low voice; Rif's lieutenant leaned in to listen.

* * * * *

Amrabat's face puckered in horror as Rivera spat.

The rest of the men in the room recoiled; the man bearing the handcuffs paused mid-stride.

Rif's men had grown up ragged. Their feral childhoods had shaped them into perfect products for what the boss required. But their style was one of swagger and intimidation. It was governed by a curious set of rules. Rivera had no rules: for him, fighting was a simple matter of economy and survival. Once a fight began, time slowed for the ex-soldier. Muscle memory kicked in; he moved without thinking, as if in a dream.

The hesitation caused by him spitting was all he needed. Street fighters tend to fight like movie actors, with big swings and posturing. Rivera's approach was different: his thunderbolt-like fist moved in a straight line from his hip. Amrabat was almost lifted off his feet. But as his head snapped back, the ex-soldier was already moving – he knew speed was key. The man carrying the handcuffs stepped clumsily forward with all his weight on his front foot. Rivera grabbed his wrists, and half-threw, half-flung him across the room. He clattered into one of the gunmen just as he pulled the trigger. The shot caught him, blowing away half of his face and leaving one of his eyeballs hanging on a thread. But, though his head swung like a broken pendulum, his body fell forward, knocking the gun from his killer's hand.

The remaining men were almost hypnotised into a freeze-frame by Rivera's speed. Raheem – the man with the strop – recovered fastest. He swung the heavy length of hard leather at the ex-soldier, but misjudged the angle. His target dodged the arc and launched himself, driving upwards from the floor. His outstretched elbow caught Raheem in the throat, crushing his larynx and sending him plummeting onto the bare concrete. As he fell, Rivera grabbed the strop from his hand and, in a fluid motion, turned and swung it at the other gunman. The armed man was frantically trying to aim his weapon while disengaging the safety catch. It was too much for him – he hadn't spent countless hours practising that very action until he could do it in pitch darkness while under fire. And he certainly couldn't accomplish the task at the same time as avoiding a leather strop swinging towards his temple.

As the strop smashed into the man's temple, the light went out in his eyes, and his legs crumpled. Rivera was already rolling along the base of the wall, away from him, towards where the nearest Uzi was propped. Bullets from the third gunman thudded into the brickwork above him, sending shards of shattered masonry ricocheting across the floor. Though the shooter had succeeded in discharging his weapon, his aim – at such close quarters – was poor. Reaching the gun, Rivera rolled, turned, and fired. He hit the man in the centre of his chest. Turning, he then aimed his rifle at the first gunman, whose weapon remained tangled in the lifeless limbs of the man who'd tumbled into him. For a split-second, he glanced up, looking the ex-soldier straight in the eye. As Rivera pulled the trigger, his head exploded in a red mist, rendering the wall in an avant-garde montage of blood, bone and grey matter.

For the five seconds the encounter had lasted, Ismail hadn't moved from the electrical supply. The man looked at the ex-soldier with a frown. He was still frowning when Rivera shot him. The ex-soldier then put a lucky bullet into each of the corpses that now littered the basement.

As the echoes died and the cordite smoke drifted, Amrabat slowly stood and raised his hands in surrender. 'Will you shoot me?' he enquired, his voice wavering slightly.

Rivera didn't answer. Instead, he reached up for the rope that hung from the ceiling pipe and threw the looped end around Amrabat's neck. Then, he tightened it and pulled hard, hoisting the other man off his feet, and dragging him towards the ceiling. Amrabat's eyes bulged, and he gargled. His hands wrenched at the makeshift noose while his legs kicked wildly like the limbs of a panicked frog.

'Freeze!' came a voice from the doorway behind.

'Raise your hands!' another voice shouted. 'Both of them – put them where I can see.' The order was accompanied by the metallic sound of a round being chambered.

Rivera looked up in disappointment at the not-quite-dead form of Amrabat and slowly raised his hands. As he did, he let the end of the rope slip through his fingers. The hanging man crashed to the ground as strong arms forced Rivera to the floor.

Chapter 118.

'In here!' Francisco hissed at Pancho and Nour. He held the card on the end of his lanyard against a sensor for a moment. It glowed green and a dull click sounded as he ushered them through.

The opulence of the vestibule had nothing on that of Rif's private quarters. The visitors were greeted with a floor-to-ceiling oil painting of the owner dressed as a sultan. In the depiction, he was surrounded by topless women who all stared up at him with eyes narcotised in worship. Golden chandeliers glittered; gold-leaf wallpaper clung to the brickwork, and garish golden ornaments bedecked the enormous lounge in an orgy of Midas-like tastelessness. The centrepiece was a huge golden fountain, above which two jewel-encrusted golden mermaid statues were entwined, embracing.

'Wonder what is his favourite colour is?' Pancho muttered in disdain.

'This is fucking obscene!' Nour sighed.

The trio gazed around the room for a moment before Francisco snapped them out of their reverie. 'Let's fucking get on with it. Rif's bed chamber is through that door.' The Segovia Palace employee drew out a handgun.

'You're not coming with us?' Nour frowned.

'No.' Francisco shook his head. 'I'll cover you from out here. Just unload your bags into one of his wardrobes and then disappear.'

'Won't he be in there?' Pancho enquired, pausing close to the door.

'I shouldn't think so,' Francisco replied. 'If Tatiana has any sense, she'll have taken him into the en suite. There's a thing he likes to do – one of his little fetishes.'

'Won't they hear us?' Nour asked.

'Not likely,' Francisco winked. 'It's the biggest bathroom I've ever seen – more like a bloody aircraft hangar.' He paused by the doorway, breathed deep and turned the handle, before poking his head into the adjacent room. 'Clear!'

Chapter 119.

Mühren's eyes roved: wing mirror; rear-view mirror; side view; front view; watch. His mouth was sandpaper dry, and he could almost hear his pulse beating in his brain. Protocol meant he'd had to send Thijssen with the new recruits. He, meanwhile, was stuck. Waiting. Blood pooled over his thumbnail where he'd subconsciously clawed at a step-mother's blessing.

Twelve minutes had passed since Rivera had gone inside. He'd sat, parked at the edge of the road, close to the entrance of the Segovia Palace for that time, counting the seconds. The red hand of the dashboard clock seemed to hang suspended.

When he and Fletcher had talked through the plan, he'd set fifteen minutes as the absolute maximum time frame for their various charges to carry out their tasks. Fletcher had argued for twenty, but the Dutchman had insisted.

Right now, Mühren thought, fifteen minutes felt like an eternity. The Interpol agent looked again at his watch; the second hand seemed to linger, dancing between the marks of each increment as it moved onwards.

Three... two... one...

Thirteen minutes gone.

Mühren was a stickler for procedure. But something told him this called for a different approach. He had a niggling feeling. A sense of impending doom. Besides, he reasoned, it would take the best part of sixty seconds for him and his squads to move from their covert positions to surround Rif's property. And in a hostage situation, sixty seconds was a long, long time.

The Interpol agent swore, thumped his fist into the dashboard, and then grabbed the radio. 'All units... calling all units... Go! Go! Go! Remember, priority one is to secure November, Papa, Romeo, and Tango. Take the Sultan alive. All the others... do what you've got to do...'

Chapter 120.

Rif had just been removed in a police van when Fletcher arrived. He'd been led out of the building in shackles by four armed guards. The British officer was decked out in his customary Costa del Sol camouflage – an unashamedly garish Hawaiian shirt and a leather-like tan.

'You took your sweet time!' Mühren laughed.

'Well, that's what happens when you're only invited to the after party,' Fletcher grinned. 'Anyway, I had some of it on Rivera-cam.' He paused. 'Are they – er – all present and correct?'

'Yeah,' Mühren replied. 'You'll never believe what we found in the Sultan's quarters.'

'No?' Fletcher chuckled. 'Who'd have thought it? So, bang to rights then?' He pulled out a cigarette.

'Yeah – let's just hope a jury will see it that way,' Mühren nodded.

The police officer lit his cigarette. 'And Rivera?'

'Ask him yourself,' Mühren answered, nodding beyond the policeman towards where the ex-soldier was emerging from the main door of the entrance. The man's expression was somewhere between a disgruntled grimace and an angry scowl. He was naked to the waist and had two bloody welts across the middle of his back. Purplish bruises were already beginning to form across his torso.

'Here he is!' Fletcher announced. 'The main fucking man!'

'I needed another sixty seconds,' Rivera grumbled. 'Letting that bastard down from the gallows was a fucking travesty. Are you working for Amnesty now or something?' He reached out, removing the lit cigarette from Fletcher's mouth. He claimed it for himself, inhaling deeply.

'Help yourself.' Fletcher shrugged.

Silence.

'You alright?' the policeman asked. 'I mean – *really?*' He paused. 'We thought maybe you'd need our lads to lend you a hand...'

'Piss off!' Rivera grinned and shook his head. He turned to Mühren. 'Well?'

The other man nodded. 'Full house.'

Exhaling, the ex-soldier shook his head. 'Who'd have thought it – Fletcher as a tactical genius?' He paused. 'I wish I'd been that lucky when I used to bet on the horses.'

Mühren smiled. 'I want you to head down to the ambulance, please, Mr Rivera.' His tone was kind but insistent. He regarded the casualty with genuine concern.

Rivera shook his head. 'No, no – I'm fine. I swore off hospitals a long time ago.'

'Even so,' the Interpol agent continued, 'it's procedure – let them at least give you an ice pack for the bruises, huh?'

'Yeah, get them to bandage you up,' Fletcher agreed. 'You know, one of the nurses looked pretty hot. See if she can rub in some ointment.' He winked. 'You're a bloody hero – you might even get special treatment!'

'Is he always this angry?' Mühren asked, turning to face Fletcher.

'No, Frans – he's normally much worse. I think it's the shock that's made him docile.' He turned to Rivera. 'Go on, mate. Seriously – the least they'll do is give you an aspirin. And who knows – that nurse might give you a blow job.' He shrugged. 'You might even get something better!'

Rivera frowned. 'Where's Tatiana?'

'Rehab,' Fletcher answered, bluntly.

'Already?'

'Yeah – we're not pissing about with those girls. In two weeks, they'll be pink-skinned and glowing.'

Mühren frowned and turned to the policeman. 'Is he in love with her?'

'Lust really, Frans,' Fletcher replied. He turned to Rivera. 'Remember, in about five hours' time, cold turkey will kick in. She'll be throwing up everywhere and involuntarily shitting through the eye of a needle. I'm not sure even your standards are that low... are they?'

The ex-soldier shrugged and made his way painfully towards the waiting ambulance.

Chapter 121.

As Rivera descended the steps, Mühren turned to Fletcher. 'He's something else – that boy of yours, isn't he? He's like a one-man army - we could probably have sent him in on his own!'

'Yeah,' Fletcher nodded. 'But between you and me... I was a little worried before. I thought they'd have butchered the bastard by the time we got to him. I mean, people I spoke to said he was good, but nailing all those blokes like he did is ridiculous – it's like something from the movies!'

The Dutchman nodded. 'He's a tough old sonofabitch alright.' He paused. 'What next then, maestro – for you?'

Fletcher sighed, reached into his pocket, and pulled his pack of cigarettes out once more. He removed one with his teeth, lit it, and then shrugged. 'I don't know. I reckon I'm done here, though. Sometimes I wonder if I'm getting too old for all this shit, anyway.'

'What? You're not going to hang your boots up? Surely?'

'Who knows?'

'What will you do? Take up golf? Do crosswords?'

Fletcher laughed. 'If they'd leave me out here in the sun, I'd think about carrying on. But they won't – I'm damaged goods now. Cover blown. So I should think they'll want me back in bloody Rotherhithe... but I'll take a few weeks of leave first. Stick around. Work on my tan.'

Mühren frowned. 'Rif will still have people around, though. I'd make myself scarce if I were you.'

'Yeah,' Fletcher nodded. 'But he'll want his people to lie low for a few weeks. That's my guess.' He paused. 'If he's in the jailhouse, he's not going to want any of his guys causing problems on the outside.' He looked hard at Mühren. 'You really think we've got the bastard, then?'

'I fucking hope so,' the Interpol agent shrugged. 'It's been a long bloody time coming. It's out of our hands now, but this is the closest we'll ever come if not.' He paused and his expression grew serious. 'Honestly – I'd put a bit of distance between yourself and the Costa. For a couple of weeks, at least. Wait and see how the dust settles.'

The policeman nodded. 'Yeah – maybe I'll head up to Benidorm. Blend in. Do what I do best.'

Chapter 122.

Rivera opened the door of the apartment in Latinaja to find Mühren standing on the steps. Rosie mewed loudly, brushing herself against the visitor's calves. He bent down to stroke her. It was early evening a few days after events at the Segovia Palace.

'No offence, Frans,' Rivera began, looking down at the other man, 'but I thought we were done?'

'Yeah, me too,' the Dutchman nodded, standing up again. 'Working with you seems to have a lot of risk attached to it. You all set to get out of here?'

'Pretty much,' the ex-soldier nodded. He then frowned and looked out at a large, black SUV with tinted windows that was parked on the street outside. 'This isn't going to do much for you operating incognito, is it? Driving around in that thing screams law enforcement! You want to get Fletcher to lend you a shit car like mine!'

'I know,' Mühren replied, sheepishly. 'Anyway, there's someone wanted to speak to you - you coming to say hello?'

'If I must. I guess Pancho wanted to go into the programme after all then, no?'

'Negative,' the Interpol agent replied. 'But his course in Madrid has been transferred. He's going to complete his PhD elsewhere – overseas. We reckon he'll be alright.'

Rivera nodded. 'So who've you got for me then?'

* * * * *

Saïd and Nour were seated in the back seat of the SUV. Both were dressed in clean apparel; both looked a million miles away from the dusty figures he'd first met in the shantytown. Rivera peered in as the window slid down and grinned. 'What the hell are you two doing here?' he chuckled. 'You're supposed to have vanished – Witness

Protection. Isn't that right?' He turned to the Dutchman. 'Frans – what are you playing at?'

Mühren held up his hands in mock surrender. 'They're officially documented European citizens now – they're exercising their constitutional right!'

'We wanted to say thank you, senōr,' Saïd interrupted. 'Without you, we'd still be in El Barranquete. We won't forget that. You planned it all – we just did what we were told.'

Rivera shrugged. 'Well... I wish you both well with whatever you're planning next. I guess you can't tell me your plans, though, can you?'

Silence.

'Ideally, we'll open a restaurant one day – at least that's the plan,' Nour announced. 'Arraf turned himself in to the authorities. And once they let him out, he can join us.'

The ex-soldier grimaced a little. 'Yeah – about that,' he said, uncomfortably. 'Even if he gives evidence, he was still a dealer for them. Your cousin will end up in prison unless he's extremely lucky. They'll do him a deal, of course, but he's likely to do some time.'

'We know,' Nour nodded. 'Mr Mühren has explained. But they'll definitely shorten his sentence. He's agreed to tell them everything. So we're hopeful.'

Rivera nodded. 'Well, good luck. The only shame is that I won't know where your restaurant is – or what it's called. I'd have liked to try the menu.' He shrugged. 'Never mind – you wouldn't want a *guiri* clogging the place up – I'd only make things look bad!'

Saïd smiled. 'I've got a feeling you could find it, senōr. If you *really* wanted to.'

Chapter 123.

Three weeks had slipped by. The noontime heat was still extreme, though now it lacked some of the lion-like viciousness of high summer. Nights were lengthening, and – on days when the wind came from the north - dawn sometimes carried with it the promise of cooler weather. Once the sun rose, though, the temperature climbed with it; by mid-morning, people sought shade, and the cicadas struck up their chorus. Rivera and Fletcher were back at Chas Edwards' former residence. They were seated either side of a table on the sun deck.

'So, where have you been?' the ex-soldier enquired, accepting a light from the policeman.

'Oh, you know – here and there. I had to see about a girl.' The policeman waved his wrist, which still bore a band from an all-inclusive resort hotel. 'Didn't you get the postcard?' He chuckled. 'Any word from your lady friend?'

'Which one?'

'You're a dirty dog, you are! I mean the one back in Blighty, you melon!'

'A little,' the ex-soldier shrugged. 'I think I'll need to head on home. See if I can patch things up.'

Silence.

'So...' Fletcher sighed heavily. 'I'm not too good at sentimental stuff but... I appreciate what you did for me back there. Don't let this go to your head, but... I can't think of anyone who'd have been better suited. You did well, soldier. You're a tough bastard.'

Rivera nodded.

'You got the money, right?' Fletcher continued.

'I did.'

'Good. I've told them to add a per diem on, and some insurance money too. Compensation for injuries sustained in the line of fire blah-blah-blah. All being well, you should get a bit more of a payout.

I'm not talking loads, so don't get too excited, but it should keep you going for a while.' He paused, frowning at the other man. 'Are you alright? I mean – you're kind of a weird bloke, you know...'

'Right back at you, Fletcher.'

He laughed. 'Yeah! You're not the first to say that. Sometimes I wonder if it's the shirts. But, seriously, I mean... the way you go bumming around like a hobo – it's not normal.' He sighed. 'You know, it's none of my business, but I've had mates with PTSD. It screws people up; affects them in different ways; it's not all night tremors and headaches – I know that much. He bit his lip, uncomfortable. But there are people you can see, you know? I mean it.'

Rivera nodded, pursing his lips. 'You're right.'

'I am?' Fletcher raised his eyebrows.

'Yeah – it's none of your business.'

* * * * *

Fletcher cleared his throat. 'I meant what I said – I appreciate what you've done.' He slid a set of keys over the table. 'Consider this a small gesture.'

'What's this?' Rivera frowned, the corners of his mouth curling up slightly into a nervous smile.

'Well... Carvajal Rental Cars is no more. The force will have to wind it up. We don't think its cover's been fully blown, but it's not worth the risk.'

'So?'

'So Manuel was still on the payroll until...' he checked his watch '...about five minutes ago. He's had ten days to focus on Iris.' The officer chuckled. 'He's polished that T2 up to such a sheen you can see your face in it. Maybe not quite as good as new, but I bet she's looking better than she's ever done since you've owned her.'

'I appreciate it...'

'...there is one more thing.' Fletcher's expression grew serious. 'You've come a long way with me.' He paused. 'I thought that – maybe – potentially – you'd like to come a bit further?'

The ex-soldier narrowed his eyes. 'What are you getting at?'

Fletcher paused. 'Coffee?'

Chapter 124.

'You want the good news or the bad news?' Fletcher enquired.

'Good – always,' Rivera replied.

'Tatiana's free. Well,' he waved away a buzzing fly, 'she's finished rehab – along with Oksana. They're on a kind of supported release thing – they've got them both jobs too. *Proper* jobs. *Normal* jobs.'

'Yeah?'

'Yeah,' he nodded. 'Far away – somewhere safe from you!'

Rivera smiled.

'Torre de los Boliches has been sold to a developer too,' Fletcher continued. 'At least they've sold what's left of it. Bargain price, I should think. The land's good though - it's going to be a tourist complex. Package deals mainly.'

'Well, it's good about the girls. And that's just what the Costa needs, isn't it? More tourist lets?'

'Better than a knocking shop...' Fletcher shrugged.

'Yeah – I'll give you that. And the bad news?'

The policeman produced a newspaper and placed it on the table. 'This.'

Rivera frowned. He scanned the text for a moment. 'So, the rumours are true then?'

'They are. The bastard walked free this morning. There's still an investigation, but we all know what that'll come to.' He sighed. 'Fuck all.' He shook his head. 'The Sugarman's dead too – apparently when he was questioned about him, Rif just laughed.'

The ex-soldier shook his head. 'And what about the photo?'

'Not kosher, apparently,' Fletcher sighed. 'Don't fucking ask.'

* * * * *

The picture on the front page was of an immaculately attired Abdellah Rif leaving police custody. His team of lawyers stood to one side of him; Amrabat was in the background, beaming. Phrases like 'miscarriage of justice' 'inadmissible evidence' 'police brutality' and 'coercion' abounded.

'The law of unintended consequences, right?' Fletcher sighed.

'You mentioned going a little further?'

Fletcher nodded. 'When I was sounding you out, I spoke to Christie.' He paused. 'She said you were a man who likes to get things done.'

The ex-soldier nodded. 'Yeah – fair enough, I guess. But I think she likes me – maybe she was trying to butter me up?'

'Yeah – don't flatter yourself. She's on track to be a Commissioner, I reckon. She won't want grubby little skeletons like you in her closet!'

Rivera chewed his lip. 'So, what did you have in mind?'

The policeman smiled. 'Well, my friend, before you meander off into the sunset in that Volkswagen of yours, there's something I'd like your help with. If you're willing, I mean. Something which I think will be right up your street.' He looked hard at the other man. 'Interested?'

'I'm listening...'

Chapter 125.

People would later claim it was one of the largest gatherings of the press Fuengirola had ever seen. Representatives from the construction industry stood beside employees of the gambling commission; the mayor and his many councillors were decked out in their finery. And a selection of politicians from Madrid had been flown in for the occasion. The Rif organisation had done its best to ensure maximum publicity.

No expense had been spared: marquees had been erected on the beach; wooden-slatted walkways lay across the sand; exotic flowering plants sat in huge gold-leafed pots, and an enormous stage had been built. On the backdrop behind the lectern, a giant sign was hung, bearing the legend ¡*Una, Grande y Libre*! – it was to be the resort's name. As well as pictures of the proposed super casino, there were blueprints of the hotel; mock-ups of the redeveloped marina; plans for restaurants, and the faces of celebrities eager to endorse Rif's ambitious project. The target audience for the new development was clear: moneyed global travellers.

The crowd was kept waiting for almost an hour, plied with complimentary refreshments all the while. That was all part of the plan – the boss wanted their enthusiasm bolstered by the free booze his caterers were pressing on them. A rapturous welcome would feed Rif's ego even further.

'You've got to keep them waiting, Amrabat,' the boss explained to his assistant. 'Remind them who's in charge. Anyway,' he smiled, 'I'm not going to start until the FC Castillo match is due to kick off. If I can't steal their thunder on the opening game of the season, then when can I?' He laughed bitterly. 'That fucker Ibanez won't even know what's hit him!'

* * * * *

Amrabat had been opposed to his boss' public appearance. It was – he argued – too sudden. Too soon after his release. Too public. There hadn't been time to arrange sufficient security. He was still worried about Miletski's organisation. And he was concerned that – now there were question marks over Rif – he'd be a target.

But the newly-freed Rif was in a bullish, combative mood. He was determined to show Ibanez, and the rest of the world, that he was back. That he wasn't scared. That he'd seize the day and prevail. Eventually, the assistant had simply acquiesced.

Rif strutted out onto the stage a little under an hour after the scheduled time. He was met by healthy applause. His latest venture promised investment and new jobs. As he repeated the name of the super casino like a mantra, those assembled whooped and cheered. But then, they'd been paid to – the crowd was integral to launching a newly-minted Rif. A different man. A member of the establishment. A potential political figure.

Someone who could be trusted.

Chapter 126.

'You see him?' Fletcher enquired.

'I do,' whispered Rivera. He was lying prone, eye glued to his sniper scope. The butt of the rifle was wedged against his shoulder, immobile. It was an Israeli firearm – a DAN .388 - which Fletcher had secured. Beside him, the policeman regarded the distant scene through a pair of binoculars.

'Seems an awfully long way away...' the officer's voice trailed off.

Rivera spoke from the side of his mouth; his voice barely audible. 'I told you - this is well within normal limits.' He paused. 'What's *not* within normal limits is you yapping in my ear like a fucking Jack Russell.'

'Roger that,' the officer replied. 'Radio silence.'

Rivera lay still. Steadying his breathing. Slowing his heart rate.

Nearly three quarters of a mile away, the target walked onto the stage, waving cheerily at his audience. From where the two watchers were situated, his words were a metallic buzz. The ex-soldier adjusted his scope minutely, lining the crosshairs up with the centre of the speaker's head. Ten storeys below, muffled noises of traffic rose up from the street. Occasional screeches of tyres could be heard, along with the blaring of horns and odd snatches of conversations that drifted upward on the wind.

In the three weeks he'd been absent, Fletcher had pondered deeply; he'd realised that sometimes the only way to bring an organisation down was from the top. And that meant only one thing: he'd spent three days reconnoitring vantage points until he'd found somewhere suitable.

The late afternoon sun was positioned directly behind the deserted hotel. Demolition work had begun on it even before Rif had been released. Were anyone to look up, searching for a muzzle flash, or the reflection from a binocular lens, they'd be blinded by the brilliant yellow-orange hue of the sky.

Rivera inhaled... exhaled.

* * * * *

Rif leaned back, nodding at the applause. 'And so I say to Dubai... to Las Vegas... no – there is nothing you have that we do not possess here.'

The crowd roared its approval once more.

Rif nodded again and opened his mouth to speak. The words he intended to say, though, were lost. The crowd looked on in utter bewilderment. One moment, Abdellah Rif was speaking to them. The next, his head was exploding in a cloud of reddish-purple, and his body was flung sideways across the stage.

* * * * *

The empty shell casing pinged onto the scaffolding.

Rivera remained motionless.

Fletcher chuckled. 'I bet you were always winning goldfish as a kid, no? The fairground folk at shooting galleries must have fucking loved you!' He lowered the binoculars, looked at the ex-soldier, and shook his head. 'Bull's-eye!' As he spoke, he dialled a number on a burner phone that he'd removed from his pocket.

* * * * *

Abdellah was swiftest to react. Before screaming panic ensued, he implored the onlookers to take cover. The assistant was operating on autopilot; he knew there was no hope for Rif. For a moment, the crowd seemed to heed him. And then, his voice was cut off by an earth-shatteringly loud explosion offshore. At once the gasping assembly's attention was drawn across the water where a huge plume of fire and smoke was ascending. People stared, stupefied, unable to process what they were seeing.

* * * * *

Nearly a mile out to sea, the Semtex charge detonated. Earlier that morning, the pair had dragged a rowing boat out to sea behind a motor launch. They'd tied it to a floating buoy, packed with the leftover explosive from Chas Edwards' stash. It had been mined with the same style of charge used at Torre de los Boliches.

Since positioning himself on the tenth floor of the half-derelict hotel, Fletcher had repeatedly shifted the gaze of his binoculars between the lectern on the beach and the boatload of explosives out at sea; he wanted to make sure there were no other vessels in the vicinity. The charge was simply a decoy; he knew that blowing the Semtex would create far more of a distraction than the shot. It would also create mayhem on the beach, which would lessen the chance of any errant law enforcement officials taking an unhealthy interest in looking for him and Rivera.

Watching the chaos erupting on the sand, Rivera squeezed the trigger once more.

Chapter 127.

With the attention of everyone on the beach focused far out at sea, nobody was looking at Abdellah when the bullet struck. Like everyone else, he'd stood, statuesque, rooted to his spot on the sand as the charges blew.

And then, suddenly, he was thrown bodily towards the edge of a marquee, dead before he hit the floor. He lay, sprawled, blood pumping from the ragged hole ripped through him by Rivera's round.

* * * * *

'Bloody hell!' breathed Fletcher in admiration. 'Double whammy! Two from two! You're on fucking fire, my son!'

The ex-soldier rolled over. He swiftly broke down the rifle and retrieved the shell casings before depositing the various components in a shoulder bag. 'Shall we?' he enquired, looking at his companion.

'Yeah,' Fletcher nodded. 'I was just admiring my handiwork.' He pointed at the burning wreckage out at sea. 'I love the smell of Semtex in the early evening!'

'Idiot!' Rivera shook his head. 'Come on, let's hustle. It won't be too long before this boulevard's full of blue lights.'

* * * * *

Night had fallen by the time the two men arrived back at the villa. Streetlights cast a pale glow over the road outside the Edwards property.

'So... anything we need to remember?' Fletcher asked as the vehicle drew to a halt.

In the front seat of the police car he'd requisitioned, Mühren turned around. The Interpol agent had been waiting at the base of the derelict building where he'd collected the two men. He spoke seriously. 'Only that today never happened. And that neither of you were ever here.' He looked at them both pointedly. 'It's probably best if you disappear.'

'Roger that,' Fletcher replied.

'It's true what they say, gentlemen,' the Interpol agent nodded. 'Sometimes the old ways work best. Everyone knew Rif and the Kbir were the same thing. Hopefully, with him out of the way, the organisation will wither and die.' He drummed his hand absent-mindedly on the bonnet of the car. 'I'll cover for you for the next twenty-four hours. You've got a free pass – I'll just say you were tying up loose ends if anyone asks. But don't do anything stupid.' He paused. 'After that, you're on your own.'

The two men nodded.

'Safe travels, boys,' Mühren smiled, before climbing back into the vehicle.

As the sound of his car engine receded, the two men made their way back towards the house. 'This place is going on Airbnb,' Fletcher announced. 'Fucking unbelievable, isn't it? This is a piece of gangland history – they should turn it into a museum!'

Silence.

'Has your ticket come through yet?' Rivera enquired.

'Yeah. And Frans is right – you need to get moving too.'

'First thing tomorrow.'

'Good,' Fletcher nodded. 'Iris is ready for you in the workshop – you can have a reunion. We can even have one for the road at Jim's Bar before you vanish, if you like?'

Chapter 128.

'So... what do you think?' Fletcher asked, nodding eagerly towards Iris. 'Fucking brilliant, isn't she?'

'Yeah,' Rivera nodded, grinning. 'You were right – good as new!' He cast his eye admiringly along the polished sides of the T2 and then climbed in.

In the rear, Rosie was settling down. The ex-soldier had provided her with water, food and a bed. He knew, though, that within ten miles, she'd doubtless be asleep on the front seat alongside him.

'You'll have to give Manuel my regards,' Rivera continued, leaning out of the open window.

Fletcher nodded. 'Well, I guess this is us then, no?' he shrugged.

'You getting soppy?'

'Piss off!' the policeman grinned.

The two men shook hands solemnly.

'You going to hook back up with your old missus, then?' Fletcher asked. 'Try a bit of domestic bliss?'

'We'll see...'

'Well, *bon voyage* and all of that!' The policeman tapped on the side panel of the campervan as Rivera pulled slowly away.

* * * * *

The ex-soldier changed down into second gear. Rosie jumped through from the table at the back of the cab and then scrambled into the front. She mewed loudly; Rivera stroked her, leaving one hand on the wheel. 'Where to, then?' he enquired. The cat simply stared back at him in blank indifference before settling herself down on the passenger seat and closing her eyes.

Chapter 129.

Thank you so much for reading this novel. I hope you have enjoyed it. Should you have a spare 5 minutes and would like to leave a short review, I would be hugely grateful.
Very best wishes.
Blake Valentine

Chapter 130.

The First Chapter of *FOUR LEAF CLOVER* – the next novel in the TRENT RIVERA SERIES.

The man stood back, admiring the tableau through the gritted teeth of a grimace. He was dressed head-to-toe in black. The once grand barroom of The Diplomat Hotel was lit only by the ghostly shaft of moonlight cutting through its broken first-floor windows; they looked out upon the town of South Quay like sad, vacant eyes. Years before, the establishment had been *the* place to stay; *the* place to be seen; the jewel in the crown of the south coast. A holiday El Dorado for the superior set who wished to rattle their jewellery in the faces of those they perceived as being beneath them.

But that was long ago. It stood now, abandoned and decrepit. Wire-panelled fencing surrounded its site, replete with notices bearing vivid images of snarling, non-existent guard dogs. Signs claimed that any trespassing would activate alarms. The building's ground floor casements were boarded up, and successive layers of obscenities had been daubed upon them. Half a century before, The Diplomat's gardens had drawn admirers from far and wide. But now they were overgrown – a haven for wildlife that dwelled in the discarded detritus of a once affluent town whose way had been lost.

Removing a phone from his pocket, the man pressed a button. The screen illuminated. Its light cast his expressionless eyes in a ghostly glow, where they peered through the holes in his balaclava. One blue. One brown.

No messages.

No further orders.

He checked his watch.

It was time. He strode over to the dust-encrusted bar top and lifted down a jerry can. He was tall; strong. The weight was easy for his thick arms to bear. His lips formed themselves into the hint of a smile as he upended the vessel. Liquid sloshed onto the carpet, splashing into its worn fabric.

'Stop!' a voice rang out.

He paused. Frowned.

* * * * *

Turning, the man placed the can on a bare patch of floorboards. The petrol fumes were overpowering. He wrinkled his nose slightly. 'What the fuck do you want?' he demanded. His tone wasn't aggressive – more perplexed.

He looked back at his handiwork: there were three of them. Two with mouths bound by duct tape. One without. All three were firmly tied to a long, cast iron radiator which ran the length of the wall. The eyes of the two wearing gags were wide; they'd grown wider still as the man began pouring petrol. The third captive stared thinly, though. He'd been less cooperative. So he'd been knocked out, smashed across the side of the head with an iron bar.

The man had assumed he was dead. But the captive was evidently tougher than he'd imagined.

Much tougher.

His boss had planned the whole set-up. She wanted the victims to be fully aware of their fate – to know what was coming before it came. To feel the ferocious heat of the flames before being consumed by them. Before they were turned to ash, along with the remains of the old hotel. But he hadn't expected the third man to wake up. In fact, he hadn't banked upon him being there at all. Despite looking only a little less derelict than the hotel itself, he'd put up quite a struggle - even when faced with a pistol. For two minutes of fighting, he'd more than held his own. At one point, he'd even landed a punch that had given his much larger assailant pause for thought. But then he'd started coughing.

That had been the end of it.

The man in black frowned again and approached the radiator. His two gagged captives made frantic gurgling noises, wrenching at the ropes that restrained them. But they held firm. The man grinned a little, recalling how they'd entered the premises willingly. A little inebriated, they'd walked right into his trap. Just like his boss had told him they would. Once he'd produced the gun, they'd had no choice but to follow his orders.

By the time they understood their predicament, it was too late for them to do anything about it. The man had taken his time – anticipation was something he revelled in.

'Problem?' he sneered. The ungagged figure looked up, his eye bloodied and swollen. His head lolled as if too heavy for his neck to support. He rested it against his shoulder for an instant before straightening it. He was thin; wiry. Strong – at least he had been, once upon a time.

'You won't get away with this,' the man said. He spoke slowly, deliberately, pausing to spit a gobbet of blood from his mouth. 'People know I'm here.'

The dark figure smiled and shook his head. 'No one knows you're here, tramp. And nobody would give a shit even if they did.'

Glaring up at his captor with a look of icy contempt, the third man opened his mouth. He enunciated his words clearly. 'Fuck you!'

* * * * *

Far off in the distance, a car horn sounded. It was followed by another. The Diplomat Hotel was an Eagle's Nest above the town. In the past, it had looked down; imperious. Now it felt removed – a remnant; a symbol of the years of plenty that preceded the town's pockets being slowly drained. In its heyday, the great and good had flocked to the area's golden beaches, and frequented its dance halls and discothèques. But that was before budget flights and the lure of the Mediterranean. By the time the Chamber of Commerce realised the place was sliding, it had already plummeted.

'I think that knock on the head confused you,' the man said bluntly - his voice gravelly. He strode over and slammed his steel toe-capped boot into the side of the third man's chest. The captive shrieked in pain as the attacker brought his full weight to bear on his ribs.

They broke easily.

As the injured figure spewed a stream of expletives, his attacker tore a strip of duct tape from a roll with his teeth. He stuck it roughly across the third man's mouth, silencing him.

'Better now?' he enquired, laughing. 'It's better for me – this way I don't have to listen to you whining like a little bitch.'

* * * * *

Ten minutes later, the man returned to inspect his prisoners once more. Since leaving them, he'd poured the contents of half a dozen jerry cans up and down the staircases, soaking what remained of the carpets and covering the exposed floorboards of rooms on all floors. For nearly three weeks, there'd been hardly any rain. He knew that once the petrol sparked, it would take only moments before the place became an inferno.

The man pulled a low bar stool across the carpet and sank lazily onto it. It was one of the few pieces of furniture remaining in the bare room. Looking at the first two captives, he sneered once more. 'Miss Keane sends her regards. I thought you might like to know that.' He paused, looking at the third man. 'You're different – you just pissed me off. You weren't even part of the plan. But three's a lucky number. So, the more the fucking merrier.' He looked around the room and slowly removed a cigarette from a packet, placing it in the corner of his mouth. Then he brought out a Zippo lighter.

'Oh!' His expression changed to one of mock alarm. 'Where are my manners?' He threw a cigarette towards each of the captives. 'You see, we have our own set of laws here in South Quay. You should know that – they're Leah Keane's laws.' He shrugged. 'You broke them... you pay.' The gyrations of the bound figures were growing more violent; their gurgling more desperate. 'Me though – I *obey* the laws.' He grinned. 'That's why I'm going to step outside for my cigarette. You know – because of the smoking ban and all. Don't worry though, I'll chuck a light back in for you.'

Yawning, the man rose from the bar stool. He walked slowly across the barroom and then exited the door, making his way down the grand staircase. Opening the front door, he glanced at the wasteland of brambles and nettles before him, and then picked up the Molotov cocktail he'd prepared previously.

Stepping outside fully, he lit his cigarette, inhaling deeply. He wedged it in the corner of his mouth as he touched the Zippo's flame to the petrol-soaked rag that protruded from the bottle's neck. It ignited instantly, the angry blaze roaring and hissing as it chewed at the fabric.

Holding the burning bottle, the man took a last look around before hurling it into the vestibule. It shattered, bursting into a fabulous Roman Candle of flame. He nodded with approval as the petrol-sodden staircase followed suit almost immediately – twin paths of tangerine-hued sparks raced upwards, flaring.

Chuckling, the man flicked his cigarette through the open door. He then thrust his hands into his pockets and walked away.

About the Author

Blake Valentine is the author of the TRENT RIVERA MYSTERY SERIES. Prior to becoming a writer, he worked in the music industry as both performer and producer before moving into various roles in education. He has lived in Osaka, Japan and San Diego, California, and now resides on the south coast of England with his wife, 2 children, and a cat.

All books featuring Trent Rivera are available on Amazon and can be read for free on Kindle Unlimited. Please take a look at Blake's website for more information. News, updates and competitions are also featured on Facebook (www.facebook.com/blakevalentineauthor).

If you've enjoyed reading any of Blake's books and have 5 minutes to spare, then do please leave a short review online.

Read more at https://www.blakevalentine.com.